THE MURDER MACHINE

Also by *New York Times* bestselling author Heather Graham

The Blackbird Files

LEGACY OF BLOOD
MARKET FOR MURDER
DEATH BEHIND EVERY DOOR

The Blackbird Trilogy

CURSED AT DAWN
SECRETS IN THE DARK
WHISPERS AT DUSK

THE REAPER FOLLOWS
SHADOW OF DEATH
CRIMSON SUMMER
DANGER IN NUMBERS

New York Confidential

THE FINAL DECEPTION
A LETHAL LEGACY
A DANGEROUS GAME
A PERFECT OBSESSION
FLAWLESS

Krewe of Hunters

THE UNKNOWN
THE FORBIDDEN
THE UNFORGIVEN
DREAMING DEATH
DEADLY TOUCH
SEEING DARKNESS
THE STALKING
THE SEEKERS
THE SUMMONING
ECHOES OF EVIL
PALE AS DEATH
FADE TO BLACK
WICKED DEEDS
DARK RITES
DYING BREATH
DARKEST JOURNEY
DEADLY FATE
HAUNTED DESTINY
THE HIDDEN
THE FORGOTTEN
THE SILENCED
THE BETRAYED
THE HEXED
THE CURSED
THE NIGHT IS FOREVER
THE NIGHT IS ALIVE
THE NIGHT IS WATCHING
THE UNINVITED
THE UNSPOKEN
THE UNHOLY
THE UNSEEN
THE EVIL INSIDE
SACRED EVIL
HEART OF EVIL
PHANTOM EVIL

Cafferty & Quinn

THE DEAD PLAY ON
WAKING THE DEAD
LET THE DEAD SLEEP

Look for Heather Graham's next novel
THE SWORD OF LIGHT
available from MIRA October 2025!

For additional books by Heather Graham, visit theoriginalheathergraham.com.

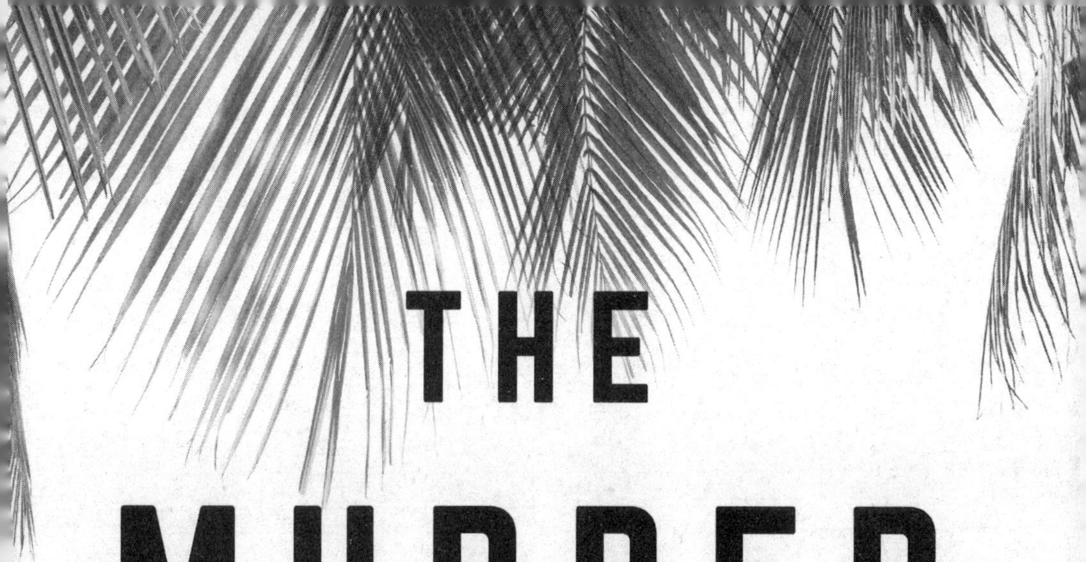

THE MURDER MACHINE

HEATHER GRAHAM

MIRA

MIRA

ISBN-13: 978-0-7783-8741-1

The Murder Machine

Mira
22 Adelaide St. West, 41st Floor
Toronto, Ontario M5H 4E3, Canada
MIRABooks.com

Printed in U.S.A.

For Monique Flores,
for the care she gives every pup in her keeping.

And for Liz Pusley,
and in memory of a small Clover with the heart of a big one!

PROLOGUE

Barton Clay was an idiot, and it wasn't going to work.

Worse, he risked them all spending their lives in jail! Yes, they had clients who were brilliant at manipulating AI. They were amazing at artificial intelligence, but the plan Barton wanted…

Crazy.

It was really his need to impress and obey Celia Smith, and Celia was always trying to prove how important she was to Nathaniel Wharton and so the game went on and on. But no matter—Barton thought his and his wife's friendship with Celia meant he could talk to her and…

No, no, no!

Marci Warden was angered by the whole ridiculous thing, and she slammed the door after entering her house. *Right! Slam the door. That'll help. Take it out on the house!*

She smiled briefly. Time to chill, to relax. Not only could her house's artificial intelligence system open and close doors for her, turn lights on and off, control the TV, even run the faucets…

The house could even behave like a real friend!

It could give her answers about movies, about the weather, the state of the world, and more, so much more! She'd given her personal AI system one of her favorite names and even chosen the voice.

"Chrissie!" she commanded the house's AI, "Turn the lights on. And go ahead and get the TV going, too, any news channel!"

Lights came on; the television sprang to life presenting the weather.

"Lights, TV. Welcome home, Marci!" Chrissie said.

"Thanks!"

Of course, AI didn't care if it was thanked or not, but what the heck? She should stay in practice for dealing with the human world.

Yep. She loved Chrissie. She *hated* Barton Clay.

Shaking her head, Marci headed on into the kitchen.

She was hungry. She looked around at the oven, the range, the toaster, mixer, coffeepot, cutting board, electric knife...

There were all kinds of things she could find in the refrigerator, but first...

Her eyes went to the bar, set up on the marble-topped counter between the kitchen and the dining room.

After the day she'd had...

A drink.

She poured herself a large whiskey, swallowed it in a single gulp, and went for another.

Then she was ready for the rest of the kitchen. She was, she knew, *very* hungry and at the rate she was drinking, food was going to be necessary, even if she was hoping the whiskey would help her sleep, close her eyes, and black out the day.

So...

"Chrissie, open the fridge," she said.

Obediently, the refrigerator door slowly swung open. She began to peruse the contents thoughtfully. A salad would be good, but not filling. But it could go with some toaster pastries. Easy. Fast.

She was vaguely aware of the weather making way for the news. Wall Street was at it again. Well, of course. The world had become a place that could be so easily manipulated!

Setting her drink down, she reached for the lettuce and grabbed the box of toaster pastries from the pantry. The fridge automatically whooshed shut behind her.

Walking past the sink, she set the food down on the large cutting board on the counter and put the pastries into the toaster.

"Chrissie, start the toaster, please," she said. "Not too well done!"

She frowned. That was all she said, but the electric knife had suddenly started whirring.

"Hey, Chrissie—hey! What's going on? I said toaster, not knife!"

But Chrissie wasn't listening.

The knife was on high, flopping all around on the counter, almost flipping about like an excited puppy. She tried to reach past it to pull the plug, but her hand hit the toaster—which was red-hot! The metal burned her and she instinctively jumped back, only for the automated refrigerator door to swing open, throwing her forward toward the counter and the wildly hopping knife.

She managed to grab it, only for the toaster to sizzle and burn with such a vengeance that it was jiggling on the counter, moving toward her, and from the nearby sink, the water suddenly began to spray wildly from the kitchen spigot.

Her stereo system suddenly came on, the music incredibly loud.

Her lights began to flash!

"Chrissie, what the heck? Stop! Shut it all off!" she screamed.

But it would be her last command. The water spray reached

the outlet, and a sizzle of electricity went surging through her body, her arm spasming and slamming the knife and its serrated edges into her chest and up to her throat.

She was going to sleep all right, closing her eyes…

But she knew, even as the world turned to darkness, that she hadn't truly been killed by the evils of artificial intelligence gone awry.

For artificial intelligence to exist…

There had to be a human mind behind it.

A human mind…filled with evil, and evil that could fester, grow, and within this new world of AI, explode into bloodshed and murder and so much more…

The darkness came. And her thoughts about the day were finally and absolutely set to rest with her last one being that yes…

The house was just like a friend.

Chrissie could and would do just about anything.

Including kill.

ONE

Jude Mackenzie stared at the scene, mentally shaking his head. He had to admit he'd never seen anything quite like it.

And he'd seen a lot.

The woman's body lay on the floor in the kitchen. An electric knife lay near her head, and the floor was an entire pool of bloody water. The horrific scent of burning flesh seemed like a whisper in the air, along with the smell of blood. Everything appeared to be saturated, but the faucet was now off.

Everything was off.

Aidan Cypress, one of the state's best forensic experts, gloved and in booties, balanced on his toes while he studied the floor near the body. Dr. Emil Dresden, medical examiner, did his best to avoid disturbing the grisly puzzle as he examined the charred and bloody body.

Both looked up at Jude as he entered the room and stood, nodding in acknowledgment of his arrival. Maybe they knew, or maybe they, too, were wondering why—as he was—an FBI agent had been called in for what appeared to be a ridiculously horrible and sad accident, a local situation, one for the

St. Augustine police force or the Florida Department of Law Enforcement.

Thankfully, he had worked with both agencies before; since he liked and respected Dresden and Cypress, he was glad he'd be getting the particulars from them even though they were state and he was federal.

"Jude, cool to see you. Well, it would be, in better circumstances. All right. There's something off and..." Aidan began, before pausing thoughtfully. Aidan was a member of the Seminole tribe of Florida and he had the striking strong cheekbones of his lineage and a talent for finding the smallest speck of evidence that had kept him in demand with local, state, and federal authorities.

Aidan, like Dr. Dresden, worked for the Florida Department of Law Enforcement—which again left Jude wondering why he had been called in since he was federal when it seemed the groundwork was being carried out by the state. He hoped that someone in the hierarchy hadn't demanded the feds take the case. He hated stepping on toes and in jobs that demanded the best from everyone. It wasn't pleasant to work when resentment was in the mix.

"Marci Warden, thirty-three, single, parents deceased, one sister in Nevada, no known significant other at the moment, receptionist at the law firm of Wharton, Dixon, and Smith."

"Time of death approximately eight hours ago. Exsanguination," Dr. Dresden added. He winced, shaking his head. To examine the body, he had been forced to stand in the pool of bloody water.

"This looks like a tragic and horrid accident," Jude said.

What else? A very strange murder, if that was the case. Suicide? And why am I here?

"Was she a suspect in organized crime, in serial murder, in a major federal crime?"

"No, local police checked her record. She doesn't even have parking tickets," Aidan told him.

"A romance gone bad?" Jude murmured. "Fingerprints? Skin or foreign substances under her fingernails?" Jude asked. "Have you gotten that far? In this mess of water and blood with everything soaked, can you get anything? Any signs of a break-in or other areas of struggle?"

Aidan shook his head. "The only fingerprints are hers. Scanned what the techs picked up and they're hers. Hands are clean, nothing under the nails. We do think it's a break-in, though. Just not the usual kind."

"You've lost me there. So. Someone was here?"

"Not physically," Aidan said.

"Okay. Suicide? How did she slit her own throat with an electric knife? Not that hard, I'd imagine—but then again, I must admit I haven't tried it," Jude told him, grimacing.

However gruesome, the scene truly appeared to be that of a tragic accident. He wasn't lacking in empathy; he just couldn't figure out how they were considering the scene to be a homicide.

And who would kill themselves in such a horrific manner? Had the knife done the trick, or had she been bleeding out when the spraying water and flying cord caused a lethal electric jolt? Exsanguination, Dr. Dresden had said.

"Not physically. But if not a suicide, then someone, somehow, made her do this to herself? They would have had to come in here in some physical manner, right?" Jude asked.

"No. We've been asked to investigate this as a murder," Aidan said. "By, um, your people."

"My people—as in the Bureau? Hey, I'm always happy to work with you guys," Jude said, "but a single incident that appears accidental or even suicidal but may have magically been murder…why bring in the feds?"

"As I said, the powers that be—local, state, and federal—are suspecting something else," Aidan told him. "We don't understand everything. A neighbor called it in when they saw the house behaving weirdly—"

"The *house* was behaving weirdly?" Jude asked.

"Horrendously loud music, lights flashing... Anyway, he called his headquarters right when information had come in. They called state, Dresden was called in, I was called in, and—"

"This whole thing is confusing, but it will all be straightened out as far as chain of command. Or responsibility," Dr. Dresden said dryly. "But I need to be able to call my people in and get the body to the morgue," he continued. "I'm willing to bet my preliminary assessment is correct—yes, what's obvious is obvious. She would have bled to death if it hadn't been for the electrocuting jolt that I believe stopped her heart. I don't think I'll find anything other than that, but we won't know until the full autopsy is complete."

Dresden was a good man. Jude had worked with him before, and his preliminary assessments tended to be right on, but he was always determined to know everything before ruling a death as natural, accidental—or homicide. He was a man in his late forties, lean and fit, just beginning to go gray, and on the nerdy side with steel-rimmed glasses. He had been working as an ME for over twenty years.

"All right," Jude said. "Forgive my confusion. There's no indication anyone was in the house with her. The method of death is an electric knife that only she handled. The cause of death is exsanguination or electrocution, both brought about by an electric knife and a faulty faucet—"

"Boy, you are old-school," a voice murmured from the entry.

Jude turned quickly to see that a woman was there, a young brunette in a dark blue pantsuit—hands in gloves and feet in crime scene booties. Her hair was rigidly coiled as if even a single escaped strand might suggest inexperience.

"I'm old-school, and pardon me, but just who the hell are you?" he demanded.

"Special Agent Victoria Tennant," she said, walking toward him. "Or Vicky. And yes, pardon me, but you're missing the big picture here."

He looked down at the corpse and the pools of blood, then back at her.

"Oh, I'm seeing a pretty big picture. There's the corpse of a woman who died a horrific death. But the finest forensic expert I have ever worked with is telling me that there is no sign of a break-in, no unidentified fingerprints, partial or otherwise, no evidence by the body, and no marks from self-defense—no suggestion that another person did this to her," Jude said.

"Again, you are missing a bigger picture," she told him.

He frowned. "Again, I've worked this area for several years, Special Agent Victoria Tennant, and I'd like to understand why we've never met."

"I was sent for this specifically because I've worked in both the profiling or behavioral science unit and the Geek Squad—sorry, Cybercrime—divisions," she told him.

"We couldn't even get in here until Vicky got things…settled," Aidan told him.

"What?" Jude asked, frowning.

"I hacked in to take Marci Warden's system offline because we couldn't take a chance on the doctor or Aidan or any other member of the forensic crew winding up in the same way—"

"You've been in here already?" Jude interrupted.

"Yes. No. Not exactly. Look, no, I only just got here and I'm not trying to step on toes," she said. "The patrolman called it in. Information on a few other situations just hit the desks of the higher-ups across the nation, and the patrolman was ordered to stand down because the entire house was still in motion. I was called to deal with it."

"The house was in motion?" he repeated. "And you were called."

"Yes," she said, and though she was trying to appear as if she was giving him due respect, he could almost hear her inward sigh of impatience. "Sir, you must have heard about these systems. Every major tech company out there has one. Artificial intelligence that turns your lights on and off, manages security systems, music, water…you name it. Most people just use it for their televisions, phones, lights, and security but Marci had everything in her house geared up to work by voice control. She called her system Chrissie, and it appears that Chrissie went crazy—glitched."

"All right, so we're looking at an accident," he said. "A computer glitch."

"No. Yes—"

"And I'm missing the bigger picture?" he asked dryly.

"All right, I'm trying to explain. We believe there is someone out there causing these computer glitches, and *we're* here—federal agents—because this is the third time that we've come across such a similar situation," she told him.

"What?"

She took another deep breath as if explaining anything to him was going to be far more difficult than solving any crime. "They all look like accidents."

"But computers do have glitches," he said.

She nodded. "Yes, things can go wrong. A computer is a machine. That's why people backup their work to the cloud or when you're driving an automatic car, you must still be sober and you can't go to sleep."

"But people do drink and/or fall asleep," he said.

"Yes, they do, and that will be a problem as we move into the future, and there will be more and more on the road. But it's not…okay. Most of the time when there's a computer glitch in these systems, someone just needs to turn the lights on manually and check the problem. Defense can be simple—good firewalls, antivirus protection. But the rise of technology has brought about a new breed of criminal, the hacker. Anyway, three incidents were brought to our offices—and yeah," she admitted dryly, "we were alerted by a computer system. We began to believe there was a serious problem out there." She hesitated. "There's the standard meme—technology is wonderful—when it works. But..." She looked at him earnestly. "There are those people who can breach just about any firewall and even hack into some car computer systems. It's possible to cause a car to crash, or at the very least take control of it. There are those who fear that major transportation fields—trains and planes—can also be hacked. Major businesses can be hacked by anyone who can manipulate code, break firewalls, understand algorithms, and get behind any technological security. Therefore, it's more than possible to take control of a home computer system."

"Okay, let me see if I understand this," Jude said. "This poor woman was murdered because someone took control of her home computer. Someone made her knife jump out and attack her? Turned her water on to make sure it would soak an electric outlet and cause her to be electrocuted if the knife didn't do the job."

"Exactly," she said.

Dr. Dresden cleared his throat and spoke again. "Aidan has done what forensics can. So, am I going to call my people in to retrieve the body?" he asked.

Jude, still looking at the newcomer, nodded.

"We'll step out, they can step in. And then, Special Agent Tennant, you can explain to me more of what is going on here," he said.

"You weren't told you were meeting me here?" she asked him.

"I was told I'd be meeting another agent. I'd assumed—

never mind. Let's get out of the way and the doctor can bring his people in," Jude said.

She turned around and walked out to the front lawn. He followed her. And the situation seemed even more bizarre to him.

Inside, the scene was so horrific. Yet, outside…

It was a beautiful day. The sky was a brilliant blue and their victim had kept up a charming yard with flower beds in small brick planters that enhanced the entrance and a few towering trees by the walkway. As he'd noted, a crystal blue sky with little puffs of clouds floated overhead.

She walked to the side as the peaceful vision of the day was slammed back to reality when Dr. Dresden's people entered with their gurney to collect the corpse.

Yes, he *had* known he'd be meeting someone from the main offices up in DC. That hadn't been any kind of a surprise. Since the case in Colorado, he'd been working with a new partner or team wherever he was assigned.

So, no surprise. She simply wasn't what he had expected—starting off by telling him he was old-school and a house had killed a woman.

Young and impatient. She was professional to a fault…yet she still appeared to be more likely to walk down a runway than take on deadly cybercriminals. And he wasn't an idiot—their cybercrime units were huge across the country, following money trails, breaking through firewalls, finding the online evidence needed to take down the biggest thieves, scammers and manipulators out there.

But a house that killed?

She was looking at him. Awaiting his questions.

"All right. I need to understand more of what is going on. And go slow. Old-school, you know," he told her.

She nodded. "Just like most of the world," she told him, "people are worried about AI, and in a way… Well, here, of course…" She looked toward the house. "People don't realize how much AI they're already using. There's a combination of tech and AI in almost everything we do, down to simple editorial assistance in writing programs. Anyway, AI and tech can be combined in some instances, and someone determined to play havoc can do so. New cars may have computers which can work wonderfully by warning a driver when something mechanical is necessary, allowing for warnings when something is near, or when danger is imminent. There are well over a thousand internet service providers out there, some huge, some small...but a brilliant hacker can get into any of them, no matter the firewalls or virus protection."

"I understand that computers—just like social media—can be a benefit and a detriment," Jude told her. "What I'm still not getting is...what are you implying? My God, computers committing crimes? I understand—I think. I was at a meeting recently where we were discussing the changes in the Bureau. We were once fighting organized crime, major 'families' and other criminal concerns. And now we investigate drugs, try to control the cartels if not stop them, and we still have major organized crime. But the cyber division is huge and dealing with white-collar crime and big money. When someone is seen as a danger to the major players in a drug cartel, they usually meet a bullet."

"And a bullet is obviously murder. Proving that a situation like this isn't an accident is difficult. And yes, to most people, it might look like a technical accident—a glitch. But I told you, we're looking into two other cases. A car accident—"

"A car accident?" Jude asked.

"New cars run on computer systems. And systems can be hacked. The car accident never should have happened. It was in Tennessee on a quiet road that led out of Nashville toward Nunnelly. The driver was just driving straight on a road that maybe sees a hundred cars in a day. Surrounded by farms and ranches and...trees. The driver suddenly picked up speed and crashed straight into a massive oak at the side of the road. The airbag didn't go off," she explained.

He shook his head. "That's tragic. But wouldn't the car company be at fault?"

"In the world of the law, yes. But..." She hesitated. "All right, look. I am a field agent, so I don't understand everything that one of the truly brilliant technical analysts knows, but for everything that went wrong to go wrong...there had to be interference."

"You're telling me any hacker can—"

"No, no, not any hacker, just a *really* good hacker. No, a brilliant hacker. And that's—"

"All right, you believe you know that someone hacked into a car system in Tennessee—"

"Exactly."

"And you can prove this?"

"It's a new world, so, as I said, things are often hard to prove, but it wasn't just the accident. It was who it happened to."

"And who did it happen to?"

"Judge Ian McFarlane, known to many in the area as the Hanging Judge."

"All right, a man who might have many enemies. And I assume anyone he handed a harsh sentence to might have reason for revenge, and someone on the outside might be able to find vengeance. But this woman, this poor woman, she wasn't a judge. She was a receptionist," Jude said. "I hardly think anyone would kill over being told they had to wait to see someone for a few minutes. Then again..."

"Sir!" Vicky Tennant snapped, somehow making him feel very old. "She was a receptionist, yes, and that's part of the point here. She was a receptionist for Wharton, Dixon, and Smith, one of the largest law firms in the area. That means she might have known something that made her dangerous to someone. And before today, law enforcement was baffled by another incident that took place out at sea."

"A boat went crazy?" he asked. "Wait. A little while back, I think I saw something about a speeding boat wrecking, but I'm not sure they thought it was anything other than a drunken boater or an accident."

"It was a yacht, a forty-two-footer called the *Lucky Sun*. Again, it just suddenly picked up speed and slammed straight into a jetty in Matanzas Bay. The captain, Ronald Quincy, chef, mate, and a party of three were killed. The *Lucky Sun* was owned by the captain, a man suspected of having found the wreck of a speedboat carrying a huge cache of fentanyl and selling it rather than reporting it."

"And therefore, someone might have wanted to kill him for the fentanyl having killed a loved one?" he queried.

He knew about the yachting accident. He'd seen it on the news; people had talked about it at the office. But the agency hadn't been involved and everyone had assumed it was a sad accident. Or they'd thought maybe there's been a little too much alcohol or other mind-altering substances involved. Living near the water, they'd seen too many accidents caused by alcohol or drugs. And the captain of the *Lucky Sun* had been a suspected dealer, so…

She was studying him. "Exactly," she told him.

"A house, a car, and a boat," Jude said. "And you believe the computer systems on each were hacked, and the 'accidents' were caused by a hacker."

"It didn't come from me. It came from Assistant Director Arnold."

Jude nodded. He knew, of course, because his field director had gotten word to send him out straight from Arnold.

But he still shook his head.

"Old-school!" he told her. "I can't begin to understand—"

His words were cut off as a shot suddenly rang out. Instinctively, he shouted, "Down!"

Of course, Special Agent Victoria Tennant might look like a runway model, but she had made her way through Quantico—she was already down on the ground.

He stayed down himself, drew his gun, mentally tracking the trajectory of the shot and rising with his Glock out.

More shots rang out; a blue van was moving down the street. He aimed at the van, as did Special Agent Tennant.

"Tires!" he shouted to her.

"Got it! The plate muddied, purposely, no readable number," she shouted back.

She had given him heed; her shots slammed into the tires as well.

They didn't need a computer. The van careened off the side of the road. They saw an armed man hop from the driver's seat and take off into one of the neighboring yards.

They tore after him. The wrecked van was just three houses down. Jude motioned to her, and they tore around the house closest to the vehicle and each took a side.

They met coming around the back. Their suspect had disappeared.

"The house?" Victoria Tennant asked quietly.

"Or the fence," Jude suggested. He inclined his head toward the rear of the yard. The fence that lined the back of the property was wooden and about seven feet high.

"Only if he's a red kangaroo or something like that," Vicky observed.

"No, vines—"

"I'll take the house—you look in back," she suggested.

He nodded. They split. Vicky headed toward the rear door of the ranch-style home; Jude took off for the rear of the property.

Vines laced the far elm by a giant banyan tree. He knew how their suspect had escaped. He grabbed hold of a vine, which wasn't strong enough for his weight, but with it, he could maneuver his body against the tree easily enough to push himself up to catch the top of the fence and hike himself up and over.

He'd barely hit the ground before he heard Vicky's voice quietly calling to him.

"The owners are fine, the house is empty. I'm also playing kangaroo," she said.

"Going forward, back of the house here," he told her.

She was fast; he had to give her that. She landed on her feet at his side in a second, indicating the home here on this side of the fence. He nodded, knowing from the incline of her head that he should take the back while she walked around to the front.

He headed toward the rear of the property as she ran around.

There was an open pool there along with a screened patio. He noted the screened door into that patio was ajar.

He slipped in quietly.

As with so many such homes, there were double-glass doors leading to a family room at the rear of the house. Down a small distance was another set of doors—the kind that usually led to the master bedroom. He heard the doorbell ring and then a woman's muffled cry.

He eased against the glass, trying to carefully see what was happening inside.

And listen.

The man, their shooter, was there holding onto a woman. She looked to be about fifty, gray-haired, casually dressed…

As if she'd just been home relaxing for the day.

"Answer it! Answer it and get rid of them. You're alone here, all alone. If you had a problem, you'd dial 911 immediately. But you don't have a problem. Get rid of them now, or you get a bullet in the back of your head! Do you understand?"

"Yes, yes, yes, please!"

Jude watched as she walked to the front door. She opened it cautiously. The man stood behind her.

He couldn't imagine what Vicky Tennant intended to say. Surely, the suspect had seen her and had to know who she was. She couldn't pretend to be the Avon lady.

"Hi!" Vicky said cheerfully. "We're just checking on people, making sure they're all right. We're afraid we have a fugitive in the area, and we're just going door to door!"

He didn't dare break the glass here or even try the door. He'd be seen instantly and that might well kill the man's hostage. But there was a cup on a small table just outside the glass doors to the bedroom.

He hoped Vicky could keep talking; he just needed a few seconds.

As he'd hoped, the doors to the bedroom were open. He slid in quickly and headed to the hall, moved along it, and paused at the end with his Glock pointed at the suspect. He had a shot; he could only pray that it was clear enough.

"Well, that's it!" Vicky was saying cheerfully. "As I said, we were just checking up on people!"

"FBI! Let her go!" Jude shouted.

He'd had the element of surprise. The man turned to stare at him. He seemed an unlikely suspect, no more than in his mid-twenties, with long unkempt hair; he looked more like a skateboarder than a desperate fugitive.

Why is he a fugitive? Why the hell did he go by the house to shoot at us? We're in plainclothes. But under the circumstances, with the morgue vehicle still in front, it had probably been obvious we were the law enforcement looking into the incident.

Split seconds. Split seconds could mean everything.

Startled, the man had moved the gun from the back of the woman's head. But he was going to act and act quickly.

Jude took aim, but even as he did so, the door suddenly slammed inward.

Hard. Slamming the woman and the man against the wall.

Vicky stepped in as the man's gun flew from his hand. The

woman fell back on the floor screaming, and the man—minus his weapon—took off around the now open door, slamming her hard against it as he flew out, making it impossible for her to stop him.

Jude ran after the shooter. And he was faster. Vicky was on his tail, but he knew he'd get the man before he reached the road.

And he did. But even as he catapulted at their strange attacker, the man put his hand to his mouth.

Jude slammed him to the ground, face down, then rose above him and demanded, "Hands, behind your back, now."

There was no response.

Vicky had arrived; her gun was aimed at the suspect.

Puzzled, Jude rolled him over.

The man's eyes were open wide. Foam was forming on his lips and dripping down his cheek.

"My God!" Vicky breathed. She had her phone out and identified herself. She asked for an immediate ambulance.

Then she dropped down on her knees by the man's side, trying to talk to him. "What did you take? What did you do? Whatever is going on, whoever these people are, they're not worth dying for!" she told him.

He'd started to shake. More foam was forming.

But Jude could swear there were suddenly tears in his eyes.

Just what the hell is going on?

He obviously couldn't talk; he wasn't going to tell them anything. But beyond a doubt—knowing that he was cornered, he'd chosen to take his own life rather than talk.

Vicky glanced at Jude. "Cyanide?" she asked. "Did he take a suicide pill? Why? Why would he do this?"

"Because he's been threatened with worse than death," Jude said.

He was glad to see Dr. Dresden and Aidan were hurrying

toward them, even as they heard the sirens coming toward the street.

Dr. Dresden was quickly down by the man, studying him, searching his eyes. “Injection in my bag…speed can matter, hydroxocobalamin. Man, I’d love to keep this one off my table!”

“Doc, when you can, I need his ID, wallet, phone…after you’ve saved his life, if possible!”

“Yeah, let me get the injection in him… I’ve got a living patient. I’d like to keep him that way.”

“Definitely!” Jude agreed. “He’s still…”

They were all quiet for a second. Then Dresden said, “We made it just in time.”

“Thank God you were close,” Jude told him quietly.

Dresden smiled, and Jude imagined that saving a life instead of investigating a death was a good moment for him.

“He’s still got a rough road ahead of him, but he’s got a hell of a chance. Doesn’t appear he’s abusing drugs or alcohol and…”

He frowned. He’d been checking the man’s pockets. He looked at Jude, shaking his head. “Nothing. No phone, no wallet, not a scrap of paper.”

“Thanks, Doc. Make sure they check his prints, dental records—”

“Of course,” Dresden said.

“I’m going back to check on the woman,” Vicky said, rising and nodding to Dr. Dresden. “She may need medical help, too.”

She walked back to the woman’s house. Jude waited for the EMTs to arrive and for Dresden to tell them what he had done and what to report to the doctors at the hospital. He was glad to see the EMT was already radioing the hospital to inform them of the situation.

As Dresden attended to the medical information needed, Jude called his SAC regarding the events. Then as the EMTs and their patient took leave, he looked to Aidan and Dr. Dresden.

"Every time I think I've seen it all," he murmured.

"You realize you never will," Aidan finished for him. "Dresden is headed in. I'm going to find out whatever I can about that van. You'll have our reports by morning."

"I'll wait a few minutes for the ambulance to arrive. Call if anyone else needs medical help," Dresden told Jude.

"Thanks."

He nodded and headed for the house. Vicky had the woman comfortably seated on the sofa; she had gotten her a glass of water. She didn't appear to be injured, just shaken.

"Jude, this is Mrs. Gail Meyers," Vicky said. "She works at the supermarket, but today is her day off. Her husband has been out of town on business, but he's on his way home to be with her now."

"I'm glad to hear that," Jude said.

"Never, never, never..." the woman was muttering. "This neighborhood... I've lived here for thirty years. It's a good neighborhood. We watch out for one another. And then... then right before, there was something on the news... They weren't using her name, but they showed the house and, of course, I know the house and... Oh, it's all so horrible. I don't understand, they were saying her house went crazy. I didn't even know that a house *could* go crazy but..."

"Right now," Jude said quietly, "the important thing is this, are you all right? When the door opened—"

"I took the chance and fell!" she exclaimed. "His hold on me eased... I think he knocked his head against the wall, and it made him dizzy and... He was going to kill me! He didn't care if he died. He just wasn't going to be caught. He swore that he'd kill me! Why? Why... I'm so scared, so scared, so scared!"

"He's on his way to the hospital—" Vicky began.

"He did hurt his head?" the woman asked.

"He's in bad shape, but...that's not his main problem. He

took something. He was terrified of being caught," Jude told her. "We don't know if he'll make it or not."

"He didn't look good," Vicky said.

"Is it terrible? I hope… I can't hope he dies. I'm too, um, religious for that, except that, God forgive me, in my heart of hearts… But, of course, you're trying to save him?" she asked.

"We need to find out why he was shooting at us, why he attacked you, and why he would be so desperate that he would try to kill himself rather than allow himself to be arrested," Jude explained. "But he can't hurt you."

"So," Mrs. Meyers looked confused, "he broke in here because he'd been shooting at you? Why was he shooting at you?"

"That's what we don't know," Jude explained. "But you don't need to be so afraid. No one who bribed him, threatened him, or hired him by whatever method to attack us will ever know that he fell at your house. And frankly, they'd have no reason to hurt you. Still, we can see to it a patrol car keeps an eye on you, or—"

"We're going away!" Mrs. Meyers said. "My husband and I… We'll leave as soon as he gets home, and we'll go visit my son in New York."

"That sounds fine. We'll just need a bit of paperwork first," Vicky explained. She tried to smile and speak lightly. "There's always paperwork, you know that. Simple. Just your statement!"

"Of course, of course, thank you! Thank you! You saved my life! I guess… I take it that you are cops?"

"FBI," Vicky said.

"Whatever," she told them. "Thank you!"

"We're just happy you're okay," Vicky assured her. "So… local police are on the way, and they'll speak with you and…"

"And we'll have to go in to do our paperwork," Jude said wearily. He glanced at Vicky. It was late, but there was no helping it.

"Don't leave me, don't leave me!"

"I won't. Not until someone arrives," Vicky promised.

Jude nodded.

They waited for the local police to arrive; when they did, they left the house at last. Vicky paused to stare at Marci Warden's house.

"What?" he asked.

She shook her head. "Working on the *why*. But I'll bring you up to speed on everything else as soon as we get through the paperwork here at the local headquarters. We've been assigned dedicated space in the city for the next few days—or however long the duration of our case. The Jacksonville office isn't far, but we'll be needing to move quickly—"

"The investigation of the shots fired and our suspect will be at the precinct here," Jude said. "No problem. As far as this incident went, we need to debrief at the local station. I know the captain there and he knows… Well, *he* knows what is going on here, though he turned it over quickly. But our strange suspect shot at us on a neighborhood street, and he's heading to a neighborhood hospital and… Damn, it's getting late."

"We both have cars here," she told him. "I'll meet you there."

He nodded. "Debriefing will be fine but then tonight, no matter how late, I need every file and everything you know about these cases and any possible connections… I was sent out so quickly I wasn't aware of everything that had happened before I got here today and—"

"Because we didn't connect the previous cases to this house until today, and today…it all happened *so quickly*!" Vicky explained, interrupting him. "But, um, you're okay with this, right? Working with me."

"I do what I'm asked and give my best as a sworn agent," he said.

She lowered her head, looked up at him, and shrugged.

"Well, as you might be able to comprehend, this case is

complicated. I'm understanding the logic of the powers that be," she told him.

"Oh?"

"Well, I believe I'm the brains of the operation. And you're the brawn," she told him sweetly.

And he was surprised.

Because it had been one hell of a day. One he was still trying to grasp in its entirety, and the hour was late, indeed.

But even so…

She had managed to make him laugh.

TWO

Everyone was tired and confused, which oddly enough Vicky thought made their time at the local precinct go quickly—simply because everyone was determined to work as quickly as possible and get out.

Dr. Dresden was still working and trying to find an ID for the man now fighting for his life in the hospital—the man who had shot at them before taking a suicide pill.

But there was no information yet—except the poison in the pill had been cyanide. His prints weren't anywhere in any system. Dresden would work on dental impressions, and the man's image would be run through facial recognition software.

A computer working again, she thought dryly.

The van that he used to sweep by the house and shoot at them had been stolen days before from an elderly gentleman living in South Georgia. What should have given them something to work on had given them nothing.

Captain Larry Ormond was at the precinct himself and apparently, the man knew Jude well. He shook his head at the events and told them he was glad they were taking the lead;

but, of course, he knew the local police and Florida Department of Law Enforcement would be working and assisting them in any way possible.

The paperwork went quickly. There was little choice—their information was filled with more questions than answers.

Ormond was a large dignified man with snow-white hair and a hard-lined face—evidence, probably, of his rise through the ranks to his position. He had a no-nonsense manner about him and was also capable of common courtesy.

"We've coordinated with our various agencies," he told them as they each signed their last pages. "We have a dedicated workspace that's just on the other side of St. George Street. Jude, you know it. You worked there before during the kidnapping case last year." He shrugged. "It's not quite the Casa Monica, but it's been set up with internet. FDLE is providing the full-time services of Aidan Cypress, and we're sending Cary Simmons first thing in the morning. She is, while local police, truly brilliant on a computer."

"She is," Jude said, nodding, glancing at Vicky as if to make sure she knew they had heard of computers before. "She cracked the codes the kidnappers were using on that case the captain mentioned and gave us a location, and we brought that little girl in alive and well. We'll be delighted to have Cary. Tomorrow morning, we'll be at Marci Warden's office—finding out why in God's name anyone would go through that kind of machination to kill a receptionist. The why can give us the who."

Vicky glanced at Jude again. He might know these people, but he hadn't asked her yet how she'd managed to be involved here so quickly when she worked out of the DC offices.

"And we'll get on that boating 'accident,'" she said.

"Great. Well, our help is a call away at any time. And, of course, it's my city, so keep me in the loop," Ormond told them.

"Absolutely," Jude promised.

"Special Agent Tennant," Ormond said, handing her a slip

of paper. "This is the address of our dedicated space—don't know what else to call it—but it is all set up. I believe you'll find the working conditions there excellent even if it isn't the Casa Monica."

She smiled. "I do love the Casa Monica Hotel, but, sir, I am comfortable just about anywhere."

"Hopefully, you can get some sleep. And hopefully, I can, too."

As they left the office, Jude looked at her. "You've stayed at the Casa Monica?"

"Yes, and I do love it. But I've stayed at some cool bed-and-breakfasts here, too. They were all great as well. I love this city."

"So, you do know it."

"I do. And you?"

He looked straight ahead, smiling. "Yeah, you could say I know it."

"Do you live here?"

"Not now. But I was born here."

"Oh! Well, then, I guess you know it better. Anyway, this place we're going—was it a home?"

"Strangely, once upon a time. It was a funeral home, too. The last owner was a shopkeeper on Aviles Street. He was being robbed at gunpoint—with his daughter in the store—when an off-duty policeman tricked the robbers, brought them down, and saved the man and his kid. In appreciation, the man willed his home to the police department, and the city helped them turn it into dedicated space for law enforcement in the area. It's okay as far as sleeping—the beds are hard, but hey—and the old reception area has desks, state-of-the-art computers, any old-school print periodicals land lines, you name it." He looked her way. "Are you already checked in somewhere?"

She shook her head. "I was just getting here to investigate the boating 'accident' when I got the call about the situation at Marci Warden's house. I had to, um, borrow an office at the airport—"

Jude laughed. "You mean you *commandeered* an office at the airport."

She shrugged. "The powers that be made all the arrangements. Anyway, first up, I got through to the internet provider for Marci's place and got the house taken offline and then drove there, and then…there you were."

"And I guess I was sent because I do know the area, though in this—"

"Two events have now occurred in this area," she reminded him. "The boating accident occurred in Matanzas Bay."

"Right. Now that I'm here, of course, I remember that I saw it in the news—we weren't assigned to it. The local police and the coast guard investigated, and it was chalked up to…well, an accident, a glitch in the yacht's system along with human error," he told her. "You do know, it's a big world. And as you've told me, the world kind of runs on computers these days. So, with all this artificial intelligence going around, is it so surprising that we've had glitches?" he asked her.

"Glitches happen," she said with a sigh. "But you tell me—how many times have you seen an electric knife go crazy and head straight for the jugular?"

He shrugged. "Okay, you've got me there. You've got a car—you know where you're going?"

She nodded. "I might not have been born here, but yes, I know where I'm going. And if not, wow, my phone *does* have GPS."

He groaned. "See you there."

As they left, she winced and hurried to her car.

Great. They've partnered me with a Neanderthal.

Vicky mentally shook her head as she slid into the driver's seat of her company SUV. The strange thing to her was that Special Agent Jude Mackenzie just wasn't that old. He'd grown up in the computer age, too. She'd briefly studied his file; he was thirty-three, he'd worked in the Jacksonville office for the last three years, worked DC before that, and done a stint down in Miami as well. He had received a few commendations, one for bringing down a large drug cartel, another for defusing a situation in which hostages had been involved during a bank robbery, seeing to it that every hostage came out alive *and* that the would-be robbers were arrested.

So…

He was a good action agent. But for this…

He didn't seem to understand the extent to which AI had entered the world.

Well, if nothing else, he had a sense of humor. And he did know the city, but was that going to help them when one of their victims, the judge, had been killed in Tennessee? She wasn't sure a physical location was going to matter, no matter how much hands-on work they could do on the victims and their lives. These crimes needed the expertise of their "geek" squad, and they had a heck of a good crew working at the main office.

Of course they were still working. She could handle a good amount on a computer herself, but she was far from the "brilliant" some of their people offered.

And that they would need.

Then again, she thought dryly, in their age of tech, they could all be together virtually in a matter of seconds.

But on the ground…well, maybe…

They needed an agent like Jude Mackenzie, one who knew people, variables, and the landscape.

Marci Warden's law firm and home were both in St. Augustine. The drive to the office they'd call home for the next few days wasn't far. But as she drove, Vicky noticed a dark SUV just like hers had been traveling close behind her for some time. That made her smile. Special Agent Jude Mackenzie was on her tail every step of the way. She was tempted to see if she could lose him, but playing games at this point didn't seem like a good way to start a working relationship, especially after she had told him he was the "brawn." Now, brawn itself wasn't bad—suggesting he hadn't the "brains" might not have been that polite. But he had laughed. So maybe that was okay. And chasing their shooter...

They had communicated easily when dealing with the shooter through nods and looks that were easily understood. It was going to be a decent work situation, except...

They were traveling into relatively new territory. Virtual territory that translated to murder. Handling a situation on the ground with flesh and blood suspects and physical buildings was one thing. Stopping a machine...

That was another.

Except there was someone out there manning the machine. And only by following the clues could they possibly discern just what was going on and who was commanding it all.

Now, it was time to study the victimology, to use everything the computer age they were investigating could possibly give them.

She was surprised when her phone rang. She'd been given Jude Mackenzie's number earlier, so it pinged into her directory.

"We're almost there," he told her. "This place is right off Aviles..."

"The oldest street in America," she told him, unable to resist letting him know she knew something about the area as well.

"It has a horseshoe driveway where we can park. No gates, though there's an old coquina wall around the place, open at the driveway and the walk."

"Gotcha," Vicky assured him. "Any security?"

"An alarm system and a code for the door."

"Ah, AI at work!"

He groaned and added, "Ormond just told me he heard from Cary Simmons. She and Aidan are already inside, and they'll be working anything we get from the brilliant folks in cybercrime and elsewhere, and they will also be chasing down leads themselves. Oh, and we're within easy walking distance to both St. George Street and Aviles so we're conveniently near lots of food."

"That's always good," she told him. "Meet you there. I have folders—my computer and some print files—"

"For us old, old-school people, huh?"

She laughed softly. "Paper is good stuff when you've been staring at a computer too long," she told him. "See you."

Ten minutes later she had parked. They were across the road, but as Jude had mentioned, she could see they were near to both St. George Street and Aviles, which made sense since the streets were close to one another. Getting out of the car, she thought about the many times she'd been here with her family when she was a child. St. Augustine wasn't a huge city like nearby Jacksonville or Ft. Lauderdale or Miami down in the south of the state. But to her, it had always been magical. She loved that it was the "first" city in so many ways, including being the home of Potter's, the first wax museum. She also loved the Pirate and Treasure Museum, and especially the Lightner Museum, which was housed in the old Hotel Alcazar, an amazing gilded age resort and spa commissioned by Henry Flagler. And for hardier souls, there was even the Medieval Torture Museum on St. George Street.

Of course, St. Augustine also offered beaches, beautiful beaches…

Jude had parked and gotten out of his car as well.

"Uh, are you okay?" he asked her.

"Yeah, fine. Just thinking about different times here."

"The city is rich in history," he agreed. "And sometimes, when it's two in the morning as it is now," he added dryly, "you can look down the old streets and feel as if you've really traveled back a few centuries."

He stood still, just looking out into the night.

"Jude?" she murmured.

He shook his head and then turned to her. "Sorry. I was just thinking. We're in the oldest city in the United States—or more technically, the oldest continually inhabited European settlement in the United States—investigating a murder that might have occurred because of the most modern technology we have in the world today. Where does it lead?" he asked quietly.

"I guess we fight new battles every decade," she said. "Everything new has its wonders and its detriments."

"I know, but this AI—"

"Your smartphone is AI!" she reminded him.

"Right. Yeah. Sorry. Again, just thinking. There's a viral ad I'm sure you've seen about a guy who can't remember where he parked his car. He presses a button on his phone and locates it immediately—and with the press of another button it starts and drives to him! So, it makes sense. If he can control his car with his phone..."

"Then someone else can control his car by hacking in on it, right," she said quietly.

"Right. So, the judge who ran into a tree at a zillion miles an hour could have been murdered. And a modern yacht? I guess you're right, and it could have had such a system, too. So someone could have broken into that system and murdered all aboard. It just makes me curious. How do we—"

"Firewalls. Encryption. Spyware, all kinds of protections—"

"Those can be breached," he reminded her. "According to you, anything can be breached by a good hacker."

"But not by many people. And usually those who can are not homicidal. Tech departments are trying to get through all the IP networks connected to various sites, but we're the ones who need to find out why anyone would want to do this to someone else."

"And we think it's the same person or people," Jude murmured. "All right, then, let's get to it. We're going to have to go to Marci's law offices—"

"When they're open. It is late, you know. Sorry. Now it's early. Too early."

He laughed at that. "Good point. Need any help with your things?"

"One suitcase, my shoulder bag, and a briefcase. The Bureau taught me never to travel with anything I can't manage myself."

"Ah, but never turn down help when it's offered," he reminded her.

She laughed. "It's okay. Get your stuff—and get us inside!"

They gathered their things, and Jude punched in the code to open the front door. The house had been set up for office work with no frills. They entered to see a long stretch of desks with computers and good swivel chairs. A large screen was attached to the far wall, which allowed for pertinent information to be shared by all—*even the nearsighted*, Vicky thought. But it was a good place.

And they weren't alone in it.

She'd met Aidan at Marci Warden's house. He was now working beside a young woman with short dark hair and a quick smile. Both had been busy at their computers when they'd entered, and both rose to welcome them.

"Hey, welcome to Motel Hell!" the young woman said.

"Oh, come on, it isn't that bad!" Aidan protested. "I was particularly fond of the fact there is a kitchen and they stocked it. Sorry, after what we saw this morning… I was still starving by the time we got here. There's food. I doubt if you guys have eaten."

"We have not," Jude said, stepping forward to meet the young woman. "Cary Simmons?" he asked.

"Yes, sir. Just Cary. I'm not a special or any kind of agent. I'm tech," she said, still smiling, shaking his hand, and looking past him to Vicky. "Hi!"

"Cary, hey. And you and Aidan are still awake. So, you're dedicated—or simply crazy," Vicky told her, smiling and shaking her hand as well.

"Both," Aidan assured her. "We've gotten all the information regarding the case in Tennessee. We've been trying to find a connection between the accidents."

"Anything yet?"

"Well, the judge and the captain of the boat were both hated—so we have long lists on them. Not to mention that Captain Ronald Quincy's first mate of the *Lucky Sun*, Jeremy Hart, was just paroled out of the federal prison down in the south of the state—he'd been convicted in a child pornography sting. The chef seems to have been nothing other than a chef—no criminal record. And the other three men aboard appear to be tourists out for a day's fishing, but they were prosecutors from Virginia, so..."

"Who was the target, the drug pusher, the pornographer, or the prosecutors?" Jude murmured.

"We're trying to pin down associates or anyone that all of them may have known," Aidan assured him.

"Or it was an accident. As in one or two of the incidents were accidents, and just one person was targeted, or computer glitches can kill—" Jude said.

"No! Don't start!" Vicky moaned. "Artificial intelligence is just that—computers can juggle all kinds of information, work off algorithms, and so much more. But they are also fed information. And a good hacker—"

"Can get past any firewall or security," Aidan finished for her, grimacing at Jude. "That's the point—*artificial.* A computer—or system—must be fed information to work."

"Sorry, okay, whatever," Jude murmured. "Sorry!" he said to Cary who had sat silently, just looking distressed, throughout their discussion. "Okay, let's pretend I'm totally convinced there is a person or a cult of brilliant people who are killing others through artificial intelligence systems. Either there's a connection through victims, or they have a murder-for-hire thing going on. That's something we need to be looking for."

Vicky nodded, still doubtful that the "brawn" was really on their side.

"That's true. But if so…"

"It's terrifying for the future," Aidan said. "Luckily, it's difficult to get so good at all this that you can hack through systems easily. But for now, we'll keep seeking the connection. On the one hand, someone might have gone after the fishing boat captain because he caused a loved one to die through his tainted drugs. The police were gathering evidence and it seems he was a pusher. So. Revenge. But there could be something else, so…"

"You're looking into the three fishermen, the prosecutors? There is something there. A judge, prosecutors—and a receptionist from a law firm?" Jude suggested.

"Of course, we're on it!" Cary assured him.

"And sleep?" he suggested.

"Well, the accommodations aren't so great," Cary said. "But there are two bathrooms. Aidan said it was all right when I claimed the front bathroom, but of course you two are the field agents—"

"And you are probably much more important on this case than either of us," Jude assured her. "But the sleeping—"

"Go check it out," Aidan said dryly.

Jude looked at Vicky, arching a brow. He indicated she should go first to choose a sleeping place from what was left.

She nodded and headed for the hall.

The place had, indeed, been outfitted for work. The old house had been transformed into something of a dorm—with fewer amenities. There were several rooms with a small closet, a small dresser, and a bed with a pillow, sheets, and blanket.

"Um, not much different. Guess I'll crash in here," she told him, choosing a room on the left.

"Guess I'll take this across the hall." He shrugged. "I am tired enough to drop so this should work."

She nodded. "Me, too. I guess. I'll tell Aidan and Cary good-night—and suggest they're better at their work when they're awake, too."

He nodded as he went into the small bedroom he'd chosen. But he turned back around to follow her.

"Don't get me wrong," he told her. "I might not be Mr. Cyber Genius or even Mr. Cyber Fairly Intelligent. But I do have tremendous respect for those who are. And Aidan is one smart man, and I'm sure Cary is equally as talented."

She smiled and nodded at him. Maybe he was finally really getting it.

They walked back out to find that both Cary and Aidan were busy at their computers again.

"Guys, great minds need sleep!" she reminded them.

"Oh, yeah, well, we've got this thing going so one of us needs to be watching at all hours," Aidan said.

"I'm on now for a while," Cary told her. "Aidan started early. I was already on the night shift. Make him get some sleep."

She looked at Aidan.

"Yeah, yeah, I'm going!" he told her. "Just…yeah. All right, Cary, I'll take over at eight, sound good?"

"Lovely," she assured him.

Aidan looked at Vicky. "Sometimes…if we're on the right track, we might see something going on that can be stopped."

"Then you two need to work, work, work!" she told him. She shook her head in a way that assured them both she knew just how hard they *did* work. "It's always incredible when you get to stop something bad before it happens!"

"Yeah, like us getting shot," Jude said thoughtfully.

"And if only we could have stopped that man…"

"Yes, I agree," Jude told her. "I certainly didn't expect the man to stuff a pill in his mouth. And still, I'm glad to be standing here. And we know any situation with a shooter could be them—or one of us. Well, I'll be happier when I'm lying down somewhere. So, you guys…figure it out, sleep when you like, as for me…"

"No cyber genius," Vicky said sweetly. "But he does think you guys are great!"

"Thanks!" Cary said, smiling.

Aidan grinned. "Jude's all right. We are on it. And we're not alone. FDLE, police, and feds are all in the game, too. We're sharing information—very carefully. When we know something, we don't want the hacker to know that we know what we know—no problem at this particular moment since we don't know that much yet!"

"You'll get there. And I'm getting to bed," Jude said. "Good night, all."

He disappeared down the hallway. Vicky looked after him.

"Hey, he really is a topnotch agent," Aidan said quietly.

"Oh, of course, I'm sure!" Vicky said. "Anyway, I'm getting some sleep, too." She started for the hallway but paused. "I'm still disturbed about that guy taking a suicide pill. And I'm worried. Someone only does something like that if they're afraid of something worse than death. Like a loved one being tortured or killed."

"Or because they really believe some ridiculous dogma that someone has been spouting," Aidan said. "We've been involved with cults where…where very bad things can happen just because people believe something they've been told."

"I know," Vicky agreed. "I just…" She paused and shrugged. "I guess I'm just worried."

"Because you're somehow an experienced agent and a decent human being. Of course, we all know that we can't—"

"Get personally involved, right," Vicky said.

"There's a fine line. Trust me, we all walk it," he said.

She nodded. "Okay, now I'm really out of here. Well, out of this room and into bed."

"Me, too!"

Aidan walked with her down the hall. They parted ways at the doors to their tiny dorm-style rooms. But as much as she wanted to crash right down on the bed, she opted for a fast shower. The "girls' bathroom" was little more than sufficient, but the water was hot.

And that was what she wanted and needed.

That would help her sleep.

But even crashed onto her bed, she lay awake and relived the incidents of the day. She wondered how well she and Jude would work together once they were able to begin interrogations.

Of course…

She'd called him the brawn.

And when they'd been in trouble, he had had her back and trusted she would have his. That might be the most important key in any such working arrangement.

And still…her mind twisted and turned with the situation.

What they did know. How much they didn't know.

But at some point, she did fall asleep.

And that made it a tremendous jolt into wakefulness when she heard the hard tap at her door.

She had no concept of time, but it couldn't be too late in the morning. The person at her door was Cary Simmons.

"I'm sorry, it's just that I know you were worried and I'm going to call it in, but I wanted to let you know right away. I found your 'dead' man."

"Pardon me?" Vicky said, shaking the last sleep from her mind.

"Facial recognition. Most pictures of the shooter had him with different kinds of facial hair, so the program took a little longer than usual. But the man who took the pill is a fellow named Samuel Hutchins. There's no current address—he was divorced. But his last known address is where his ex-wife, Jessy Hutchins, is living now and I thought—"

"You thought right! Text me the address—"

"I've already got it. She woke me five minutes ago," a voice claimed from the hallway. Jude appeared behind Cary at her open door, fully dressed, professional, ready to move.

"I only need two!" she assured him. "Thank you, Cary!"

She was already closing the door.

Because, as she had promised, she did want to be out of the room in less than two minutes!

Samuel Hutchins had tried to kill himself, she was certain, to protect others.

So, unless there was someone else around on someone's payroll, they shouldn't be in any more danger…

And he had shot at them hours ago.

And still…

Moving quickly seemed to be not just expedient…

Urgent. Desperate…

Whatever. They just had to get there!

THREE

"You do know this fellow's family may have no idea about what he was doing," Jude reminded Vicky.

She nodded, staring straight out the windshield of the car. He was doing the driving today and she couldn't help observing the new and old of the city that had grown from America's oldest European settlement. "I'm not expecting much from them, either. I'm more worried about whoever paid or arranged for this man to kill Marci if she escaped the house. I mean, I'm assuming that's why he was there, for cleanup if necessary. They may go after his family, thinking he might have chickened out on killing himself. And you can't threaten a second round of minions if you don't carry through with the first."

"Whoever is manipulating this may not know the man didn't die," Jude reminded her.

Vicky shook her head. "We live in the information age. With all the events going on yesterday, I'm sure the news has picked up the tragic story of Marci's 'accidental' death, whether they had access to the scene or not. So, they will know they accomplished their goal, but when they don't hear from their man…"

"Why kill the family if he accomplished his goal?" Jude asked. He looked her way quickly. He was concerned but not *worried.* "Vicky, there really shouldn't be a reason that anyone would go after his ex-wife. What other information do we have? You were texted the address—anything else?"

She looked at him grimly. "Two children, five-year-old Chloe and seven-year-old Justin."

"We're almost there. It's going to be all right."

She nodded. "Right. Not that much time has passed. Maybe…it's early. The kids are probably in school, but they might not have started out for the day yet. They need to be in protective custody, Jude."

"Right. We have safe houses in the area. They'll be fine."

The address led them to a section just on the other side of the oldest part of town, a small home but one that offered a Victorian charm from gables to pillars and the small balcony porches on the second floor.

Vicky was unbuckling her seat belt and opening the door before the car was fully in Park. He hurried to join her as she walked up the little tile path to the house.

She knocked quickly, drawing out her ID and calling to the woman inside. "Mrs. Hutchins, we need to speak with you! We're law enforcement and—"

"Show me your badges!" they heard. There was a peephole in the door. Obviously, Jessy Hutchins was being careful.

Why? Is she always smart and wary? Or has her ex given her a reason to be nervous?

They both held up their IDs so she could read them.

The door opened slowly.

Jessy Hutchins was a tall slim redhead, an attractive woman in her late twenties or early thirties. Or she would have been attractive if she weren't so fraught with tension; her features were drawn into a taut knot of apprehension.

"What? What is going on? I… What did I do?" she asked anxiously. "Or…"

"Or what did Samuel do?" Vicky asked gently.

"I… Sam! Is he okay? He's not a terrible person. I mean, he's a good person, we just started fighting so much, and I… He's a good father… Oh, dear God! Please tell me that he's okay. He's not—he's not…" the woman began as tears streamed at the catch in her voice.

"He isn't dead," Jude told her. "But he is fighting for his life in the hospital."

"No!" Tears slid down her face as she stared at them, not wanting to believe what she was hearing.

"Money! Money was tight. And Chloe needs therapy. At first, he kept assuring me he was onto something…he didn't like it but…he didn't understand yet quite what the job was, he was just confused, but then… I think he was worried and then horrified and *scared*, and then he said he didn't like what he was doing but he had no choice, and then he called to tell me I needed to be careful, and…now you're here!" Jessy said.

She was shaking. Jude could imagine that someone had approached the man with a job—just something a little illegal maybe, but one that could give him what he needed for his child.

But then he'd been told what the job was, and if he didn't follow through correctly, if he gave anything away…

His family was dead.

"What is going on?" she whispered.

"We don't know. But we are afraid you and your children might be in danger. And we'd like to set you up in one of our safe houses where you'll be under guard and secure."

"But what happened to Sam?"

Jude glanced at Vicky. She was already looking at him.

The hardest part of the job was dealing with stricken family members. They all learned that lesson, and it was never easy because empathy was a natural reaction. But they couldn't allow themselves to become too personally involved.

"All right, we believe what you're saying is exactly what happened," Vicky said gently. "Someone told Sam they had a job for him that was a little illegal, and it would be explained. Then—"

"Then he was threatened by someone powerful enough to scare him, and—" Jude continued.

"He was afraid he was going to be caught. Even if he kept his mouth shut during any kind of interrogation, you might be in danger," Vicky said. She looked at Jude again and then at Jessy. "I'm so sorry, I can only imagine how painful and frightening this is, but we believe he was dealing with very dangerous people. He knew that and felt he couldn't risk being interrogated." She caught Jude's eye once more, and he knew they were in agreement.

The woman needed the truth.

He nodded and turned his attention to Jessy Hutchins, speaking quietly and gently. "We believe your ex-husband truly loves you and the children. He attempted to take his own life rather than take any chance that you or the children might be in danger," he said.

"Oh, God," she whispered. "Then he..."

"He may make it. The doctors are optimistic," Vicky told her.

"I have to see him!" Jessy said.

Jude shook his head. "Right now, whoever is doing this will assume he's dead. At the very least, they'll believe—or know—that their main mission was carried out as planned. We have agents watching very carefully at the hospital, and we're taking you and the children to a safe house."

"But if they believe—"

"Mrs. Hutchins, we're talking about saving lives here," Vicky reminded her.

"Of course!" the woman said, looking aghast as she stared back at them. "Of course, what am I thinking? Fine—"

"What's a safe house?"

Jude turned. The little boy peeping around the corner to hallway had to be seven-year-old Justin, of course. He was a cute kid with shaggy sandy hair like his dad's. And an inquisitive little face.

Explaining the situation to an adult was hard enough!

But Jude didn't need to worry. Vicky was already on her way over to him, smiling as she knelt to his height. "Justin, right?" she queried first. "I'm Vicky. Your dad is sick at the moment, and I'm afraid you can't see him right now. But we want to take you to a place where you'll be able to see your dad as soon as possible."

"What's the matter with my dad?" Justin asked.

"He's just recovering from some stomach troubles," Vicky supplied. "So—"

"We're going to a safe house place," Justin said. "Mom, we need to pack, right?"

"Yes, we do!" Jessy said.

"Can I have friends over?" Justin asked.

"I'm afraid not," Jude told him.

"That's okay. I can play on my tablet," Justin said. "Right, Mom?"

"Of course—" Jessy began.

"No, I'm afraid not," Vicky began.

Justin was seven. He immediately appeared to be devastated.

"But," Jude said quickly, "we're going to get you a brand-new state-of-the-art tablet, and it will be so, so cool!"

"Oh, wow!" Justin said. "And Chloe, too?" he asked.

"Of course. Chloe, too," Vicky said, looking over at Jude.

Nice to feel that some of my moves and words are appreciated! he thought.

Then Jude looked at Jessy and told her, "No phones, computers, tablets, or anything electronic. We'll supply you with a burner phone and—"

"Get down!" Vicky suddenly shouted.

She threw herself over little Justin as she hit the floor; Jude covered Jessy Hutchins with his bulk, bringing them both to the floor as well.

They barely made it. The front windows of the house exploded inward as the thunderous sound of automatic gunfire sprayed bullets across the walls.

Jude quickly rolled off Jessy, warning her to stay down as he crawled to the front of the house in time to see a blue van disappearing down the street. It was filthy, being covered in dirt and dust that, of course, obscured the license plate.

It would be impossible to chase. He pulled out his phone and called it in quickly to Aidan, knowing Aidan would have every law enforcement officer and agent in the area looking for the dirty blue van.

Jessy was sobbing. Justin was trying to reach his mother.

Vicky was up. "I must find Chloe!" she whispered to him as she quickly made her way down the hallway.

The little girl. Just five years old. He winced but headed out to the front yard. Sirens were blaring. The agents who had been assigned to take Jessy Hutchins and her two children to safety had arrived along with three patrol cars from the local police. He quickly explained the situation; the patrol cars left the matter of the house in the hands of the FBI and went in search of the van he described.

The agents were David Sanchez and Ella Goldman, and they already understood the situation.

"They're shaken, of course. And I haven't seen the little girl myself yet, but..."

"Oh, no, since the shooting?" Ella Goldman asked him. She spoke with empathy but had the look of someone who had been around—and she had been, he knew. He'd worked with her before. She wasn't particularly tall, about five-five, but her face showed lines of past tension, of having been on the job a long time and her dark hair was drawn back severely.

She'd managed to be all the right things, kind and tough as nails all in one.

He shook his head. "Ella, I'm not sure yet. Vicky Tennant is on it."

Ella closed her eyes and winced. "Oh, dear lord—"

"It's all right!"

The call came from the door; he saw Vicky there, stepping out to join them.

"That little girl had some kind of instinct! She got scared when you and I arrived, Jude, so she hid in the closet. She's fine. They're just grabbing a few things and they'll be ready."

"We'll follow you to the safe house and watch for anything around us," Jude said.

"This is so strange," David Sanchez said, shaking his head. He was a young agent, probably a few years younger than Jude, dark-haired, serious. "We've been briefed, of course. But I don't understand. If someone was trying to kill Marci Warden, and it wasn't an accident—which given the circumstances was most likely murder—the woman is still dead. And if Samuel Hutchins was sent in as cleanup, as far an anyone knows, he's dead, too. Why go after his family if he carried out his assignment?"

"Appearances," Vicky said. "Fear factor. A real warning that things must be done exactly as ordered or no quarter will be given."

"But who would want to work for them if they know they'll die if the slightest thing that goes wrong could be a death sentence?" Sanchez asked.

"Desperate people," Vicky said simply.

"Or those experienced criminals they've brought in from elsewhere, perhaps promised that a plan they've wanted put into action for a long time might be carried out as well," Jude said. "For the moment, we've just got to get these guys here to safety and then get on it."

"I'll see what I can do," Ella said. "Maybe I can help with the packing."

"Jessy is good—they're about ready," Vicky said.

Jessy appeared in the doorway as they spoke, just peeking her head out.

"Let's move," Jude murmured.

The four of them went into the house. First, the agents brought out the three bags Jessy had so quickly packed. Jessy also swore to them she'd made sure all electronics had stayed behind. Then with Jessy at David Sanchez's side, Justin with Jude, and little Chloe between Vicky and Ella, they made it out to the agency vehicle David was going to drive. They loaded the family and then were quickly back on the road again. Jude and Vicky followed closely behind, keeping a close eye out for any signs of trouble.

The safe house had a driveway that led behind a high stone wall and security gates. When the group in front of them was through, Jude turned to Vicky.

"Okay?"

She nodded.

"But you were right," he said. "Your instincts are great. I'm not sure what might have happened if we hadn't been there."

His phone rang; it was Aidan.

Jude answered it through the Bluetooth connection in the car, causing Vicky to murmur, "Your technology at work!"

He shrugged as he answered Aidan. "We're both on," he said briefly.

"Cops found the blue van, abandoned, of course," Aidan said.

"And you're going to tell me it was stolen from someone recently," Jude said.

"You got it. Reported stolen from in front of the house of

a Mr. Joseph Kramer just last night. An APB was out on it, but…obscured plates, the dirt actually darkening the color of the BOLO…"

"Naturally," Vicky murmured.

"But I'm heading out with a team. I doubt we'll find fingerprints or anything helpful, but…we'll get into the Hutchins' house as well, collect the bullets… You never know. We may find something helpful…anything."

"Thanks, Aidan. Keep in touch."

"Right."

"Cary will be at the computer, searching IPs, you name it, and…"

His voice trailed.

"And what?"

"She'd never do anything illegal, of course," Aidan said.

Jude grinned. "Of course not."

Cary was probably hacking into Marci Warden's legal firm, or perhaps the judge's private accounts, or those belonging to the men who were killed on the *Lucky Sun*.

"We all know that you two would never dream of anything illegal," Jude assured him.

"Keep us posted, too," Aidan told him.

"Oh, wait, anything new from the hospital?" Vicky asked.

"Nothing new, but the doctors believe they are getting the situation under control and they may be able to bring him out of it and keep him stable as early as tomorrow," Aidan said.

"And the hospital is well-covered. People who know enough to make sure that the hospital staff are really the hospital staff?" Jude asked.

"Yes, absolutely," Aidan said. "Federal, state, country, city—the best of the best are being brought in on this. I've been assured."

"Great. So. We'll let you in on our plans as soon as we've solidified them," he said.

They ended the call and he looked at Vicky again.

"Where do we start?"

"Marci Warden's legal firm," she said. "And—" she shrugged "—from there, well, it is a beautiful day. We can head out to the island and discover what we can at the wreck site."

"Do you dive?" he asked her.

"I do." She frowned. "What do you think we'll find in the water?"

"I never know what we'll find anywhere," he said with a shrug. "A boat wrecked horribly on a jetty. Whatever didn't splinter into a thousand pieces or blew up may still be at the bottom of the bay."

"Police divers were in the water," she told him.

"They were probably hoping to find someone alive—not thinking the yacht might have been hacked. Hey, I'm from here, remember? Cops and coast guard alike spend a lot of time grumbling about the drunk boaters out on the water all the time. Anyway…"

"It's a nice day. You just want to go diving," she said.

He saw she was grinning. He grinned as well.

"Might as well mix business with pleasure. But…"

She frowned, turning to him as he set the car into motion again to head for the law firm.

"What do you think we can find? If I—and other minds above my pay grade—believe the yacht's navigation and controls were hacked, what could be in the water?"

He turned to her in response, grimacing.

"The elements of the navigation and control systems—proof that they were hacked."

"I wonder if that's possible."

"Hey! It's the technological age. We have a few magical technical analysts among our numbers, and you of all people—"

"I can manage my way through many things in the computer age, but I am far from a magician!" Vicky told him.

He grinned. "Thankfully, Aidan is a magician. All worth a good try, fighting in the technological age with technological weapons."

"So, you do get that."

"I get it. I get it. And we're here," Jude said, pulling into a parking space.

He looked up at the building. It was a large modern facility with windows on its many floors that let in the sunlight of the day.

"The firm has floors seven to twenty—including what they call the 'penthouse,'" Vicky said, reading from her phone. "Wharton, Dixon, and Smith are the partners. Nathaniel Wharton, Donald Dixon, and Celia Smith. The firm has been around for thirty years, always the same partners. Twenty attorneys in all, specializing in just about everything including family law, marine law, personal injury, and criminal law." She winced, glancing at him. "This could take some time."

"Concentrate on the biggies."

"Okay, so...partners and heads of the departments."

"Right. A good start, anyway. Divide and conquer or go after them together?" Jude asked.

"Let's see what kind of resistance we get when we go up," Vicky said.

"There's a plan. I'll let Aidan know where we are. Just in case we disappear into a computer," he wisecracked.

Vicky groaned. He made the call, and they headed in. It was a busy building. The lobby was filled with people coming and going.

But they quickly located the elevators. Jude found himself staring at the call buttons, interested in the other businesses with which the firm shared the building.

"Typical," Vicky murmured.

She looked at him, inclining her head in a nod. "Dentists,

another law firm, cosmetic surgery, investment firm, two more doctors, and…"

"Sledge Incorporated," Jude supplied.

"Wonder what that is," she murmured.

He laughed. "Easy."

"We drop in on the way out?"

"Easier than that. We ask Cary or Aidan."

"Of course!"

The elevator arrived. Jude noted it was equipped with cameras—as he assumed all the hallways in the building would be.

They arrived at reception—at the desk where he believed Marci Warden would have sat.

Had she not been killed by an electric knife in a house run amok.

A young blonde was there today. She was barely in her twenties, Jude thought, but very attractive.

An excellent face to welcome people to the firm.

As once Marci Warden's had been.

"Hello! Welcome to Wharton, Dixon, and Smith. How may I help you?"

They both produced their credentials.

She looked at them as if stunned. "I, um, I'm sorry—I don't understand."

"Really?" Vicky asked sweetly. "The woman who sat in this chair just yesterday is dead and—"

"Oh, I know! I know. And I'm so sorry. I didn't know Marci, but what a terrible accident! I…got rid of the AI in my house—I'll turn my own lights off from now on!" she said. "And, of course, the entire firm is in mourning…we're at half-staff, so…"

"How about we start with Mr. Wharton, Mr. Dixo,n or Ms. Smith?" Jude suggested politely.

The blonde winced. "I'm afraid Mr. Wharton isn't in today.

He hired Marci years ago, and I believe he is truly broken-hearted. As are so many! We are a family here."

"A family. But you didn't know Marci?" Vicky said.

The blonde lowered her head. "I just started. I mean, I'd seen Marci… I saw her when I applied for an assistant's job here. I was on the list, and this morning I was called in and…"

"Okay. Who called you in?" Jude asked.

"Ms. Smith," the young woman said.

"Then you can point her office out to us, please," Vicky said.

The blonde glanced toward the back. "Well, let me give her a call—"

"That's all right, we've got this," Vicky said, starting toward the rear hall.

"Wait! You can't just—"

"Feds. Yes, we can," Jude said pleasantly.

The blonde leaped to her feet, running like a gazelle ahead of them, bursting thought the door with the plaque that designated the office as belonging to Celia Smith.

They let the blonde precede them, entering directly behind her.

"Ms. Smith, I am so sorry—" the blonde began.

"We do apologize, but we are racing against time!" Jude interrupted.

Celia Smith was in her early sixties, Jude surmised, with her hair cut short and kept at a shimmering white-blond color. It didn't appear she went out of her way to seek cosmetic surgery or turn back the hands of time; she was an attractive and well put together older woman.

"Nancy, it's fine. I can see you were given little choice!" Celia said. She didn't rise; she remained behind her desk, studying Jude and Vicky curiously. "How may I help you?"

There were chairs in front of her handsome highly polished desk.

They took them.

Comfortable, nicely upholstered chairs, not the usual business rollers. But the entire office was impressive. It also offered a large viewing screen, accessible, he imagined, for information on important cases. There was a handsome sofa across the room with two matching—once again, comfortable—chairs. And the upper walls were lined with pictures of the partners and the heads of the law firm's various departments.

"We're here about Marci Warden," Vicky told her, producing her badge again as they sat.

The woman looked truly stricken.

"Marci!" she said softly. She looked down, wincing, and looked up again. "You must realize...we're in mourning for her here. Many of my colleagues... Well, I'm afraid the law doesn't take holidays, so we needed to have a skeleton crew in, at the least, and still..."

"We're so sorry for your loss," Vicky said.

Celia Smith nodded.

Then she looked up at them, frowning. "We heard it was a terrible, terrible accident. That she lost control of her electric knife and she had water on at the same time and... A truly and horribly tragic accident!" She shook her head. "You think it was something else?"

"What was she working on?" Vicky asked.

"Working on? She was our receptionist, a wonderful one," Celia said, "but she didn't handle any of our cases. She directed people to the right departments, the right attorneys. Oh, and she planned the business luncheons we had on our penthouse level, a few parties...but nothing else at all!"

"All right, then. How about your infrastructure?" Jude asked.

"Our infrastructure?" Celia countered, confused.

"Have you had any difficulties with your computer systems, with work being lost—have there been cases where the other party knows things they shouldn't?" Vicky asked.

"No, not that I know about. And if there were any problems, I know our attorneys would come to either me or one of my partners," Celia said.

"No difficulty with malware of any kind?" Jude pressed.

"No, our people know what they're doing," Celia said.

"You must have a department here for technical analysts, right?" Vicky asked.

Celia shook her head. "No, we, um, call in our national experts when we have a problem. You see, many of our people grew up with computers and technology—they're very savvy all on their own."

"Well, we'd like to speak with your most 'savvy' people and the heads—" Vicky began.

"That's impossible," Celia said.

"Oh?" Jude asked.

"None of them are here today. I'm not trying to be argumentative. We loved Marci. But I just can't understand how what happened could have been anything other than…tragic. But if you want to speak with the heads of our departments, I'm afraid you'll need to find them at home or come back," Celia said. She seemed sincere.

Jude smiled.

"We'll do that," he said.

"You said your employees are young and cyber savvy," Vicky told Celia. "We're going to need a list of them, please."

Celia suddenly sat back, shaking her head, pursing her lips.

"You're forgetting something," she told her.

"What's that?"

"We're a renowned national law firm, emphasis on the word *law.* I was trying to be helpful, but now you're digging into things that may be harmful to this company—"

"Not as harmful as they were to Marci Warden," Vicky said.

"Warrant. You want to harass my employees, you're going to need a warrant!" Celia told her.

"And you said you wanted to be helpful," Jude said.

Celia let out an impatient breath. "Marci died because of an accident! A tragic one, and my people are in mourning. We should leave it to you all to turn it into something else entirely. Please! Get the hell out of my office or I promise you, I'll be bringing a harassment suit against your entire department!"

Vicky looked at Jude and smiled. "So helpful! She clearly cared very much!" she said.

"Right," Jude agreed, shaking his head.

He turned to smile at Celia. "That's fine. We'll get a warrant. And well, I didn't go to law school, but… I do know how to be creative. I can create rolls and rolls of red tape."

They headed to the door.

"Wait!" Celia called.

They turned back. "I'll get you a list of our employees with asterisks by those who provide technical help when necessary. If you leave a card, I'll put together what I can. Truly, I loved Marci. But I honestly believe that—that you're desperately trying to make her death something it wasn't!"

"Your help will be greatly appreciated," Jude said, walking over to her with one of his cards. "Don't email the information—create the list with a pen or pencil on paper, and we'll have someone by this afternoon to pick it up."

She took the card and nodded.

The two of them left the office at last. As they passed the reception desk, the blonde stood and stared at them as if they were deadly aliens who had just arrived from a hostile planet.

He glanced at the nameplate on her desk.

It still said "Marci Warden."

He smiled and walked back to her despite the look she was giving him.

"Thank you, thank you so much for your help today, Miss…?"

"Nancy. Nancy Cole. And I'm hoping you didn't get me fired!"

"Then you file a suit against the company for unlawful dismissal," Vicky said sweetly. "We'll be happy to testify at any trial! Special Agent Mackenzie, shall we?" she asked.

They headed to the elevator, turning to smile as they departed the law firm at last.

"Well, that was almost worthless," Vicky murmured.

"Almost?"

"There's something up with that blonde!" she told him, turning to him.

He frowned. "Little miss sweet, young, and innocent-looking?"

"She was on the phone when we left Ms. Smith's office. I believe she was telling someone we were here, and we were about to leave."

"So, who would she be telling?" he asked.

"Someone who isn't in the building today. Someone mourning the death of Marci Warden with so much sorrow that they had to stay home. And someone who might be dismayed but not shocked to know that someone in the world might suspect there was more to Marci's death than just technology run amok!"

She stopped suddenly, staring at the wall.

It was covered with headshots—Wharton, Dixon, and Smith themselves at the top of the pyramid of pictures.

Beneath them were the various heads of the department, some alone, several with spouses and presumably their children.

The company dealt with corporate law; Wharton himself was the head of that division. The maritime law division was headed by a Mr. Lee Chan who was appropriately pictured on a boat along with his wife, Gina, and a son who appeared to be about ten named Jason. Next, came the division of personal injury headed by a Mr. Barton Clay pictured with his young and lovely blond wife, Belinda. The firm also specialized in criminal law headed up by a Ms. A. Taylor, a woman of about forty, pictured all by herself.

"Well, we know who we're looking for!" Jude murmured.

"Interesting—I don't see what Mr. Dixon and Ms. Smith are heading," Vicky said.

"Maybe they're the overseers," Jude suggested.

"Such a family affair!" Vicky murmured. "And we're dragging a list out of Ms. Smith!"

"They may be guilty of nothing, and they may be guilty as hell, but..."

"But what?" Vicky asked.

"This is a law firm. We're going to need to be careful—"

"If they're guilty—"

"We sure as hell don't want anything thrown out of court," Jude finished.

She nodded. But she suddenly turned back to look at the pictures again. "Strange," she said.

"What's strange?" Jude asked.

Vicky shrugged. "May have been, may not have been... The lobby was so busy when we arrived, but..."

"But?"

"I thought I saw a couple of the people pictured on that wall in the lobby."

"Attorneys who weren't here because they were in mourning?" Jude asked.

Vicky nodded. "Well, one attorney and one wife. The pretty blonde woman... Belinda Clay. I think I saw her come out of an elevator. With another woman, the head of the criminal division. Um." She paused, turning to study the wall again. "Ms. A. Taylor, as her picture on the wall tells us."

Jude was thoughtful. "The blonde looked different? Hair up in a braid or a knot or a twist or something. And Ms. A. Taylor... I think you're right. But she was really different, wearing jeans and a sweatshirt?"

Vicky nodded. "I think we saw them, Jude. I think that was them."

"Maybe. Again, just seeing them in an elevator..."

"Is not evidence of guilt."

"And we need to be very, *very,* careful."

"Right! You are *absolutely* right on that!"

Attorneys. They would know how to use the law…

And while he wasn't sure why, Jude was convinced that someone here knew something.

They were all tech savvy?

Maybe someone was just a bit more savvy than the others.

FOUR

With Jessy and the kids safe—and knowing they would need to be very careful and within the law at every turn—Vicky and Jude made the decision to return to their dedicated headquarters to see if their cyber sleuths had any new directions in which to go. Although Vicky knew Jude was determined they needed to get in the water.

She thought it was more of a hunch than anything else because salt water could quickly destroy whatever evidence might have existed. But sometimes hunches were the backbone of what they did. He was, she thought, probably an excellent diver as well. Beyond a doubt, he was a man who kept himself in shape. And while she remained skeptical, he was proving to be a decent enough partner, though she understood he often worked solo and had been doing so most recently. He probably did well enough; he was an imposing enough figure, at least six-three, she reckoned. But he was also capable of looking like the handsome young fellow next door with his sandy brown hair and green eyes, a man who could quickly turn on something like college-boy charm when necessary.

She had to admit, the cyber skills required to find the truth behind this situation were beyond her expertise as well, which was, of course, why Aidan and Cary might be the most important people assigned to nothing else but the case at hand.

But unless the two of them had something else for them to be doing now…

They would be getting into the water.

It was possible something had been missed by the police when the *Lucky Sun* had crashed and, according to reports, exploded into pieces with a fire erupting at the scene. But due to the watery state of the "accident," the fire had not lasted long.

"Anything on the law firm or anything else yet?" Vicky asked.

"Nothing that we've been able to find," Aidan said, "but—"

He turned to Vicky and Jude and solemnly added, "Cary is one of the best technical analysts I've ever met, so…"

Vicky nodded, smiling. She was becoming well aware they were very lucky in having Cary and Aidan for their tech team.

"Hey!" Cary said. She was seated in their workroom at her computer. "Don't let Aidan fool you—he's a top dog. The point being, between us, we'll get what we need. But I will be the one working when Aidan needs to be working forensic magic in the field."

"What have we got so far?" Jude asked. "Anything that will take us anywhere? Have you found any connections between the judge, the receptionist, and the crew on the boat?"

"Nothing yet, but we have information on all the players," Aidan told him. "Oh, and we've sent you an email, Jude. Just some terminology so that you—"

Jude groaned. "Hey, guys, come on! I do use a computer every day. I admit—I haven't tried to hack into any sites, so no… I'm not great at hacking!"

"Well, it's a good thing our Cary is on the side of law and order and justice," Aidan said lightly.

Jude laughed. "And you, too, Aidan, I imagine," he told the man.

Aidan shrugged. "I'm gainfully employed. I think. I don't need to hack my local grocery store. Anyway, we've found a few instances where something could tie in. Our judge wasn't called the Hanging Judge for nothing. The death penalty is supposedly set by jury in the state, but the judge certainly has the ability to sway it and approve it. Three men are now on death row from cases he presided over, and a fellow named Gilbert Miller was executed about a month ago for the murder of a couple in their home when a robbery went bad. Miller claimed his innocence until the very end. I'm doing more research into him now. The three sitting on death row are Marcus Suarez who was convicted of an execution-style killing and suspected of being in the Arroyo cartel out of Colombia. Benjamin Morton was convicted in the murders of two off-duty police officers. And Lawrence Jennings was convicted of killing his wife and mother-in-law. Many people side with the judge, feeling that those who commit such murders are not worthy of any mercy, but many people don't believe in the death penalty, period. We're looking into all known associates of these men, but so far we can find no connection."

"Cartels are pretty powerful," Jude commented.

"And weren't a few of those on the boat involved with drugs? That could be a cartel connection," Vicky said.

"And we are looking into it," Aidan promised. "The crash and explosion of the *Lucky Sun* have us digging all over. Every man on it might have been wanted dead by someone. Captain Ronald Quincy, drugs. His mate, Jeremy Hart, just out of federal prison. And the chef, Gene Walters—nothing on that man at all, not even parking tickets. He was single, an only child, and his parents died in an automobile accident six years ago. It appears that he was just in the wrong place at the wrong time, but at this point… Anyway, then there were the passengers—

three attorneys. Ansel Thornton, Walter Roderick, and Claude Hathaway. They've won and lost cases. They've sent a few bad guys to prison. We're looking for any connection between any of these people. The weird thing is..."

"That we have evildoers, those who go after evildoers, a most likely innocent chef, and Marci Warden, a receptionist," Vicky murmured.

"But," Jude reminded her, "she worked for a law firm."

"True. So, someone is after someone..."

"Or several someones are out there working their trade. There could be several hackers out there, right?" Jude asked.

"Not ruling anything out, but...to get this good? I don't know just how many someones there could be," Aidan said. "The car... Well, perhaps that was the easiest hack. And I'm sorry as hell, but this takes time and..." He paused, frowning. "Oh, something I discovered this morning. Reading files the public most likely doesn't have access to—"

"In the interest of justice and saving lives?" Vicky suggested.

Aidan shrugged. "I believe we will be given access to everything, anyway. Arnold had a brief discussion with Mr. Wharton. We have his blessing to find out what's going on. The agencies here are working together. So, they found enough body parts to put together the corpses of the captain, the mate, the chef, and two of the attorneys. But for the third fellow, they found all kinds of ripped up and bloody clothing, but not his body. Now, mind you, this happened in Matanzas Bay—"

"Slaughter Bay," Jude said dryly.

Aidan shrugged and continued, "Precisely. But the body of Claude Hathaway hasn't been found, in whole or in pieces, though there is blood on the clothing. And while forensics had a hell of a time discovering anything from bits and pieces collected out of the bay, what forensics they have suggests that the blood is Hathaway's."

"And the thing is, there are enough predators in the bay to

see that a body was completely…destroyed. However…" Jude murmured thoughtfully.

"You think he might be alive?" Vicky asked.

He looked over at her. "I did want to go diving. The police thought it was an accident. They wouldn't have been looking for evidence of a crime when it happened."

"You've been to the law firm. You've seen to it Jessy Hutchins and her kids are safe and just in the nick of time. Samuel Hutchins is still being maintained in the induced coma," Aidan said. "Every agency is sharing in extreme protection for the man just in case. Okay, so, on another front. Who knows? Maybe you can find something, anything, in the wreckage of the *Lucky Sun*."

Jude looked at Vicky. She shrugged. "I can dive. I just prefer the Florida Keys, Grand Cayman, the Bahamas…"

"But Slaughter Bay it is!" Aidan said cheerfully. "Don't worry. We're tirelessly working away here and will give you anything and everything the minute we have it!"

"And," Cary said sweetly, "we are very, very good. It's probably a good thing we're not criminals!"

Jude looked at Vicky. "Let's use the daylight, shall we?"

"Oh! I didn't bring my scuba equipment!" she told him. "Maybe—"

"Maybe you have nothing at all to worry about," he assured her. "Trust me. Every agency in Florida plans for water investigations, so not to worry! We'll get you set up with some great stuff. I helped with several buys for the equipment out of our offices here. You're going to be just fine."

"Great. Okay…"

They said their goodbyes and left headquarters.

They stopped by a facility where diving equipment was kept.

In minutes she was ready to go, and Jude was right—vests, regulators, masks—all were of the highest quality but she wished…

She wished she were diving in the Keys or the Bahamas instead of looking for...

The proverbial needle in a haystack.

Except this was like looking for a wet needle in a wet haystack!

An officer showed Jude and Vicky to the location where the *Lucky Sun* had gone down. Down not far from where they found themselves was a beautiful beach.

However, this point of entry was tricky.

"You okay with this?" he asked Vicky.

She nodded. "I'm actually more coordinated than I look, I guess."

"No, rocks are tricky for anyone."

"Hey, come on. We are entering Matanzas Bay. Slaughter Bay, Massacre Bay—I understand you can translate it either way. And either way, it's sad," she said, shaking her head. "In the year 1565, King Philip of Spain was incensed that the French were creating a settlement at Fort Caroline. There were two incidents...he had Pedro Menéndez de Avilés attack Fort Caroline and kill all the men but did allow the women and children to go to Havana—and he was then ordered to attack survivors. The Spanish were Catholic, the French were Huguenot, but a few were spared because they professed to be Catholic. As I understand, a few Britons had been pressed into service and they were spared. But hundreds died and thus..."

"Massacres and slaughters," Jude said, frowning as he looked at her. "I admit, I don't know that much about you, but you know some Florida history?"

She grinned, finding a good rock to sit on so she could slip into her flippers.

"You've been working out of Jacksonville, and I surmise you've spent a lot of time in St. Augustine. But I was born just down the beach in, hmm, a tiny place called Crescent Beach.

I spent a lot—a lot—of time here in the nearest *big* city, and I always loved it. Besides slaughters, some good things happened here, too. Technically, the first Thanksgiving took place here in 1565—that magic year of bloodshed. Pedro Menéndez de Avilés again. Thanksgiving in celebration for the founding of the place, and he set up a major feast for the Savoy, the Native American people in the area at the time."

He nodded. "Things every school kid knows, right?"

She shook her head, laughing. "Hey, I don't know what is going on. Some is good, I imagine, some very, very bad. History is history. We cannot change the past. And it has alarmed me several times when people my age and younger believe they need passports to travel to Alaska and Hawaii!"

Again, he grinned, shaking his head and pulling his mask and regulator into place.

"Well, maybe they're going through Canada on their way to Alaska? Now, Hawaii...you never know. A few foreign islands could pop up on the way!"

She laughed, too, following suit and preparing to enter the water.

And he thought as he slid down into the shallows first, it definitely wasn't like diving in the Florida Keys or the Bahamas. Rocks and murk were right here by the jetty. The proximity of the shore caused a stir of dirt that hampered visibility.

He flicked on the light accessory that, thankfully, they'd obtained through the office for special underwater situations. He saw Vicky was competently moving along the collection of rocks and debris at the base of the jetty. They were in approximately fifteen feet of water, but the debris field stretched out at least thirty feet into the bay. While she worked the close area, he was determined to get down deeper.

Bits and pieces of wreckage were everywhere, making it difficult to decide if anything was useful to explain what had happened. A yacht like the *Lucky Sun* would have had a "black box," or a voyage data recorder, sometimes simply called a maritime black box. And if they could find it...

Something swam close by him. Instinctively, he tensed, but he quickly realized he was being observed by one of the bay's curious bottle-nosed dolphins.

He wished they were diving for fun. Sometimes, the animals warily kept away from people; this one had evidently had good experiences with human beings in the water. It seemed the creature wanted to play. Maybe it liked the show of light coming from his mask attachment, like how a cat loved to chase a laser beam.

He allowed himself a second to run a hand along the animal's sleek topside, but even as he did so, he saw Vicky was coming his way and beckoning to him.

She had found something.

He followed her and saw what she was pointing to. Something metal and partially cylindrical was wedged between rocks toward the bottom of the jetty. Bits and pieces of red paint had survived the blast, but the item showed signs of blackening by fire.

Damage to the object was probably extensive, but he thought it might be the yacht's VDR, or voyage data recorder.

And like an airplane's black box, this one might tell them quite a story—if it had survived enough to do so. But...

Like an airplane's black box, its function was to record; for that reason, they were usually strong enough to survive quite a bit.

It was wedged deep in the rocks. He pulled out his diving knife and began to chip away at the rock that was holding it in. Vicky was by his side, ready to grab the object as it broke free.

It was a split second after she caught and held the VDR that he felt something whizz by their heads. Through the feel and sound of it, he instantly realized they were being shot at from the surface. He looked at Vicky; there was no panic in her eyes. She gave him a slight nod and dived deeper toward the heart of Matanzas Bay.

Slaughter Bay, Massacre Bay!

He instantly dove deeper himself, checking his gages. They still had plenty of air.

But how long might someone be willing to wait to see them rise from the depths?

He could see the bullets strike and whizz through the water as he turned to look back. Whoever was doing the shooting must have been concentrating on the area directly by the jetty. Naturally, perhaps? That was the area where something might have lodged after the explosion right there on the rocks?

He carried a P-11 underwater pistol, but he needed the correct range for its use—and a sense of his target. He was angry with himself; he'd carried the weapon naturally for underwater defense against animal predators since he'd had a few cases in the area that involved underwater discoveries, but he hadn't expected anyone to come after them from above. He chastised himself, knowing he should have been better prepared.

He looked at Vicky, somewhat surprised to see she didn't seem to be distressed. She was grim and aware of their danger but looked at him as she waited for his determination on a way out of their situation. He showed her the pistol that had been attached to his belt and she nodded; she had known he carried it.

He motioned to her, telling her to remain where she was while he went around the other side of the jetty. Keeping extremely low, he almost crept along the bottom. The bullets kept coming—but around the other side. Almost flat against the rocks, he moved upward toward the surface and lifted his mask and spat out his regulator.

He was able to see the shooter at last—at least the form of the shooter. He—or she—was wearing an encompassing dark jacket with a hood.

It was a lone shooter. They were concentrating on that one area of the water, assuming he and Vicky would be searching on the side of the rocks where the boat had hit and then exploded into an inferno. The shooter had likely decided they would need to surface eventually.

On the road, not far from the shooter's position, was a nondescript dark sedan.

The range wasn't good; his position wasn't good. But Jude knew he had to take a chance. They had an air supply. But it would run out.

He fired.

The shooter let out a grunt of pain. They didn't go down, but Jude could see they'd been clipped good in the upper arm—their right upper arm.

The person's weapon fell; they stooped to retrieve it awkwardly with their left hand.

Jude swore inwardly. *Damn!* If the gun had been left…

It had probably been stolen, anyway. Criminals didn't tend to use registered firearms.

And whoever it was doing the shooting, they were smart enough to duck low, almost flat to the ground, and move like a bat out of hell to the sedan waiting on the road. There was no way in hell Jude could get in another shot.

With a roar of the motor, the sedan was gone.

And by then Vicky—cradling the discovery that might at least send them in the right direction on the case—emerged by his side and removed her regulator and mask.

"A better shot and we'd have someone," he muttered, still angry with himself.

"Hey, we're alive. I'm opting for that at the moment," Vicky told him. "Do not beat yourself up! We found this. Maybe, through the magic of Aidan and Cary, we'll get something. And we weren't dealing with a pro here—no automatic weapon. Whoever it was fled at the first response."

"Injured," Jude murmured. "If we had a suspect… But I think that these 'lesser' would-be assassins may all be like Samuel Hutchins. Bribed and threatened."

"And Samuel Hutchins may be able to speak soon. If so, we'll have more leads if nothing else," Vicky said.

Jude turned to her, nodding grimly. Even soaked, he realized, she was a beautiful woman. Or maybe it was because she was soaked that he could finally see the sculpted perfection of her face.

And body.

"I did get the first three numbers on the license plate of that car," he told her. "The rocks were obscuring the rest."

"Brilliant!"

He pulled his phone from his belt, and she stared at him.

"Your phone works in the water," she murmured.

"It's one of those durable things. As the mission progresses, we should get earpieces and make sure Cary and Aidan can hear us if we get into any trouble."

"You are full of surprises. But let's get out of here and get this black box thingy to the right tech people!"

He nodded, hefting himself onto the rocks and turning back to help her. Their tanks and equipment were heavy. Getting into the water was easier than getting out of it.

But Vicky was out, turning to him for help in removing her tank, and ready to give assistance in return.

"Hey, for someone who didn't want to go diving, you're not a bad diving buddy," he told her.

She grinned. "Dad was a navy SEAL. No way I wasn't going to know my way around water."

"Gotcha. All right, then…"

As they packed up their equipment, Jude put through the calls necessary to get their team, the FDLE, and the local police on the hunt for the sedan with what little information he could give them. Aidan was going to start calling up the local hospitals to find out if anyone had come in with a gunshot wound in the right arm.

Jude paused for a minute then, shaking his head. Looking across the bay, he could see that bathers were out on the beaches. It was just another beautiful sunny day.

And that's what the world should be, he thought. People getting to appreciate the natural wonders to be discovered across the planet.

"Back to the ranch," Jude murmured.

"Ranch?" Vicky queried.

He groaned. "Headquarters. Shower. Delivery of our black box. Shower. Check on Samuel Hutchins. Find out what the hell is going on."

"Oh, yeah, shower, shower! But! Do you think they will be able to get something out of this device?" Vicky asked.

"I do. The thing is, that's the function—to indicate where there's trouble, to show location, navigate. So like an airplane's black box, they should be hardy things. The biggest trouble with them—which confirms our suspicions that something's going on—is that they are susceptible to hacking."

Vicky nodded thoughtfully.

"Cars, too," she murmured. "Remember? You mentioned it to me. There's that ad…the guy at a game who can't remember where he parked his car so his 'clicker' shows him *and* starts the car. Hack the little clicker, or even get a hold of a little clicker, and the car shows you where it is and starts up for easy stealing. Well, they do try to install fail-safes," Vicky said.

"Arnie."

"What?" she asked, confused.

"Arnie. Arnold Schwarzenegger. *The Terminator.* The day that the machines take over," Jude said.

"The rise of the machines," Vicky murmured. "But!"

"But?"

"Artificial intelligence has someone behind it. A human being. Someone is manipulating all this."

"And how far can it go? Will the machines take over?" he asked.

She turned to him. "For this case? No! Jude—"

"I know. We are chasing a human—or humans. Someone with power and money. And yet…what is the motive for all this?"

"Murder for hire," Vicky said.

He glanced her way. "I hope it's that simple," he told her.

She turned to him, frowning.

"I admit, I don't know how to hack any kind of site. But I worked a case as a field agent where we traced it back through a high school and a man pretending to be a high school student. He was really twenty-four, and he'd been raised a diehard jihadist. He easily managed to make a brilliant young tech fall in love with him and hack into access military codes. We were incredibly lucky to arrest him before he got the codes to those who could have used them."

"And hopefully, they have since changed the codes," Vicky said.

Jude nodded. "But you must first know that you've been hacked before you change anything." He shook his head. "For some people, it seems so incredibly easy. And then, those we know who are also brilliant still have trouble tracing them!"

"Okay, there are dozens of servers and kinds of servers as hardware in computers and even as software. And…"

"And?" he asked her.

"Then you have malware and viruses. Now if you want to really mess someone up, you can easily email them, be so intriguing that they open the email, and voila, there's a virus in their computer. That's also a way to dig into someone's information such as their email and—as in the case you're talking about—delve into information that only they are supposed to have. Malware, now…" She paused, looking straight ahead, and letting out a long breath. "Malware. While all viruses are malware, malware is specifically designed to attack a certain system. Malware is a specific threat category. It's all… Well, it can all be deadly. It's the terrorism of the future."

He nodded. "Who knew?"

"Pardon?"

"Computers. Great things. Smart phones—wow! Hey, my grandmother lived in the south of the state and used to travel across Tamiami Trail and what was then Alligator Alley—"

"Now I-75," she said.

He nodded. "Yep. And they had their AAA cards and a pack of dimes at the time, but phones were miles and miles apart. So back then, if you wound up stuck in the Everglades, well you were stuck until a Good Samaritan came by."

Vicky laughed. "Now you just need to hope you get a signal. And trust me—you can't get a signal everywhere in our great River of Grass!"

"Don't I know it!" he murmured. "Anyway…"

"Jacksonville. The offices there. They'll be best equipped to find whatever might be found from this black box."

"Jacksonville it is," he said. "But… Well, we are soaking wet, and…"

"That's okay. I wasn't expecting us to stop by a five-star restaurant. We'll do drive-through, get that there, get back…and see what's happened. And maybe, hopefully, get some sleep!"

He smiled. She'd leaned back. Relaxed. Confident. Not caring who drove.

He kept quiet.

Maybe having a partner wasn't going to be so terrible.

Their phones rang at the same time as he drove. He glanced her way, and she picked up quickly. He could see that it was Assistant Director Arnold calling them.

"We're both here, on speaker, sir," Vicky said quickly.

"Good," Arnold said simply. "Just so you know the car with

your shooter has already been discovered. No shock here—it was found abandoned."

"But the owner—" Jude began.

"No shock again," Arnold told him. "It was reported stolen early this morning when the Vero Beach owner discovered it was missing. But we have a forensic crew going over it with an old fine-tooth comb as they say. If there's anything, we'll find it."

"We know that the owner—"

"A twenty-year old girl, college student who lives with her parents. Their security cam has her home last night about ten and out this morning at about seven," Arnold said.

"Security cam? Did it pick up—"

"Oh, yeah. No possible facial recognition, the person who took it is estimated to be about five-ten, and we know little else. Their coat or jacket or whatever the garment was had a hood. But they did estimate five-ten."

"Right," Jude murmured, shaking his head. "Of course. But I know that I winged the man—or woman. We're still—"

"Checking doctors and hospitals across the area, yes. We're on this. You guys did good, though—get the box to the lab. I think I may send you up to Nashville, just to take a look at the crime scene there, get a feel for those who might have has a grudge against the judge—"

"Sir—" Jude began.

"Don't worry about any other assignments at this time, Special Agent Mackenzie. You two are on nothing but this until it's solved!"

"I was just going to say I think someone at that law firm knows something," Jude said. "And now we do have the navigation box for—"

"Yes, but our tech people will continue the online investigation. You're in the field. I'd be happy if you saw the entire field."

"Right. All right, sir. Just tell us when we're doing what," Vicky said, casting a quick glance his way.

Jude smiled.

She was watching out for them both.

"As you say, sir," Jude agreed.

"Tonight—sleep," Arnold ordered. "Overtired agents are worthless."

"Yes, sir," Jude said.

He glanced at Vicky. They could both agree to that.

"We'll all be back with anything that anyone finds," Arnold promised.

"Thank you," Jude said.

"Copy that," Vicky murmured.

"Good a good evening," Arnold said, and then was gone.

"Well, that's not so bad. We've been ordered to sleep," Vicky said.

"I just don't think we need to be leaving."

"He'll get us one of the Bureau's private jets. We can go and come back in a flash," Vicky said. "Tonight, sleep. Tomorrow—"

"We need to hope to hell we start to figure out what's going on before someone else dies," he said grimly.

"Jude, we will. We will get to the bottom of this. We have the best help in the world. No matter how brilliant AI may be, there's a human mind behind it all."

"A killer," he said quietly. "A killer who seems to reach across time and space. But…"

"But?" she asked.

"Gut feeling. That killer—the mind behind the AI—is right here. We're going to find him—or her—right here."

FIVE

Once the remnants of the black box were delivered to technicians, Vicky and Jude returned to the house by the old district.

Vicky wasn't surprised to find Aidan and Cary still at their computers despite the hour. They'd all learned long ago that criminal endeavors seldom worked by a schedule or timetable. And the two technical analysts working with them on this case were dedicated. Something that was not just valuable at this time, but necessary.

"So, you two had quite the day, eh?" Aidan said, leaning back as they entered.

"Nothing like a dive into Slaughter Bay!" Vicky told him cheerfully.

"And dodging bullets," Cary said, wincing.

"Still hoping they can catch him at a hospital or medical facility," Jude said.

"Vet," Aidan said.

"What?" Jude asked him, frowning. "You think the shooter might be ex-military, or even current military, and that he would have gone to a veteran's hospital?"

Aidan grimaced, wrinkling his face with a touch of amusement. "No, I've put a call out to veterinarians—animal doctors."

"Right, right, of course," Jude said, shaking his head. "Yeah, let's see... Get shot and don't want to get reported? You either know, bribe, or threaten a veterinarian. But—"

"Like Aidan said," Cary offered, "we tried everything. But if someone has been bribed or threatened, and they're still afraid of being shot themselves, they're not going to report it."

"Of course not," Vicky said. "Anyway, we were given direct orders to go to bed. I'm thinking I know you two a little better now, and I'm thinking you probably need a few direct orders to go to bed, too. We're not alone on this," she reminded them. "But, of course with that said—"

"Do we have anything new?" Aidan asked, amused.

"Do you?" Jude asked.

Aidan sighed. "Nothing telling. So far, we've been concentrating on dossiers for everyone involved in Marci Warden's life. But all she's done lately is work, so it seems. And we've gathered what we can on the fine esquire types at the law firm. We've been accumulating all the info we can on those who were on the exploding boat. We've also done a list of those who the judge sentenced harshly in the last few years, focusing on those with relatives on the outside who either have computer expertise or a lot of money."

"And you've—" Vicky began.

"We sent you all the files about ten minutes ago. Especially the files on the collision case in Tennessee once we were informed you might be making the trip up to Nashville," Cary told her.

Vicky glanced at Jude who had already turned toward her, shaking his head.

"It's not going to hurt us to spend a few hours there, though..." Vicky said.

"Hey, we think it's all centered here somewhere, too," Aidan said.

"Centered here. And I seriously believe it's murder for hire," Jude said. "What better way to get away with it? A computer goes whacky and someone is dead. Who do you blame? It becomes not who, but what. Technology."

"But—" Aidan began.

He didn't finish. Jude had lifted his hand. "But the educated and informed know that technology is fed what it has, and in this case, a devious mind is pulling strings."

"Hey, the old dude is coming around," Aidan told Cary.

"I protest that! I'm thirty-three," Jude said, shaking his head. "I just never… I never suspected someone would murder someone else with technology."

"It's happened before. We're just beginning to suspect that some accidents in the past might have been preplanned," Aidan said. He sighed and looked at them both. "Cars. GPS. Great. Law enforcement has often been able to track cars suspected of being used in a crime, and that part is just great. But now… you can find your car by pressing a key on your phone, and you can start your car and cars even drive themselves. But that kind of a computer system isn't really all that hard to hack, so… there have probably been more incidents than we know about. We know for a fact that many cars have been stolen that way."

"I'm going to bed," Vicky said. "Because you know, I was ordered to get some sleep!"

She smiled to the group and waved and started down the hallway but paused and looked back.

"Hey! We were ordered to sleep!"

"Yeah," Jude said. "That's easy enough. I can go to bed. I'm just hoping to hell I can turn my mind off."

"The human brain—the deadliest computer out there!" Aidan said.

Vicky groaned. "I don't know, guys. Assistant Director Arnold told us to go to bed. I have a feeling that means we're going to get a call at the crack of dawn giving us more orders. So…hmm. I'm going to beg my brain to let me go to sleep!"

She headed on into her bedroom. It was late—she was exhausted—but even still she showered. After the water and the day, she felt like a salt lick.

The hot water was delicious, but…

Jude was right. She kept thinking. Thinking about everything. Murder for hire. Easy enough—because a machine was going to do the murdering.

And still…

She finally got out of the shower, dried off, and curled into her bed. She lay awake staring at the ceiling. Then she forced her eyes to close.

When she did so, she saw pictures. The pictures of the heads of departments at the law firm of Wharton, Dixon, and Smith.

But exhaustion claimed her at last.

And as she suspected might happen, her phone began to ring at the crack of dawn.

Assistant Director Arnold was on the phone.

"The judge's legal aid is ready to walk through his recent hardcore cases, and police are ready to show you the crash site. You can also speak with the mechanics working on the car's tech," he told her. "There's a small private airport fifteen miles north of your location. A plane is waiting. It will deliver you to the Nashville area where a car will be left for you. The plane and pilot will be ready to fly back when you are."

"Yes, sir," she murmured, hoping she sounded as if she were semi-awake.

"Are you in agreement with your partner?" Arnold asked her.

"Pardon, sir?"

"Convinced that the heart of all this is resting near you somewhere? I don't understand his determination. Servers seem to be bouncing back and forth from all over the world. Here's the thing—I have you on the ground, other agents are checking out possibilities, Aidan and Cary and a host of people in DC are all working on this. But the heart of an AI scam could be…"

"Anywhere in the world," Vicky said. "Yes, sir. There's just…

All right, sir, we've discovered that cars are easy to hack—if you're an accomplished cyber hacker. And a boat's system is much like that of an airplane. Yes, not as easy, but again, an accomplished cyber hacker can get in and do a number on it. But Marci worked for a law firm where one of the partners assured us their people were young and able and computer savvy."

"All right, then... But it's important to find out everything that you can in Tennessee. We never know when one lead might lead to another. And—"

"It was a judge who was killed," Vicky murmured.

"No life is more valuable than another," Arnold said firmly, "but we don't want to create an open season on people in power, either. If the judge was killed in a revenge plot, and there's word on the dark web, then..."

"Right. We'll get to the bottom of this, sir. We won't stop until we do," Vicky promised. She hesitated. "I do understand my partner's reasoning. Marci Warden was a receptionist. She had a record so clean it sparkled. No drugs, nothing illegal in her past, no questionable friends or acquaintances. She had to have known something that someone was worried about her sharing. And that brings us back to the law offices."

"Your logic is good. But if you can discover anything in Tennessee, it may lead you back to the law offices—but with a better idea of where to start. Anyway—"

"I'm up!" Vicky promised.

And she was, but not much further along when there was a knock on her door two minutes later.

She had her clothes out on the bed, but she hadn't changed out of the flannel gown she loved—even in Florida. Air-conditioning could be freezing at night.

Of course, when she opened the door, it was Jude standing there.

"I take it—" he began.

"Just hung up. Give me five minutes," Vicky told him.

He nodded. "Coffee is brewed. That might help."

"Oh, yeah, thanks!" she told him, and studying his face she added, "You never turned your brain computer off last night?" she asked.

"I lay awake awhile," he admitted. "Hot shower…another hot shower. I know, I know—it must sound like I'm obsessed with showers, but they relieve tension. So! I got some sleep. Enough to really want coffee now. See you in the kitchen. I did bring an overnight bag, just in case."

"Right. Hey, I always have a to-go bag packed. I'll see you in the kitchen."

She was ready in five minutes. Being part of what was described as a "fly team," Vicky had learned from the beginning to be ready to go at a moment's notice.

In the kitchen she saw Aidan was up as well, speaking with Jude who listened to him gravely.

"I've just sent some files to your phones," Aidan said. "Cary and I think we've discovered an individual for you to investigate."

"From what I understand, Judge Ian McFarlane was tough—almost beyond tough," Jude said. "He'd give the harshest sentences the law allowed, even going so far as to—"

"He's known for doling out the death penalty in cases of first-degree murder," Aidan said. "He was a man who believed that the victim deserved justice—and those who took a life owed a life. But here's where I think—following some of the logic I gained from the two of you—that this whole cyber thing might be an exceptional murder-for-hire plot. In fact, considering the many planes, weapons depots, navy vessels, and more that might be targeted by a hacker, murder for hire might be the lesser of many evils. But here's the subject that caught my eye. Carlos Rodriguez."

Vicky frowned, pulling out her phone, finding the file, and looking from Jude to Aidan. "Ah," she murmured. "So, this

Carlos Rodriguez has been on the DEA's watch list for years. But—"

"Keep reading," Aidan said.

She did.

And she winced as she did so. "Carlos's son was convicted on two counts of first-degree murder. He...chopped up his wife, Peggy, and her sister, literally killed them by dismembering them slowly...and Judge McFarlane gave Victor Rodriguez the death penalty." She winced, looking at Aidan. "He's on death row now. His attorneys have filed another appeal."

"You don't need to see the crime photos—you know enough. But Carlos Rodriguez apparently thought his daughter-in-law was a cheating whore and deserved horrible things happening to her. But, of course, he's maintaining his son's innocence. And he's rich. Drug money, the DEA believes. But catching him has proven difficult because of his offshore accounts, and he seems to be the director of everything and never gets his own hands dirty. Anyway, there's more. But we thought you might want to start by concentrating your efforts on this man. If you can find a way to see him."

"We will," Jude assured him.

"And we're online, on call, available anytime you need us," Aidan assured them.

Jude nodded. "Thanks, Aidan. If anyone is really going to crack this thing, it's you two." He turned to Vicky. "Ready?"

"Yep. Coffee in hand, thanks," she said.

"Hey, Aidan even brewed the coffee," Jude said.

"Strong enough to move mountains," Aidan said, amused. "I know Jude, and I'm coming to know you, too, Special Agent Victoria Tennant!"

She grinned. "Thank you! And we're off!"

It was early. They had gotten out before the workforce and students that began morning rush hour, meaning they would avoid any long delays.

They easily found the small private airfield where they'd been directed, then they located the plane that had been commandeered by Assistant Director Arnold for their trip.

"Hmm," Jude murmured as they settled in.

"Hmm?" Vicky queried.

"I guess I was thinking of something more..."

Vicky laughed aloud. "Elegant?"

The plane wasn't miniature, but it only allowed for a pilot and no more than four passengers.

Their pilot, a young man of about thirty, laughed.

"Hey, she's not a bad plane," he promised.

"Yeah, you know, private jet. I was just thinking of lounge seating, a fully stocked fridge, you know... Pillows, maybe," Jude said.

They all laughed.

"Ah, but here's the thing—this baby will get you there quickly and safely. How's that?" the pilot asked.

"Brilliant!" Jude said. "Just what we need."

And it was. The flight didn't seem to be a full hour and a half. As Arnold had promised, a car was waiting for them along with a patrol car and two state officers.

They'd both taken the time to study all the information Aidan and Cary had accrued for them. As Aidan had said, Carlos Rodriguez was the man with the money—and possibly the contacts—to have arranged for a death through the dark web.

They quickly met the officers who were there to show them to the crash site: Grant Como and Franci Banks.

"Who's driving?" Como asked. He was a man of about forty with a quick and easy smile along with an easy manner.

Jude and Vicky looked at each other.

"Just throw the keys," Jude said.

He let Vicky catch them, but she grinned and handed them to him. "Ah, you can drive!"

"So you can sleep?"

"Something like that!" she assured him.

He knew she wouldn't sleep. He knew she'd be inspecting the crash photos on her phone while they headed to the location.

"Country roads," Franci Banks said. "John Denver knew what he was talking about, but you'll see," she told them. Like Como, she appeared to be in her early forties, and a woman as easy as her partner—someone more than willing to work with others.

They started out.

The plane had landed at an airfield west of Nashville, and they were quickly on their way, continuing on a southwestwardly route toward Nunnelly and the crash site.

They drove about thirty minutes.

Despite the removal of the body and the car, they could easily see the crash site. And while the area had been cleaned up after the crash, to the right of the road the small grove of oak trees wasn't enough to dispel the violence of the event with several trees bowed almost in half, rents and tears in the bark of every spot that had been hit.

Vicky and Jude walked the area, looking from the road to the crash site. There was no explanation there for a car simply going off the quiet road to slam into the tree.

And there had been no sign of alcohol or drugs in the respected judge at autopsy

Something or someone other than the driver had caused the crash.

"Trees are still alive and," Como told them, shrugging, "in this area, the flora and fauna are respected. The people brought in to inspect the damage believe the trees will live. As it happens, because of these trees, you can see…it's been estimated the car was going about seventy-five miles an hour. There were no skid marks, no attempt by anyone to slow the car down. Of course, our people studied the car's computer. They believe it was hacked. You might have noticed we're in a small place here, and the local sheriff wanted the Bureau called in because of the judge's…position."

"I know our tech people have seen the reports," Vicky told him. "And—"

"He was respected by many, many people. And hated as well," Banks told them.

"An eye for an eye kind of judge?" Jude asked.

Banks shrugged. "I don't think the man was particularly vicious. There were cases I read about when he was merciful, when he looked to psychiatric help rather than pure punishment. But some of the murder cases that went up before him…"

"We heard that a man chopped his wife up alive along with his sister-in-law," Jude told her.

"It had to have been one of the most brutal and torturous deaths imaginable," Banks told them. "The ME said she—and her sister-in-law—finally died by exsanguination. But the cruelty! He started with fingers and toes, went on to hands and feet, calves, lower arms. It's almost impossible to imagine one human being doing that to another. He's appealing the death penalty right now. But even with Judge Ian McFarlane dead, I don't see a reprieve. And I don't care how much money Carlos Rodriguez has to try to save his son."

"We hear the DEA has been watching him a long time," Jude commented.

Banks and Como both nodded solemnly.

"But…the elder Rodriguez is suspected of being a drug lord, not a computer whiz," Banks told them, shaking her head. "Of course, there are others the judge sentenced harshly. He was a man with no patience for defense attorneys that grasped at straws—not that defense attorneys aren't invaluable! The innocent are sometimes accused as well."

"Is there any possibility the younger Rodriguez was innocent?" Jude asked.

"Well, he was caught leaving the house and the bodies with the murder weapon in his possession and blood all over himself, so…it seems unlikely. Also, he was screaming about his wife deserving everything she got…that no woman did to a real man what she had done to him without paying the price."

Jude looked at Vicky, arching a brow.

"He does not sound like a nice guy," she said. "But—"

"Does the father hang out anywhere specific?" Jude asked.

"Oh, yeah. There's a bar back in the city—back in Nashville, I mean," Como said. He glanced at Banks. "We keep an eye on it—the DEA keeps an eye on it. We believe Rodriguez is responsible for the majority of fentanyl that makes its way into the city. But we've never caught him. Banking is offshore in places that don't honor our warrants or subpoenas. We've staked out the bar several times. A good old boy named Jeffrey Lemming is the titular owner, but you can usually find Carlos Rodriguez there at night in the corner seat at the bar. We've tried. Several times—just as the DEA has tried. And we're still just watching the drugs hit the street," Como told them.

"And what about the son? The killer on death row?" Jude asked. "Victor Rodriguez?"

"He's being held at the federal prison," Banks told them.

"And what about visitors?"

"Well," Banks said, looking at Como. "He sees his attorneys."

"And here we go…attorneys," Jude said, looking at Vicky. He grimaced. "Trust me! I know."

"Every man is entitled to his defense," Banks said. "I wouldn't have it any other way."

"I'd like to see him," Jude said, looking at Vicky. "Victor, that is. Without his attorneys, if we could make it happen by any wild chance. What we have is on paper. There may be more behind it all."

Vicky frowned, looking at him. It sounded as if the prosecution had been in possession of enough evidence to give them an airtight case.

But…

Jude had been right about the scene where the *Lucky Sun* had crashed when the "black box" showed them that the yacht had been sabotaged. Still, she wasn't sure what he thought he might gain by seeing Victor Rodriguez. It was apparent that the police here had already tried to talk to the man. They might have evidence on the son, but if they didn't have anything solid on the father, they couldn't arrest him.

And even if they could arrest him, they couldn't force him to talk.

"I'm not sure he'll agree—"

"I'll check in with his attorneys," Jude said. He shrugged. "I have a law degree, maybe…"

He let off with a shrug and then added, "We can't thank you two enough. We'll start at this all from the other end now. And thanks—you gave us your cards. Hope it's okay if we call you—"

"If you need anything at all!" Banks assured him. "I'll see to it the information on the Rodriguez legal team and anything else is sent to your phones."

"Perfect, thanks," Jude told them.

Vicky echoed his thanks, and they headed back toward their own car.

In the car, she stared at him incredulously and asked, "You have a law degree? You're just mentioning that now?"

He sighed. "I have a degree, yes. But I wanted to be an agent. I haven't practiced law, so it didn't really seem like something that important."

"We're looking into a law firm!" she reminded him.

"And if my degree can help at any point, I'll use it!"

She shook her head, smiling and looking down. Then she said, "Okay. Just what do you think we can get from Victor

Rodriguez? The man was guilty as all hell according to the evidence and what he said—"

"But what if he wasn't?" Jude asked.

"What? You heard what they told us. Jude, we have all those records, and the man was screaming about the woman when the police nabbed him."

"From what I understand—and you can read the records again—he kept screaming she got what she deserved. He didn't say he'd done it—just that she had gotten what she deserved."

"But he had the knife. He was covered in blood—"

"He could have picked up the knife. And anyone near a scene like that might well be covered in blood," Jude said.

"But...why? Why would he let himself be tried, go on the stand, say things that sounded a hell of a lot like a confession unless... Oh!" Vicky said.

He smiled, nodding as he drove.

"You're getting my drift. I read the records. Victor Rodriguez grew up in Tennessee—he was born in America. His father was born in Colombia—born into a cartel family. That's why I want to meet them both. Maybe Victor would have been fine with a divorce. But when you get into a man who is pure cartel and powerful enough to laugh at the DEA, you may discover a man who wouldn't tolerate the least indiscretion from a woman. And..."

"You think the son might have admitted to the murder—in lieu of his father? Why?"

Jude shrugged. "Maybe to make the old man proud of him at last? And maybe because they both believed Carlos could get Victor freed while Victor didn't have his father's influence, money, or power among other murderers and thieves."

"And when Judge McFarlane wouldn't budge in any way, shape, or form..."

"He had to die," Jude said, looking at the road ahead. "It's just a theory. But... I think we need to meet both men."

"So, I'll go after the father at the bar while you take your law degree to the prison. Wait! Do you really have a law degree?" she asked. "I mean, we don't want to do anything that won't stand up in court if we can get someone to charge!"

He shrugged and smiled. "Yeah, I really do have a law degree, and I have passed the bar in Florida. Loved the law before discovering I loved criminology more and that I wanted to be in the field. I'm not going to lie. I do keep up with an association that deals with 'innocence' work because more often than we'd like to believe, we do get the wrong person for various reasons. And when things are brought to us… Well, you don't want to keep a real killer out on the streets. And you don't want to keep innocent people in jail. Oh. And yes—and no," he told her.

"What?" she asked. "You know, I'm learning to follow that very strange mind of yours, but I can't follow that one!"

He smiled again. "We're not going anywhere alone. If I go into the prison as an attorney with one of the innocence projects, you'll come in as my assistant. And when you go into the bar—you are gorgeous. You'll be able to flirt easily, charm the old bastard, but…"

"But?"

"I'll be at the bar, too. We aren't splitting up on this."

"And here I thought you were the great loner!"

He was quiet, still staring straight ahead. Then he apparently decided it was time to explain himself to her.

"I worked with a fellow named Matt Reid when I started with the Bureau. I was the junior in our twosome. But…we were working a dual case with the DEA as it happened. I knew something wasn't right at a meet—I told Matt not to go in alone. He thought his undercover identity was completely solid. I just—knew something was wrong. I followed him, and I saw the dealer draw his gun, and I got a shot off. But just at the same time that he did. The dealer went down but so did Matt. He was a great guy, but he didn't think he needed backup. And now..."

"I'm so sorry. He was killed?"

"Matt is alive. In a wheelchair for the rest of his life."

"I'm truly sorry."

He nodded. "So—"

"So, when you learned just how important backup was, you went off on your own?" she asked dryly.

He turned at last to smile at her.

"You've reminded me there is nothing in the world like having a partner you trust in every aspect of the job," he said quietly.

"And you'll also be damned if you won't have my back?" Vicky asked.

"You got it," he said. "So...let's give Aidan a call. He can set us up with Victor Rodriguez's attorneys and pave the way for all that's needed. Tonight... Hell, I could use a drink!"

"Wait! You're going to a bar to drink and have my back?"

He laughed. "Nonalcoholic beer tonight. Fear not!"

"I wasn't afraid," she assured him.

Vicky made the call to Aidan and was surprised Aidan didn't seem at all confused. But then Jude had been working out of a Florida office, and he and Aidan knew one another...

So Aidan probably already knew about all the mysteries behind Jude.

And it did seem there were several.

With her call completed, she leaned back against the seat. The sun was bright. It felt as if the day had been long already. But Arnold had, indeed, called them at the crack of dawn.

They'd flown here. They'd driven...

And it was barely noon.

The day had just begun.

She closed her eyes. He was fine driving; she could rest. If he wanted her to drive, he'd let her know.

But she had barely closed her eyes when her phone began to ring.

Aidan. Of course. He'd have been working right away on her request, and he and Cary seemed to have a special magic with communication.

"You're all cleared. You can head straight to the prison. Federal, because the sister-in-law who was killed was kidnapped from Georgia, so you're talking about crossing state lines, which is how the FBI wound up involved from the get-go. I have you heading straight to the prison," Aidan told her. "And then at four, you have an appointment with Special Agent Enrique Torres. He was there for the arrest and the trial."

She glanced at Jude.

"Putting our address into the navigation," she said.

"GPS," he murmured.

"Well, right."

"AI," he said.

"Well, a form of it, of course," Vicky agreed.

He was frowning.

"Call Assistant Director Arnold. Tell him we need a different car. Something old—something without a computer," Jude told her.

"Jude. This is a Bureau car—"

"And as you've taught me, anything can be hacked."

"Oh? But now, today, here? You think someone—"

"Yes. They may well know why we're here and exactly what we're doing. Country roads! The judge—"

He broke off.

"Out! Get out—just jump out and roll. Now!" Jude said.

She could feel it. The car picking up speed…

As he had commanded, she threw open her door. She halfway jumped and halfway rolled out of the car, wincing as she hit the ground hard before rolling toward the softer embankment.

And it hurt, of course. She'd have bruises and scrapes and scratches, but...

The car she had leaped from careened off the road at a stunning speed...

Crashed into a grove of trees...

And exploded with a fiery thunder.

SIX

Jude felt it, naturally, when he hit the ground and rolled.

But he quickly leaped to his feet, grateful he had felt the subtle change in the car when he was no longer in control of the vehicle.

Vicky had moved quick as a whip. But…

She was rising from the soft grass of the embankment even as he anxiously rushed toward her.

"Are you—"

"Fine. A scratched knee. Two scratched knees. I'll live. Oh, my God, Jude, if you hadn't…"

She broke off, staring at the smashed-up car and the fire still burning in the trees.

"I could feel it," he told her. "I was forewarned because we knew what had happened to someone else. The judge wouldn't have known what was coming."

"But same place, same thing?" she asked him. "Maybe we were wrong! Maybe what has been happening has more to do with what happened here."

"Or what's happening extends wherever it needs to go," Jude

said. "I can't shake it, though. There's just something about the law firm where Marci worked. Shady!"

"Right, but we're here now..."

"And local police will be out, hopefully aware of what's going on so we don't spend the day in long explanations and can get going on what we need to get done." He smiled suddenly. Somehow, she still looked great. She'd been wearing a navy blue pantsuit. It barely looked the worse for wear—especially considering the "wear" it had just gone through.

But a long lock of her hair had swung crazily over the top of her head. Without thinking, he reached out to return it to its normal place.

He winced inwardly; maybe not the politically correct thing to do.

Thankfully, she just laughed. "Thanks! I'm going to guess that was an interesting hairdo I had going there!"

"Eh. You could have pulled it off," Jude returned lightly. Then he grew more somber. "You're sure you're okay? Should we head to a hospital? The health and well-being of an agent—"

"I'm seriously fine. What about you?"

"Scratches, nothing more and I do not want anyone to suggest we waste time heading in to be checked out if it's not necessary. So..."

Vicky arched a brow to him.

"Country road!" she reminded him, drawing out her phone.

"Oh, ouch, yeah—who knows when someone may be by."

"Calling Aidan," she assured him.

Either Aidan really did possess magic, or the state police they had so recently parted ways with had seen the explosion in their rearview.

Vicky had barely finished her call to Aidan before sirens were blaring, and Como and Banks were back. They were soon accompanied by the arrival of the forensic and arson crews they had called in from the state.

As Jude had feared, Banks and Como—after being appropriately horrified and worried that they were all right, began to talk about reports and paperwork. And because the vehicle they'd been in was in fragments that were still smoldering, they were at the mercy of the state police.

At first.

But Aidan was proving to be magic. A car arrived, driven by a man who introduced himself as Special Agent Tom Conner of the Nashville office. He'd been given orders to collect them, to bring them to the federal prison, and to leave them with the vehicle he'd brought—a fully restored '57 Chevy.

A vehicle created long before computers controlled everything on four wheels.

"I don't think I've ever seen such a beautiful car!" Vicky assured Conner. He grinned in return. He was a young agent, probably had not been with the Bureau more than a few years. But she imagined he, just like Jude Mackenzie, might be a true asset in an undercover situation.

"Yeah. I'm going to be heading to my dad's garage for an old baby like this myself, until all this is figured out!" Conner told him.

Banks and Como were looking from Conner to Vicky and Jude.

"Maybe..." Banks murmured.

"How many of these puppies do you think are out there?" Como asked.

Banks shrugged. "I never heard of two cars taking off like demons to crash into groves of trees before, so I admit, I haven't looked into purchasing classic automobiles lately. But I will. And forgive me, my new friends, but we must have the proper paperwork—"

And that's when the magic of Assistant Director Arnold kicked in.

"They'll be by the precinct in a few hours. I have direct orders—federal orders—to get this duo where they need to be. We can't stop a minute on this—as you can see by that fire of twisted metal still burning in the trees. They'll get their paperwork done," Conner promised, "just not right this second."

With a wave to indicate the classic Chevy, Jude and Vicky both thanked Como and Banks as they hurried to the car. Jude slid into the back, allowing Vicky to take the front passenger's seat.

As he drove, Tom Conner glanced at Vicky and then through his rearview mirror at Jude.

"I understand you're going to see Victor Rodriguez about all this. You know what the man did, right? Most horrendous murders in my career, certainly. But he's been in prison, and I'm not sure how he could have caused any of this. His father has been under investigation for years, but no one has pinned anything on him yet. He knows how to use money to keep his hands clean."

Jude leaned forward. "It's our understanding nothing changed with the death of the judge. Victor remains on death row, and all his father's machinations haven't managed to change anything for him yet," he said.

"That is correct," Special Agent Conner said. "Carlos Rodriguez has managed to stay above the law time and time again. People go to prison, terrified to talk, or they wind up dead. In the judge's case it was Assistant Director Arnold who was suspicious. Otherwise, everyone was assuming it was an accident—the judge's brakes simply failed, something that does happen. But we're all aware of everything going on now—the woman killed in her home by electric knife and electrocution, the boating accident, the judge, and now this," Conner said seriously. "Doesn't take anyone on the top tier of brilliant to hack a car system. Many cars have been stolen through their computer systems because all a hacker needs to do is get into a phone system, find and start a car, and off they go. Thankfully, it's usually thieves rather than murderers who seem to be the best car hackers, but…since it is possible to hack car computer systems, then it's easy enough to do what's now been done twice. Disable the brakes and set the speed at a zillion miles an hour, and there you go." He glanced at Jude in the rearview mirror again. "Man, you two are lucky!"

"We are," Vicky told Conner, looking back at Jude. "Very lucky!"

He shrugged. "Someone knew we were here and why we were here. We do, seriously, have some of the best people working with AI today, but whoever is doing this is using servers from all over, bouncing through systems all over the globe. But our people will prevail, I believe it with my whole heart. I'm just hoping we stop them before more people die."

"Amen," Conner murmured. "Almost there."

Jude had been to the prison in Nashville before, but he saw Vicky was looking closely at everything as they moved along with the three of them being required to show ID and badges before getting the car through the gates. Once parked, Conner handed the keys to Vicky and leaned against the driver's door.

"I'm being picked up. Bosses say you're good on your own so long as you can drive a car that doesn't wind up in a tree. But the administration has sent you my info. I'm a call away and a homegrown boy. I know Nashville and environs all the way across the state when necessary. If things should get settled, I could take you to hear some of the top new music in country western, but…"

"If we get through this, I'm coming back to Nashville to take you up on that," Jude assured him.

"You bet!" Vicky echoed.

Tom Conner pointed for them. "Head straight that way, kind of a given. They'll have you check your weapons, verify your IDs and badges, and get you on through. What you're expecting, though… Well, good luck with whatever! The cartel scares the hell out of even the cartel!"

"Right. But then again, how can a death threat be scarier than the certainty of death?" Jude asked.

"Unless you have a wife or kids," Vicky reminded him.

"Okay, good point," Jude agreed. "But—"

"Victor Rodriguez isn't married anymore. His wife is already dead. They'd only been married about a year. She was just twenty-four. The couple had no children," Conner told them. "I guess they never really got the chance to have a family. Well, I hope you get somewhere we haven't managed to get!"

He waved and left them. Jude looked at Vicky.

"Ready?"

"Let's do this," she said. "I'm not at all sure, but…"

"Do you think she was cheating?"

Vicky hesitated and shook her head. "No idea whatsoever. But…wow. That was a violent death. One would think…"

"Yeah?"

"Well, we've had files on these people. The younger Rodriguez—hey, he never even got a parking ticket. And along with his dad, he was obviously on the DEA's radar. No record. On paper…he just looks like any other kid who majored in business, met a girl, fell in love, got married. I don't know. You do have crazy hunches, but…" She broke off, shrugging.

"Carlos Rodriguez is not just old-school—he's cartel old-school. Drug lord. Rich man, smart as a whip, knows how to keep his hands clean, but…from what I've read, there seemed to be a lot of corpses falling around him. He always had an alibi, but…"

"No way out of the fact he's a violent man," Vicky agreed. "We're here, so…"

Jude didn't understand what he was hoping for. It was unlikely this man would rat out his father, especially since he'd been found with the knife that had killed the two women, covered in their blood. But…

"Nothing gained if nothing tried," he murmured.

Of course, the authorities knew they were coming; it was quick business to show their badges and IDs and turn in their weapons.

Aidan had evidently spoken with Assistant Director Arnold who had in turn spoken with his bosses. And it seemed true this case was uppermost among cases in the country, even if it seemed that they were the ones working in the field. Alone.

But it was a cyber case.

And Jude knew the "cyber" portion was being investigated nonstop.

They arrived in the interrogation room. Through the window, Jude could see Victor Rodriguez was already there with his handcuffs attached to a bar on the table.

A quiet, somber, and courteous guard waited at the door and opened it with a nod and allowed them entry. They took the chairs opposite the table from Rodriguez, studying him as he studied them.

He was young, mid-twenties. A handsome young man with dark hair and eyes, and a good face. Among young women, he probably did quite well.

But he'd had a wife, a beautiful wife, Jude thought to himself. *Had he loved her? Had the machismo thing in him raged with such a fury that he'd really cut her to ribbons?*

Or…

"Mr. Rodriguez," Vicky said. "I'm Special Agent Tennant, but you can call me Vicky. And this is my partner, Special Agent Mackenzie, but you can call him Jude. Thank you for seeing us."

The man grinned. "Yeah, you know, it wasn't easy fitting you into my calendar here, but… Okay, it's boring as all hell, so… Well, you know. Why not talk to you?"

Vicky smiled graciously at him. "Well, I'm certainly glad we could break up your boredom."

He shrugged. "Right. Except… I don't see what you're going to get out of me. I thought you were with some kind of innocence project. I admitted I was guilty."

"Did you love you wife, Mr. Rodriguez?" Vicky asked.

He lowered his head.

Yes, he had loved her, Jude thought.

"You were born in this country, weren't you?" Jude asked him.

"Yes, I loved my wife. Yes, I was born in this country. Grew up with great country music, beautiful little farm with horses and dairy cows…all that good stuff. No excuse for what I did except…well, I was in pain. She cheated on me!"

"You caught her cheating?" Vicky asked.

He leaned back in his chair with eyes lowered again. "I… Well, you know. Where there's smoke, there's fire. And my dad's friend, Mark Mason, heard about Peggy being with Tony Alvarez and he told my dad so that my dad could tell me and…"

"Let's see. Before that, you'd never even gotten into a bar fight," Vicky said.

"Matters of the heart," Rodriguez said.

He wouldn't look at them. Vicky glanced at Jude and he almost smiled; she believed him. It was the older Rodriguez who had done the killing. For his son's honor.

But the son, either through respect or coercion or even fear, hadn't been about to let the blame be placed on his father.

"You loved this woman, but she cheated on you. And loving her, you still dismembered her bit by bit until she bled to death?" Vicky whispered. "And then her sister."

He shook his head suddenly. "Ada just happened to be there. And, um, I guess, I mean, she would have known what Peggy was doing, and Ada…" He broke off, shaking his head. "What does it matter? It was horrible. I did it."

Jude nodded slowly and then leaned forward, causing the man to look up. "I don't think that's true at all. First, you didn't know for certain your wife was cheating on you. And the whole thing of being a man, a true chauvinist… Your father might have seen it somewhere else, in his sphere of people in his old country, but this is Tennessee, the old USA. We have our problems. But the marital kind, those end with divorce most of the time. You didn't kill your wife. You walked in when it was all over. You saw her and the blood was all over you because you had to hold her, had to caress her torso, maybe, whatever was left, touch her face—because you did love her. You couldn't believe what you were seeing."

"No, no, I had the knife on me," he protested, shaking his head.

"Because you picked it up from where it was lying by the body," Jude said quietly.

"And you knew the cops were there. And by some old country ways, your father did what he did because he didn't think you had the balls to do it, but it needed to be done," Vicky said. "And you believed he could get you out of all this, but you had no power to get him out of it. Also, you figured that pretending you did the crime would restore some of your honor—come on, seriously! By the old ways, she deserved what she got. Women don't cheat on men. Makes the guy a cuckhold, a fool. You don't really have a violent bone in your body but taking care of business was expected of you. Except something went really wrong. The judge sentenced you to death. And even with that judge dead now, you're still sentenced to death, and it doesn't look like the appeals are going well. You may spend some time on death row, but then… Well, who knows what it will be then. Not all lethal injections have been all that humane lately…pity!" she finished, looking at Jude.

"And you're what, twenty-seven, I believe," Jude said.

"While your dad... I hear he's in his seventies, you were kind of a later-in-life kid for him, but..."

"He thinks you're expendable?" Vicky asked softly, as if she was completely confused by such a possibility. "Well, there are people like that, though it's rare. Human instinct is to protect our offspring! I mean, I'd die before I'd see something horrible happen to a child of mine, and that isn't just me. That's being a human being!"

Her words were passionate, ringing with emotion. The expression on her face was so sincere. For a moment Victor Rodriguez looked up at her, and he saw her face, heard her voice...

"You don't understand!" he cried. "I wasn't being a man!"

"So, your father thought he had to be a man for you. But Victor, being a man means you also stand up for your actions. Your father killed those women, and he left you holding the guilt for it—"

"Because *I* should have done something, *I* should have taken care of it!" Victor cried.

Jude leaned back, crossing his arms over his chest.

"No, Victor. You're an American. First, we don't presume people are guilty. When we have a case of someone said something, we investigate. Remember? Innocent until proven guilty. You loved your wife. You had no proof she was being unfaithful. Your father killed her. And you're sitting on death row," he reminded him.

Victor shook his head. When he looked up, his eyes were damp. Jude was pretty sure it was because he had loved his wife—but he'd been given such strict machismo training he felt guilty for having loved her, for having wanted to give her a chance. He might have grown up to be a good and decent human being—had he ever been given the chance.

"You—you don't understand!" he whispered.

"Oh, no, we understand perfectly. Your father was convinced he knew something—that most likely wasn't true. And because he's got an image of who he is in his mind, he decided your beloved wife had to die—in the most torturous, horrendous way possible. And then he put it all on you. That isn't being a man. As far as your father goes, Victor, that's taking a cop-out. You didn't do a damned thing. And here you are—"

"He's going to get me off death row!" Victor claimed. "He, um…he takes care of things."

Vicky leaned closer to Victor, speaking gently. "No, Victor, I mean, he may have arranged to kill the judge, but that doesn't mean anything at all. Yes, the judge is dead. That doesn't change your sentence—it only means your father committed murder. Even if he didn't physically kill the man, but rather he arranged for the judge to be killed—murder for hire, murder by machine. Victor, please you must see, none of this means he cares about you. It's what he has in his own twisted mind along with the belief that anyone who falls in his service doesn't matter at all—not even his son. Your death sentence still stands. The appeal is going to fall through. And you will rot on death row until your execution. All of this will happen to you just for having the person you loved most in the world taken away from you."

Victor put his head down and a sob escaped him. "I—I just don't care if I live or die anymore. She's gone. And what was done to her… Oh, God, I…"

"Your father apparently knew FBI agents were in town," Jude told him. "He hired his murder machine people to kill us, too. We managed to escape."

"But…"

Vicky stood and spoke gently again. "Think about all this, Victor. Please. You somehow grew up to be a good man. There's no reason for you to be here."

"I just don't care…" Victor began.

"But you should. You said you loved her. You still love her. Life isn't worth living without her. Because of that, don't you think you owe her justice? That in her name, Victor, you should see to it that more innocent people don't die?" Jude asked quietly. "Victor, think of what was done to the woman you loved, the woman you held in your arms, the woman with whom you would have had a family one day, her little ones to love and nurture."

Jude stood next to Vicky. "Just think, Victor. Think about who is owed what. And if you don't care about yourself anymore, please, think about your beautiful young wife tortured mercilessly and most probably for nothing, and then she was taken from you. We won't ask anything more of you now. Just please, think about the things we've said, and what we've talked about."

Victor winced, looking downward for a minute.

Then he looked up at Jude.

"It doesn't matter. None of it matters. Everyone knows my father ordered the killing of that judge—it was no accident. Everyone is terrified of my father. No lawyer will stand by me. No one could help me if I wanted to be helped." He shook his head. "Maybe I've been terrified of him, too. Maybe I knew from the beginning I had to 'man-up' and take the blame because..."

"You think your father could and would order your death before you ever made it to the death chamber?" Vicky asked quietly.

Victor Rodriguez shrugged. "My mother died of cancer a few years ago. My father didn't really answer to her when she was alive, but...but it doesn't matter. She's gone."

"Victor, I am so sorry to say this, none of us ever wants to believe such a thing, but in your heart, you know your father is a monster. You even know that he stole the most important thing in the world from you, Peggy's unconditional love. We will do something," Vicky said.

"I believe you mean what you're saying. But don't you understand? It's impossible. The world is afraid of my father," Victor said.

Jude smiled. "Not quite true, Victor. I'm not afraid of your father."

"And neither am I," Vicky said resolutely. "He tried to take us out already. He failed. And he brought an army against us, but guess what? We have our own army—we have the Bureau, the DEA, police, Homeland Security... We're not afraid."

Jude grinned. "The only thing that scares Vicky is when there might be an injustice—and that just puts her in fighting mode!"

"Just don't fight to the death!" Victor pleaded in a whisper.

"Oh, we might," Vicky said. "But it won't be our deaths, I promise you that! Thank you. I'm not sure you intended to be honest with us, but...you may have saved a lot of lives today!"

"From death row," he murmured.

"And that might change, too," Jude told him.

"I'd still be on death row the rest of my life," Victor said.

"WITSEC," Vicky said.

"Witness protection," Jude explained when Victor appeared to be confused by her words. "A brand-new identity that no one knows in a place where no one could ever find you. Look, we're law enforcement. We don't go after people to kill them. We go after them to arrest them and bring them to justice. And I know you think you'd be a target as long as your father lived. But trust me, a man like your father would be in solitary confinement, no access to corruptible people or computers. He can be stopped, Victor. And you can have a brand-new life as a brand-new human being."

"The good one you were meant to be," Vicky said softly.

Jude wasn't sure they had convinced the man as they said their goodbyes and left, but he was certain they had him thinking.

And he was also damned glad his hunch had paid off.

They retrieved their service weapons and left the prison. In the car, Vicky turned to him shaking her head.

"I can hardly believe this!" she said.

"That Carlos Rodriguez killed Peggy and her sister and not Victor?"

She laughed. "No! That another one of your hunches proved to be correct! What? Do you read minds or something? Sound waves, airwaves?"

He grinned, looking at the road. "No… I've just come across men like Carlos Rodriguez before. And they're not… I don't know, normal human beings? I mean, it is human instinct to protect one's offspring. But not with a man like Carlos. That a woman just may have stepped out on his son… Carlos couldn't abide such an idea and he wouldn't have needed proof—just the suggestion. I wasn't sure about Victor, but now…"

"He could have led a normal life. Or something like a crime-free life, anyway," Vicky said. "So. Now we have this information. Still…what the hell do we do with it? We have no evidence, nothing legal to stand on…"

"Ah, well, pretty girl," he teased, "that's where you come in. It's almost time for you to go flirt with the old dad at his favorite bar!"

"And that could be almost worthless, too," she murmured.

"You underestimate yourself," he said. He realized he was being truthful. Vicky was more than just a beautiful woman. She had an air about her… Professionalism, yes. But humor, too, and a smile that could charm…

"The man would need to be an ice cube not to fall for you," he said. "You're going to do just fine."

She looked over at him, arching a curious brow, and offering him a smile. "Thanks… I think! Well we have one thing going for us," she told him.

"What's that?"

"In this car, we have a real chance of getting where we're

going!" she said. "But…hmm, I should have changed for the evening. But since our overnight go-bags blew up with the car…"

"I told you. You're gorgeous, you look great."

He smiled as she leaned back and said softly, "Thanks for the vote of confidence!"

"Oh, and you can be confident, too. Trust me," he assured her. "I will be close."

"But I do sincerely doubt the man is going to fall head over heels for me and admit to killing his daughter-in-law and allowing his not manly-enough-for-his-taste son take the blame."

"Wires and earpieces," Jude said. "Again, remember, I will be right there. I think you just need to get him talking about relationships between men and women, the role of women in the world, how a man takes care of himself and his family and demands respect and…"

She laughed. "Maybe you should do the flirting!" She grew serious, then. "Jude, this is a man who diced two women into a dozen body parts. And you think he'd also hire someone to cause cars to go off the road?"

"Yes. The first one was personal. In his eyes, she made his son look unmanly."

"Do you think the poor woman ever really did anything wrong?"

He shook his head. "To someone like Carlos Rodriguez, appearances matter. I don't know what I think. I never knew Peggy Rodriguez, and we certainly can't track down her movements now. And yes, I think Carlos Rodriguez was quite capable of doing his own dirty work. But when he killed Peggy and her sister, he knew Victor would have to 'man up' and take the rap. I don't know why, but I don't think he ever expected his son would get the death penalty. Will he let him die to save his own butt? Oh, you bet. But in his warped mind, the judge needed to pay as well. And if there was a car accident, well how the hell does anyone prove he hired the kill?"

"I understand, and you have a good point…and how the hell do we prove it now? I know cybercrimes techs have been searching, and the man's money is all in offshore accounts. They haven't been able to trace anything, so…"

"You never know what he'll tell a beautiful woman he's happy to seduce."

"One he tried to kill."

"But he never saw us. He just knew agents were here, and he knew what we were driving. He has no idea what we look like. And again, if it looks as if he's about to harm a single hair on your head, you know I'll be there!" Jude assured her.

"You'll have my back. I have faith," she said.

"I swear it," he assured her, adding solemnly, "On my life!"

SEVEN

Vicky wasn't sure in the least about being any kind of a femme fatale, but she had to admit one thing: her new partner seemed to have strangely accurate hunches.

Of course, it would have been nice to shower, change, refresh her makeup...feel more the part. But she was ready to do whatever was needed to bring down a human being who could have done something so horrendous to another.

She'd learned that an agent could never let their temper—their horror regarding aspects of the unthinkable things one man or woman could do to another—become the driving focus. They never set out to use their weapons unless absolutely necessary.

Those who went out trigger happy—maybe justifiably—were no better than those they sought to keep away from the public, those innocents who too often fell prey to a predator.

But she couldn't help thinking she was glad she was well-trained as an agent.

Shooting would be too kind for a man who had done what Carlos Rodriguez had done. And still, the law was the law:

those who upheld the law couldn't become murderers themselves. Officers, detectives, agents…all were human beings first. But most were good people, and most intended to uphold the law. Every once in a while, there was a bad egg in the blend. Bad eggs needed to be ejected but, by and large in Vicky's experience, most men and women in law enforcement were good people who had sworn to uphold the law. They were just that: officers, detectives, agents, not judge and jury.

Besides, if Carlos Rodriguez wound up dead, it would be difficult for any attorney to prove his son was innocent.

At the local offices, they'd been offered any assistance they might need. Jude had wanted her wired, and he wanted the mics and earpieces that would allow them instant and constant communication. Vicky knew he was right. They needed to be tighter than hell on any move they made that had to do with Carlos Rodriguez.

Assistant Director Arnold had been in contact with the SAC in charge in Nashville, and Vicky and Jude were assured there would be undercover agents in the bar as well as agents out in the street.

Special Agent Tom Conner would be playing at the bar—in his personal life, he was a drummer with a country western band known as the Ranch Hands, and that was something intriguing as well.

Carlos Rodriguez might hang out at the bar, but it was a legitimate business. A few words from the right person, and the Ranch Hands had been hired for the night.

It was time.

And while it seemed like a wild card play to Vicky, it was good to have the backing of the local office, good to know they were well covered.

Someone else in the hierarchy had apparently discovered that many of Jude's hunches turned out to lead them right where they wanted to go.

Jude dropped Vicky off about a block from the bar, allowing them both to arrive separately. He made a face as he did so.

"What?" she asked.

"I don't even like that you're doing this and—"

"Hey, not to worry. I'm armed and I think I'm safe on the sidewalk with the guy inside drinking already, according to our sources."

"Right. I'm just—"

"If you're too nervous, if you doubt me—"

"Not for a second. It's just difficult not to think about what this man is capable of doing. Go get him, Tiger!"

He left her and drove off.

Vicky did manage to walk the block without incident. She paused before going in. Large letters announcing that it was the Cattleman's Watering Hole sat atop the entry, along with artistically rendered skeletons raising glasses and playing musical instruments.

Local charm aplenty.

Vicky smiled as she entered. Tom's band was four pieces: lead guitar, bass, keyboards, and drums. The lead guitarist was in jeans and a tailored shirt, doing a good job with a John Denver song as she entered.

The place was decently large with a huge horseshoe bar and at least thirty to forty tables seating different-sized parties, from just two people to eight and ten. The band was on a stage a good distance from the bar. The acoustics in the place were good; the music could be heard without causing deafness. She saw Tom behind the drums, giving his attention to his music, and backing up the lead singer on his mic now and then.

She saw Jude was already seated at the bar, in conversation with a man who looked like a banker or businessman on the one side and another fellow in a ten-gallon hat, jeans, and denim jacket on the other. He saw her and inclined his head just slightly. There were just a few tables on the far side of the bar. And the band could be heard from those tables but not seen.

She walked around the bar. Jude's new cowboy friend looked over at her and whistled softly; she pretended she didn't hear him and walked on around to the tables in the rear.

She was in luck.

She'd seen images of Carlos Rodriguez, but even if she hadn't, she would have known the man. He was an older version of his son, a good-looking man of about seventy, and she assumed he might have his son's charm when he chose to smile as well.

The two-top next to his was open, and she slid in sighing softly as she leaned back.

"Are you all right, miss?" the man asked her.

"Oh!" she said, straightening and giving him her best—and most awkward—smile. "Oh, I, um, yes, I'm fine, just tired. Meetings all day, you know."

"I do know, I'm afraid. But you've come to the right place. Low-key, good music. But you're not from Tennessee, are you?"

She shook her head, grinning. "Here on business. And you?"

"Nashville is my home. I travel a lot on business, but Nashville is where I choose to lay my head."

"But," she said, hopefully giving him a charming and curious arch of the brow, "you're not from here originally, right? Latin American. You have the..." She broke off and laughed softly. "My grandmother called it the 'Ricky Ricardo' charm. She loved that old show—*I Love Lucy*. Because, I think, she had a mad crush on Ricky Ricardo."

He laughed. "Okay. No, I'm not from Tennessee originally. Medellín, Colombia," he told her, "and thus my charming accent. Not so common here, eh? Texas, California, Florida... more Central and Latin American peoples among their populations."

She smiled. "Ah, so here you can make use of that Ricky Ricardo charm!"

"Ah, you say that I have it?" he queried.

A pretty young cocktail waitress arrived at her table, a frosty glass of beer on her tray.

"The lady hasn't ordered yet," Rodriguez told the waitress.

"It's a gift from the band. The drummer said they met and discussed beer while waiting for their luggage at the airport. You don't have to take it, of course, but—"

"No, no, thank you, and thank him!" Vicky said quickly.

She heard Tom's voice in her ear as his lead player announced they would be doing a slate of Willie Nelson, Johnny Cash, and Bob Dylan. "Nonalcoholic!" he assured her.

"Thank you!" she said easily.

The waitress nodded with a smile and moved away.

"And I had wanted to offer to buy you a drink!" Rodriguez said.

"Well, thank you. I am finding that in Nashville, people are very kind!" she told him. She offered him her hand. "Sir, you seem very polite and caring. I'm glad to meet you. You're so different from..." She paused, wincing. "Um, well, you know, those who are just... I'm sorry. Too much information, but... I don't know. I believe in, well, a relationship, one with loyalty and...again. I'm so sorry, we've just met and we're in a bar and I suppose one assumes in a bar... Anyway, I'm Vicky. Vicky Tennant!"

"Carlos," he told her. "Carlos Rodriguez."

"Now the young drummer—very circumspect young man, unlike so many others. But Carlos—may I call you Carlos?" she asked.

"Of course. It's what my friends call me. And I like to believe we'll be friends!"

"Me, too!" Vicky said. She indicated the chair next to her. "Join me? And if I'm awkward...forgive me. I don't know why, but I feel I can tell you anything. I'm terribly awkward. I'm just out of a horrid relationship. He—he cheated on me, and I don't believe in cheating. If something is over, it's over. Just tell a person. And then…our money was my money, family money. And somehow he knew the right people, and he managed to take a fortune from me as well. Oh, dear! I must sound so pathetic. Forgive me, and please, you are not obliged in any way to sit with me or talk with me!"

He leaned toward her. "Tell me about this man. There are things that you can do, when you know the right people."

"Oh? Oh, but…well, I may feel hateful, and I may wish that he'd fall into a vat of oil and boil, but I could never do anything," she said. "First, I'd go to jail immediately. Everyone knows how I feel about him!" She looked away, blinking back feigned tears. "I just don't understand…"

"Something can be done," Rodriguez said, setting his hand over hers. "You and I…we are kindred spirits, my dear. Friends who could be so much more. And I take care of those who are mine!"

"You could… I mean, not that I would, but maybe, and I can't help but ask… Would there really be a way to make such a man pay?" she asked. "Did you ever…"

"I am a man, Vicky, a real man. There are certain problems in my life I have handled on my own. But I know crimes when I see them. And there has been justice that I have meted out myself…and you can find justice in dark ways, too, ways that don't connect back to us. I like you," he told her, coming so close that his whisper touched her cheeks, "and I think you like me. And I think your way of seeing loyalty to a man is real and…you could be loyal to me."

"I could be so loyal! It's what I believe. A man is a man, and a woman…she is lucky when she is cared for by such a man, and she needs to give him everything!"

She felt his hand on hers.

"Are we friends?" he asked her softly. "Because we can go somewhere. My place. Yes, let's leave. And I can really show you what such a man can give you, in the physical sense, and in that of the heart and soul!"

How did she play that?

She curled her fingers around her glass, thirsty, which was fine, of course—Tom had seen to it that her beer was nonalcoholic. No chance of even getting tipsy.

She heard Jude's voice then, low and warning. "Stop everything. Don't drink that. I'm coming over. I've got it on camera. Keep away from him!"

"What?"

She hadn't meant to say the word with such surprise. She'd felt she was getting somewhere with the man, and he might have been about to give her more.

Jude was there. Tall, composed, and perhaps more frightening because it seemed that he was stoic, so very contained.

Except, as she lifted her glass to her lips, he suddenly reached out, slamming her hand with the glass back down on the table. She stared at him—truly stunned and mystified.

But he turned to the man at her side.

"Carlos Rodriguez," he announced. "Federal agent. And you're under arrest."

"For what? Like hell I am. You wait until my attorney gets his hands on you. Federal agent, my ass! You'll be knocking out license plates at a federal prison yourself, I guarantee it!" Rodriguez announced. "It's not illegal to speak with a woman at a bar—"

"It is illegal to spike their drinks, and we just recorded you doing exactly that," Jude said flatly. "Oh, and there would be the syringe you had in your hands a few minutes ago. I'm willing to bet it's got another narcotic or something worse in it. Spike the drink, make her agreeable, get her out here, and knock her flat with whatever is in that thing? Feel free to call your attorney. He can meet us, because you are guaranteed your rights no matter how many of those rights—including the right to life—you take from others."

"What?" Rodriguez demanded. "You're going to go on about that wretched judge who couldn't drive to save his life—"

"No. But for the record, I understand that he was an excellent driver. It's just hard to drive when a car's computer has been hacked. That's neither here nor there at the moment. If you would please stand, sir—"

"Hell, no. I don't know what you've read, what you believe, but it's obvious you don't like me. And that's too bad. Get the hell away from me!"

Jude shrugged. He stepped back.

Just to allow two of the most muscle-bound men Vicky had seen outside of a wrestling ring come up to face Rodriguez, asking politely again that he rise. When he didn't, they picked him up by the shoulders, checking him for weapons and taking the syringe Jude had spoken about, and then cuffed him before prodding him toward the door. Ironically, Tom's band was busy doing a Johnny Cash number—"Because you're mine, I walk the line."

Vicky shook her head, staring at Jude. "I almost had him saying something—"

She broke off; a woman was approaching the table, her hands gloved as she reached for Vicky's glass. "Excuse me, Special Agent Tennant. I'm Leona from Forensics."

"Hi, Leona, thank you," Vicky said, and she waited for the woman to leave with the glass before she stared at Jude angrily again.

"I almost had him!"

"What, was he suddenly going to spill everything? Vicky! Listen to me. The cowboy next to me is really Duncan Clark, undercover with the state police. They've had three rapes occur to women who had been at this bar and were left in nearby alleys, assaulted but drugged so heavily they couldn't remember a damned thing. But friends said they'd been here. He had surveillance going, but, Vicky, I saw what the man did. He's using heavy-duty hallucinogens that are knocking out thought and memory, and we didn't dare let you take a swig of that beer. It wasn't the drink—I didn't want him hitting you with what followed the drink. But beyond that..."

"Beyond that, what?"

"We have an edge with Rodriguez. We found a connection between him and the captain of the *Lucky Sun*, Ronald Quincy. Clark managed to find footage through facial recognition that put the two men together in Miami where it seemed a huge haul of cocaine slipped through the fingers of everyone working down there. There hadn't been any connection at the time to either man. The drugs were suspected of being routed very circuitously through Mexico and then into the Gulf. But while you were brilliantly chatting up Rodriguez, Aidan called. Vicky, we couldn't take a chance of you winding up in the hospital for several days. According to Duncan, one of his drugged victims almost died."

"But..." she began.

Her voice faded. She was a young woman, agent or not. She'd learned in college to keep her eyes on her drink at all times, to never accept anything she hadn't seen poured herself.

But today...

She had been so hopeful. But Jude was right.

He'd had her back.

Just as he'd promised.

"Hey, you are more than welcome to keep talking to the man. It will just be in an interrogation room. You were doing incredibly well, but then I knew you would. I'm sorry, but we couldn't risk..."

"I have no interest in losing days or dying!" Vicky assured

him. "And I'm assuming those giant fellows have Carlos moving on into that interrogation room, so…"

"Let's head on out."

She nodded, rising with him, ready to head around the bar and out the door. But she grasped his hand before he could go out, causing him to pause with her in front of the band.

Tom was drumming but he saw them there, nodded, and grinned.

The song ended and she applauded enthusiastically. Jude did the same.

"Great drumming, and the same to everyone else!" she said.

Tom Conner nodded to her, grinning.

Young agents could certainly know their stuff—and be damned good at other stuff as well!

They headed after the arresting agents and Carlos Rodriguez. Vicky stood still for a moment, leaning slightly back, closing her eyes, grateful it had taken her a long time to sip the beer—of course, she would not know until she saw the surveillance footage just when he'd managed to slip his drug into her drink, but the thought she might have swallowed down a good bit was…

Ironically sobering!

And now, of course, the gloves could be off. The man was in their territory; they would have him in an interrogation room.

They were met by Jude's new friend, the "cowboy" agent, Duncan Clark. Clark told them Rodriguez had been offered a phone call to his attorney and had also been read his rights.

"Our SAC is out of the office," Duncan told them, "called to DC on this investigation. He'll be back tomorrow. But I've spoken with him, and he's all for the two of you doing anything you can. They have rooms in DC where everyone has been working on this, but the director himself seems to believe it's important that the two of you stick close to the field and keep up with your people dedicated to—and close to—some of the major events. Seems like the director is afraid of even more than a murder for hire by AI."

"No attorney yet?" Jude asked.

"Nope," Duncan told them. "Carlos Rodriguez got angry, apparently, and assured the arresting agents he'd done nothing, they'd all pay, and when he was ready, they could be damned certain he'd have an army of attorneys who could make them go to jail themselves."

"And he believes it," Vicky murmured. "The man gives new meaning to narcissism."

Jude shrugged, shaking his head and looking at the other two.

"He did play all his activity brilliantly for a long time, and he instilled a sense of being lesser into his son that was truly… awful, for a father to a child! But his confidence that he can get away with anything makes him careless. He honestly believes he is above the law and that he'll just kill anyone in his way. He will trip himself up. He's actually let it have an effect on his mind. So, any objections with my playbook? I'll take him first, leave, and then send Vicky in? I don't believe the man realizes he was taken in by an agent yet, and when he sees you here…"

"Wait. This is completely aboveboard? He really hasn't demanded his attorney?" Vicky asked. "The way he was talking—"

"Come on, Vicky. It's not strange he changed his tune. You know every word I said was true. He's a misogynist, a chauvinist, and a narcissist. He's sure we can't touch him, no matter the evidence," Jude said, shaking his head. "When he realizes that isn't the case, like it or not, he'll need help. Now, I believe he'll be screaming for his attorney. Or attorneys. Maybe he has an army of them to be called upon when he feels he actually needs them, high-priced people. But I don't think he is aware that federal prosecutors can be damned good, too."

"Right, but if he's been arrested on the drugged drinks and the rapes, those are really state charges. And state prosecutors can be brilliant, too, but how are we—" Vicky started to remind him.

Duncan Clark stepped in. "We've got total local cooperation. Local, state, and federal agencies have been after this man a long, long time. There isn't an agency out there that won't be happy to see him behind bars—no matter where the bars are as long as they're the kind made out of metal and don't include a happy hour," Duncan said dryly.

"Did you want a crack at him?" Jude asked the man.

But Duncan shook his head. "As far as the undercover work in the area goes, I'm a rancher with whole hell of a lot of cows." He shrugged. "Helps that my family does own a ranch. But no, I'm staying undercover until we know we've got this sewn up, so I'm happy to observe!"

"And we're thankful you've been observing!" Vicky assured him.

"You bet," Jude said. "All right, I'm going in. I'll be out quickly. Vicky, then you'll go in. And remind him that he's a man, oh, what a manly man! And that he should take responsibility."

"Copy that," Vicky murmured.

He left her in the observation room along with Duncan Clark.

They watched Jude walk in, throwing a folder on the table. Vicky wondered what was in it. They couldn't really have much paperwork on the man and if they did, none of it could warrant an arrest. If so, he'd have been in the room long before now.

"You!" Rodriguez spat out.

"I know. It must be a shock, right? You tried to kill me earlier," Jude said.

Rodriguez laughed and leaned in. "If I'd tried to kill you, you'd be dead."

"Wow, that's a weird confession," Jude said.

"Not a confession at all. I said *if*," Rodriguez told him.

"Hmm. But when something is personal, when something demands that a man—a real man—takes care of something himself, you're all over it. Like when you killed your daughter-in-law and her sister," Jude said.

Rodriguez shook his head, looking truly amused. "Don't you people ever know what you're talking about? My son is doing time for that. He's on death row."

"And you really don't give a damn. You managed to hire the right people to kill the judge, but that didn't help any. Victor is still sitting on death row. But even if he's your son, better him than you."

"If you've dragged me in here for that, you'd best open that door and let me walk out. There's no way in hell you can arrest me for that crime!"

"The thing I don't understand is how a real man can let his son pay the price for what he did," Jude said. "Unless, of course, your wife was a cheater, too, and you don't know if that kid is yours or not."

"Trust me, my wife knew better than to ever cheat on me!" Rodriguez said.

"Because she knew you would chop off her limbs—toes and fingers first—arms, legs, head as a finale?"

"My son is a man," Rodriguez said. "Whores deserve what they get."

"But you and I both know you are the one who committed the murders. And Peggy's poor sister! What the hell was that?"

Rodriguez shrugged. "You're asking me to think as Victor? Well, you know, maybe Peggy met the guys she was fooling around with through her sister. Then maybe the poor girl just had the ill luck to be there at the time. Victor confessed. He got the death penalty. We're appealing the penalty. The poor boy wasn't mentally fit when he performed such a deed."

"I thought such a deed made him a manly man, taking care of business," Jude said, as if confused. "And since Victor is truly a manly man, he stepped up to take the blame. Now, in my book, that's what a real man would do."

Rodriguez looked down at his hands. "Victor...he's never been interested in the family business, and I'm afraid..."

"You see your life, already mostly lived, as more important than his? I mean, that's why I assume you were really taken in. Instinct kicks in with most people. For most people, the lives of their children are sacred, they'd do anything to save them. But...hey. Maybe you truly suspect he's nothing like you, and he isn't really your son."

"If that's why I'm in here, I'm leaving!" Rodriguez thundered.

"Oh, no, that's not why you're here. That's just a conversation we're having. I told you at the bar—we have you on video spiking a lady's drink. Right now, we're testing that drink, and we'll find out just what you put in it. She would be the fourth—that we know about. And as I think I mentioned, the one girl almost died, so that's an attempted murder charge—"

"There was no attempt to murder anyone! I told you, if—big if—I ever attempted to murder someone, that someone would be dead!" Rodriguez thundered, smashing a hand on the table.

"As I mentioned before, I'm here. And you did try to kill me today. No, wait, you hired someone to kill me because it worked so well with the judge. But tricks can get old and... Well, here I am. The car isn't in great shape, but..." Jude paused, shrugging, leaning closer to the man. "Here's the thing—when you do something yourself, it gets done. And you know what? I think you're angry and frustrated because I'm not sure you know how to get even with the person who failed you!"

He glanced at his phone suddenly.

"Oh, excuse me. Lab tests are in. We're about to know what you tried to dose that young woman with!"

He stood and exited the room. As he did so, Vicky knew she was up.

"I think I've aggravated him, and it's up to you to finish him off!" Jude told her as she passed him in the hall.

The guard at the door opened it for her; she thanked him and went in.

The look of stunned surprise Carlos Rodriguez gave her couldn't have been feigned. Even after the events at the bar, he hadn't realized he had been taken in by a woman.

He stood up instantly.

And he started around the table with a furious growl, reaching for her throat.

The door burst open almost immediately with Jude, the guard, and Duncan Clark bursting in. But Carlos never got his hands around Vicky's neck.

She'd been trained to break such an attempted hold, and she'd added a damned good kick, as trained, along with her defensive arm movements.

He bellowed in pain and rage and despite his wild attempts to attack in turn, he was quickly overpowered by the three men and handcuffed—with his cuffs securely set around the bar at the interrogation table.

"Thanks, guys, but I think I was fine," Vicky said pleasantly. She stared at the man who returned her glare with a hatred that was palpable in the room. "He really isn't much of a man. I mean, you saw, a pathetic little woman like me had him down and groaning in a flash!"

"I will cut you into little pieces, I will make you bleed!" Rodriguez roared. "You're dead! You're dead! And do you know what? I'll show you! I will do it myself this time—I will do you like I did Peggy and her bitch sister. Finger by finger, toe by toe, bloody, bloody chops at the elbows and the knees. And I'll wait until you're begging to die to slit your throat!"

"This is being recorded and it's all on video," she said pleasantly. "Such a man! You overpowered two innocent women and tortured them to death. God alone knows just how many other people you killed. Death penalty, beyond a doubt. Your son—the real man—will need his day in court again, but... Well, we've got what we need to get working on his freedom. Of course, your incarceration will be for the rest of your life." She leaned on the table, just beyond his possible reach. "Well, there may be a bit of hope for you—"

"Not much," Jude said. "The results from the lab are in. What a concoction, including hallucinogens. He'll definitely go down for the rapes and attempted murder, and now that we have his confession on tape—"

"Inadmissible!"

"Well, we'll figure that all out when we bring in our prosecutors," Jude told him. "Boy, she did knock you down a peg, eh?"

Rodriguez roared with fury, promising Jude, Duncan, and the guard that he would kill them, too, kill them himself, to trust no one else...

"Hey, you know, if you want to tell us about the person—or persons—who are hacking into systems to kill people, it could help you at trial," Jude told him. But even as he spoke, he frowned, pausing to glance at his phone.

He looked at Vicky, grimly shaking his head.

"Too late. Our people found a route to your murder-for-hire friends on the web...but the site disappeared even as they found it. Too bad. Could have helped you."

"I will kill you!" Rodriguez vowed again. "And I will have an attorney now. My attorney. He'll make a bloody legal mess of all of you. I will kill you!"

He was so angry he seemed to have lost his mind or his sense of purpose. Either that or he believed that even as guilty as he was, as he even admitted himself to be, an attorney would get him off.

Because he was who he was.

It seems almost impossible he's been managing a billion-dollar criminal empire for years!

Then again…

Maybe he hadn't been. Whoever was running the cyber-murder machine just might have known the man for a long, long time.

"Yeah? Well, whatever you're doing, it won't be tonight," Jude said. He nodded to the guard who called for backup to bring the raving Rodriguez to a holding cell.

"I, uh, think we desperately need to call it a night," Jude said, smiling at Vicky as Rodriguez was pulled away.

"Yeah, blow my cover and take off!" Duncan said, grimacing.

"What?" Vicky asked, looking at him worriedly.

Duncan laughed. "Not your fault. In fact, you've managed more in a night than I have in weeks. I wanted to stay away because of my undercover work, yet now I am afraid that he might know I'm involved with the law. So I won't be going back out again undercover for a while. We don't know this guy's connections, and since he knows who I am now, too…"

"I'm so sorry!" Vicky murmured.

"Don't be! Not your fault the man is a violent maniac—or that instinct tells us to hop in when another agent is under attack," Duncan said. "And…you caught a rapist who nearly committed murder in his dosing manner. You got him to admit he killed his daughter-in-law and her sister. I don't know where we are on the murder of the judge, but we have incredible cyber people. If a site went down on the dark web, it will pop back up again."

"It all takes time," Jude said regretfully.

"But we have to take our victories, even little ones, when we win them," Duncan said.

Vicky reached for his hand, shaking it firmly. "None of it

was possible without you," she assured him. "But we have been up and going forever and ever it seems, so..."

"Get out of here!" Duncan said. "When are you heading back?"

Vicky turned to look at Jude, who was looking at her.

"Did you want—"

"One more crack at Rodriguez," Vicky said.

"I know our SAC will approve," Duncan said. "Especially with not just the assistant director but our big director of the Bureau determining that this case may be about something even bigger. Of course, when you speak with him again, it may be with his lawyer," he added.

Vicky looked at Jude again. He smiled slightly and nodded.

"All the better," she said. "Nothing like getting to know a good lawyer."

Aidan and Carly had discovered there had been a connection between the judge's "accident" and the "accident" that had occurred with the *Lucky Sun.*

Millions of dollars in drugs. Dealers who could almost twist time and space.

And on the yacht...

Attorneys.

It might not be a bad thing at all to meet the lawyer—or lawyers—representing the man.

"So, now..." Jude murmured.

"We find somewhere to sleep for the night," Vicky said, wincing. "And a shower—so that we can put on the same clothes since our bags exploded with the car."

Jude shrugged. "Yeah, pretty sure that most malls and clothing stores won't open again until the morning."

"I can shop in two minutes," she told him.

"You know, I'm betting you can. Department store? We can both shop in two minutes—if we can get a clerk to ring us up that quickly. But for tonight..."

"I'll give you the address to the place we use," Duncan told him. "They always have rooms reserved for us."

Duncan gave them the information that they needed as they left together.

In the car, Jude murmured, "Duncan's a good guy, a good agent."

"And he was already on Carlos Rodriguez. That was really darned lucky for us tonight," Vicky murmured.

He looked over at her. "You know I have absolute faith in you, but—"

"You interrupted when you needed to, and I get that. I'm grateful. Hey, I'm going to a hotel, not a hospital!" she assured him. "Duncan is a good man, a good agent. And so are you," she added quietly.

He turned to look at her and smile. "Thanks."

For a moment there was something else there. And Vicky realized if they'd met through friends, maybe even at a party…

They'd have gone out. And there might have been more. So much more.

She smiled to herself. She'd thought him somewhat of an internet imbecile and couldn't begin to imagine what he was doing on this. But he'd shown he was amazing in the field. And while she might understand the strange and invisible world of knowledge and information that traveled through the web and servers to a greater degree than he did, she was no expert herself.

He had proven himself. And she believed she had proven herself to him and, in the proving, she had discovered she found him to be far more than capable, a man who could balance humor and integrity and…

Really good looks!

But…

They were professionals. They were good agents. They loved their jobs.

And still...

Their rooms were next to each other on the same floor. And they both lingered just a minute, saying good night, maybe both of them imagining just a little bit more.

Then they went into their rooms. It had been one hell of a long day. After a long hot shower, Vicky found sleep.

However, her sleep was filled with dreams.

And they weren't about the cyber world, criminals like Carlos Rodriguez and those with whom he conspired, but rather...

They were a wee bit X-rated, all involving the man who slept next door.

She woke in the morning with a start, wincing.

Dreams were one thing. It was time to start the day.

EIGHT

"Paul Sands, Esquire, and I have advised my client not to say another word!"

Carlos Rodriguez's attorney made the announcement the second Jude and Vicky walked into the interrogation room. He stood, straight as a ramrod, a man of about fifty with silver hair and ice-blue eyes, his hand resting on his client's shoulder as he stared at the two of them heatedly, those eyes of his seeming to burn ice fire. "There's nothing for you here," he continued. "You have nothing against this man. I will see to it that he's out on bail within the hour. If anything, you'll go down for entrapment. You, especially!" he said, glaring at Vicky.

She looked at Jude and shrugged with amusement.

Jude held a chair out for her and took the second one on their side of the table himself, heedless of the standing man and simply shrugging as he looked at Carlos Rodriguez. Then he shook his head, smiling as he spoke to the attorney but looked at Rodriguez.

"Your client was in a public bar with no expectation of privacy. Cameras are everywhere in public now, so…he shouldn't have been surprised."

"She entrapped him. Believe you me, I'm a Harvard grad, not a no-name lackey, and I've represented—"

"Some of the worst scumbags in the world, yeah, I know, I looked you up," Jude assured him. "But here's the thing: I'm just not going to have any problem testifying in court; and we will have others willing to do so, too. And you see, your client is on tape and video talking about his efforts to kill us. We believe he killed the judge—"

"What you *believe* doesn't mean squat in court," Paul Sands reminded him. "You angered him. He was saying anything at all, anything he thought you might want to hear. He should have been read his rights, given access to legal assistance immediately—"

"Your client was told he could call his attorney at the time of his arrest. As Special Agent Mackenzie said, we're happy to see you in court. No matter what an amazing attorney you might be, Mr. Paul Sands, Esquire, trust me, there are laws in this country, laws regarding sexual assault—"

"He never assaulted you!" Sands interjected icily.

"Well, I believe that in the eyes of the law, 'roofies' are illegal and considered to be an integral part of sexual assault. But," she added sweetly, "I wasn't in there alone. And the problem is your client fell too easily for what he saw as an easy mark. And the man does consider himself better than any female and way above the laws of our country. He's going to do time. I don't care what you tell a judge, and I can't even imagine the tangle of having his son's conviction vacated so that he can stand trial for murder. But, of course, we can't forget he also murdered the judge—"

"He was nowhere near that car!" Sands said. "Proving that will be impossible."

Jude smiled. "Impossible? Because someone out there knows

how to manipulate servers. They're great at encryption and they're running a murder-for-hire racket. Paying someone is conspiracy to commit murder, and he can go down for first degree murder on that—"

"You can't *prove* anything!" Rodriguez said suddenly.

Vicky shrugged. "You are such a narcissist. You really believe you are more powerful than the courts, the judges, and the juries. But—"

"They can die, they can all die!" Rodriguez snapped out.

"Carlos!" Sands said, shaking his head and pressing his hand onto the man's shoulder. "Don't talk, please, don't talk. Leave the talking to me!"

"Even a Harvard education can't help when you're representing an idiot with a god complex," Jude said dryly to Sands. "Your client is going to prison. Drugging women? Rape? Murder? Things he did on video. There's no jury in the world who will let him go. And, of course, everything he's said here is also on record, so…"

"Send me to prison," Rodriguez said. He smiled. "I won't stay."

Vicky made a face. "Last I heard, there were a number of cartels and other enterprises out there. You might not stay because…well, we can't have an officer per inmate in the prison system. It's just not financially feasible."

"Now you're on record threatening my client!" Sands snapped.

Vicky shook her head. "Nope. I just said it the way that it is."

"We're done here," Sands said. "My client—"

"Will be remanded. I guarantee it," Jude said.

"Because you've threatened or bribed the judge?" Sands asked.

"Because I know the law," Jude said. "But we can leave." He looked at Vicky who shrugged. "We were here to offer help."

"To drop all charges?" Sands asked.

"Oh, hell, no," Jude said. He smiled. "But we could talk to the DA and see if we couldn't make conditions a little better."

"One thing about being a good businessman—you never screw those with whom you do business, because you never know if you'll work with them again. And you know, some of those people are invisible, and they're so very good at what they do!" Rodriguez said.

"I don't know about that. We're still here," Vicky said sweetly. "Sometimes you don't get what you paid for."

"And sometimes you give people a second chance." Rodriguez laughed.

"Carlos!" Sands warned.

"Okay, well, your arraignment is coming up and we do have a few things to do," Jude said.

"Darkness, darkness, darkness!" Rodriguez said, as if he couldn't shut up. "Criminals have lurked in the darkness from the beginning of time! But there's a new darkness, one that's strangely more stygian than any that has come before! One that could decimate the world! Well, the world as people like you know it!"

Vicky shook her head impatiently. "Wow. Right. Gee, we would never have thought of the dark web, Rodriguez. You know, brilliant techs never think of working for the good of others. Whatever—goodbye. Have fun in your cell."

She stood and Jude did the same. They were almost out the door when Rodriguez shouted out, "I'll give you the site!"

They paused, looking at one another and turning back.

"Um, too little too late, I think," Vicky said. She turned back and smiled sweetly. "It's amazing how news travels. The site has gone down, and a new one will be up by now. Your arrest was public, and I believe one of the news stations reported on it. So...let's see, whoever is running the site will suspect you were angry that they failed to kill a couple of agents and also that you've been arrested and are being interrogated. And, of course, you only think of yourself. So, you'd be quick to talk, or if not quick—because you do so love to hear yourself talk—you'd still spill something eventually."

"Get me out of general population!" Rodriguez demanded.

Jude walked back to the table and stared at Rodriguez and Paul Sands, who was shaking his head as if he had entered a strange world of pure misery.

"Here's the deal on that. We'll speak with the DA and if you admit you killed your daughter-in-law and her sister—manly man that you are—we'll find out if it is possible to keep you out of the general population for the duration of your long, long—lifelong—sentence," Jude said, staring from Rodriguez to Sands.

"You think there's a prison that can really keep—" Rodriguez began.

"Stop!" Sands roared. "Carlos, shut up!"

He could have been about to say "keep me out of the general population." But that's not what the man had been about to say.

He was going to let them know he didn't believe there was a prison out there from which he could not escape.

And it might be close to the truth.

Wherever the man would end up, he needed to be watched—constantly.

And...

He needed to be kept the hell away from the internet.

"Paper!" Rodriguez said suddenly.

"Carlos, we don't have a deal—" Sands began impatiently.

"Paper," Rodriguez roared. He stared at Jude. "This guy is a straight shooter. He'll talk to the DA. And he's right. So we'll see just how brilliant his good people turn out to be!"

Vicky quickly had a notepad and pen out of her bag. She pushed them across the table to Rodriguez.

He wrote words and symbols and pushed it back.

"No death penalty and no general population," he said.

"We will be working on it," Jude said.

And finally they were out of the room.

Duncan was waiting for them.

"You know the man believes that if he doesn't get the death penalty, he will escape," Duncan said, frowning. "Vicky, what did he write on that paper?"

"A way in," she said. "An encrypted password, but our people can figure it out. Of course, it is possible..."

She paused, looking at Jude. He smiled. He was beginning to understand a lot of it. Maybe there were things he'd already known, but he didn't work cybercrime—not usually. So this was all a bit different for him.

"There is a site where people have been going to hire these murderers," Jude explained. "But another will probably go right up. Still, if there's any hint that a way in with a link to who is running it is suspected, the site will be down in a flash."

"Then why...?" Duncan asked.

"Because our people are good enough to follow the ghost trail," Vicky explained.

"All right," Duncan murmured. "And from what I understand, our director and assistant director and other agencies believe there's a lot more that can be done than just murder for hire."

Jude nodded. "National security," he said quietly.

"Could someone really—" Duncan murmured, shaking his head.

"Yes," Vicky told him. "All right, I'm going to get this to our people. And..." She paused, looking at Jude. "We've got some work to do. We've got to get back to the Jacksonville/St. Augustine area. But we're only a hop away at any time. There is one thing that has to happen here."

"Carlos Rodriguez has to stay in custody," Duncan said. "Got it, and our assistant district attorney is on it, too. He will be arraigned in a bit, and no judge in his right mind will let the man out on remand. Trust me, our ADA is good."

Thanking Duncan again for all his help, they left the local office. Jude called the pilot; they were ready to go.

In the car Jude turned to Vicky. "Do you really think we might have gotten something the techs can use?"

"Well, we got something."

"Do you think he might have played you? That what he gave you is gibberish."

"No, for the very reasons you gave me."

"And those would be?"

She turned to him, almost swiveling in her seat. "I have never met anyone like Carlos Rodriguez. He's not just all the things you said—a chauvinist, misogynist, and narcissist. He's got a total god complex. I think the worst to me is that he's so convinced he's superior to everyone, he would sacrifice his own son. But! Because he's so sure of himself—and even if his murder-machine people messed up on killing us—he's willing to let people follow a real trail. Screw them if we catch them. They screwed up and we should be dead."

He nodded.

"You think we're right heading back?" he asked her.

"We aren't attorneys—oh, wait, you are. Okay, we aren't working attorneys. We've done what we can do in the Nashville area. We need to deep dive now into Marci's law firm and find out why a sweet young receptionist could have been a danger to anyone, and we have the yacht's black box pieces and… I need to change clothes!"

"Ah, we never did have time for shopping!" he said lightly.

Vicky's phone buzzed, and she looked at it quickly, then frowned as she glanced at him.

"What?" he asked her.

"That was from Aidan. They are following the tracks on the dark website, but…he has other information. He says that Paul Sands did represent a man in a Tennessee case who was represented by Wharton, Dixon, and Smith in a Florida case!" Vicky said. "But how—"

"I didn't like Sands," Jude said simply.

She smiled at him and nodded. "Right. I mean, why represent a client who is miserable, doesn't listen to a word, and puts you in a terrible position unless there is something else behind it? But…okay, this could go either way. It's starting to look as if one of these legal firms is behind all of this somehow—"

"Still a long shot."

"But an intriguing one. Still, I think we've made the right move to head back to Florida. Paul Sands is involved in something big." He grimaced. "I looked him up. He represents all kinds of gang leaders and cartel members. I think he's in deep with some of these guys. That's why, despite his client being half crazy or drunk with what he sees as his own power, he is determined to represent him—even if he knows that he can't get him off this time. No matter what he says, he can't get Rodriguez to shut up. And…"

Her phone was buzzing again. She read the message and looked at him, smiling and shaking her head.

"Man, you were busy texting when I was concentrating on a cyber encryption!"

Jude winced. "Yeah, I think I asked if they could look up info on good attorneys in the area. To recommend someone who might go in and find out about proving that Victor Rodriguez was innocent and getting his conviction vacated."

"Well, Aidan did. He has someone going out to speak with Victor today, a fellow who has worked with the Bureau before when things have gotten twisted."

"Great."

Vicky nodded, looking at her phone. She let out a sigh.

"As we suspected, the site is already down, but this is beyond my expertise. They've been following footprints, and as expected, they've bounded servers across the globe. But with what they have, Aidan says they'll be a step ahead when a new site takes its place. Whoever is doing this expected they might need to take it down at some point. And while a man like Rodriguez might not have understood it, the message to get back in to a new site would be in the old key. Anyway, they're on it."

"And here we are. Back home in no time. Sorry, back home for me—"

"And it's still home for me, in a way," Vicky told him.

She leaned back and then turned to look at him again.

"Is there a point when you're going to talk to me?" she asked softly.

"What do you mean?"

"I mean, you've been working solo. You were thrown when you found yourself in this position, working the field for a cyber case, for one, and working with me."

"Hey, you're proving to be an amazing partner," he said lightly.

"But are you really okay? Really ready to trust me—as an equal? I mean, after what happened with your old partner, Matt Reid, you're still blaming yourself."

"I trust you as an equal," he said, and he was surprised to realize he meant it. "Why are you asking this now? Did I do something?"

"You didn't tell me about your suspicions regarding Paul Sands," she said.

"Only because I hadn't really had a chance!" he assured her. "You were already on to the important part. Whatever that encryption thing that Rodriguez had given you. I was going on a hunch!"

"And your hunches are amazing to me!" she told him.

"Well, thank you."

They had reached the airport. An agent was there ready to take the keys and the car. They parted ways with him, greeted the pilot, and settled in while he communicated with the tower.

After takeoff, he turned to Vicky and told her, "Vicky, in all honesty, yes, it was confusing and difficult for me at first. I do trust you implicitly. And seriously, I've never believed in this line of work that an agent's gender meant anything. A single bullet can take the toughest bully on the block. We've all seen it and we've all been taught it. And," he added, managing to add in a grin, "I have a feeling you've been through tons of training, and you're good at self-defense if and when a situation comes to it. But here is something that is true: partners become like…family. And I'd be lying if I were to try and tell you that it was possible not to worry about a partner."

"Oh, that's okay!" she assured him. "I worry about you, too."

"Now that's good. I don't want to be with someone who…"

"Doesn't care," she finished. "But seriously, Jude, I promise you—I don't play at being a lone wolf. I will always want backup."

"And so will I."

She nodded and looked out the window, then leaned back in her seat and closed her eyes.

"You didn't sleep last night?" he asked her.

"Like a log," she assured him. "I'm just thinking…"

"Here's my plan. I want to head to our little headquarters, spend time talking with our cyber geniuses, see what they've gotten and if they've learned anything from the giant room of cyber sleuths working at our main headquarters. They will find something. And anything we say could help them. Then… tomorrow, we're going to a funeral."

"Marci Warden is being buried tomorrow."

He nodded.

"And tomorrow, we find out just who was heartbroken at her death. And," he added, "just who might have caused it."

"Because Marci knew something she shouldn't have known. Even as a receptionist, or…or because she was a receptionist and knew too much about communications going on!"

"Precisely."

It was a short flight. They thanked the pilot as they exited the plane, and Jude smiled as he saw Aidan was there waiting, standing by a vintage Ford Mustang.

As they walked toward Aidan, Jude saw him grinning.

"Thought you might like this. I, um, got one for myself, and Cary is now happy driving a 1965 fully restored Corvette."

"Cool, and thank you, yes! Such a great car," Jude said.

"You should see Cary in the Corvette," Aidan said lightly.

Vicky laughed and looked at him. "So! You texted Aidan about a car, too."

"Nope," Jude said.

"Hey! I thought of this all my own," Aidan assured her. "After what happened in Tennessee—twice—it seemed necessary. Thankfully, you guys just got scratched up. Maybe it wouldn't have happened here. Maybe it would be too obvious if a car went into a tree here as well as just outside of Nashville—twice—but we can't be too careful."

"No, Aidan, thank you, it's perfect!" Vicky assured him. "Trust me, after leaping out of one moving car, I'm very grateful to be assured I probably won't need to do it again."

"We've been working hard at the house to protect our own server and, of course, our own sites," Aidan said. He shrugged. "Cary is the real genius. I'm still an on-the-scene forensics guy myself. I've just had training and some expertise that works well on the cyber situation at the moment. So, is there anywhere you want to go first?"

"Headquarters! Now, please," Vicky assured him. "Our go-bags were destroyed with the explosion and flames of the car. I'm desperate for a hot shower that is followed by clean clothing."

"Creep!" Aidan accused Jude. "You wouldn't take her shopping?"

"Hey, she says she can shop in two minutes. We just wanted

to get back here. We figured with everything on the table, talking among ourselves and tomorrow—"

"You head to Marci Warden's funeral," Aidan said.

Jude nodded.

"You really think the roots of this thing go back to the Wharton, Dixon, and Smith law firm?" Aidan asked. "Wait. Don't answer that. We'll get Cary in on it all. We'll be at the house by Old Town as fast as you can drive this sucker. Whoever wants to drive. I mean, I can drive—"

"Let Jude take it and get accustomed to it. Being the driver isn't a thing for me," Vicky said.

"It's not a thing for me, either" Jude said.

She grinned. "I know. If it was a thing with you, I'd insist on driving, too, just to show you that it shouldn't be a thing!"

Aidan laughed and shook his head.

They had no baggage to stow, so they quickly hopped in the computerless car.

"There's some argument on when computers were first installed in automobiles, and just what they did once they went in. But it's safe to say that if we pick up anything from before 1965, we're good," Aidan said. "Anyway, I'm going with the determination that cars computerized to the extent they can be manipulated as the judge's car and the car you started out in is something comparatively recent. You'd be surprised by the cars reported stolen because they can be started—and even guided—from afar. But…"

"This is a cool car!" Vicky assured him.

Aidan talked computer systems and car manufacturers as they drove, and they quickly arrived at the house, entering with the code—something that didn't make Jude particularly happy under the circumstances—and greeting Cary who was busy at her computer as always.

"What's that face for?" Cary asked him.

"Our entry—our code. It can be hacked, right?" he said.

"We'll think of some other security measures and, oh!" Cary said, looking at Aidan.

"I know what you're thinking," Aidan said.

"Fill us in?" Jude said, arching a brow.

"Clover," Aidan said.

"Clover?" Vicky asked.

Jude was already grinning, "Now there's a security system without a computer! Of course, there are things that could be done for someone to break in here, but not with us watching."

"Okay, seriously—"

"Clover belongs to Aidan's family. He's an exceptionally large shepherd/mastiff mix, and he worked with the Seminole police for several years before retiring. He's huge, and to those he cares for, he's as gentle as a newborn. But he knows who doesn't belong somewhere, and he'll go after that person with all his training intact," Jude explained.

"Oh!" Vicky said.

"I mean, if you're all right with dogs," Aidan said.

"I love dogs," Vicky assured them. She winced. "And with Clover, we just have the same fears we'd have with a human, that he might be poisoned, that he could be shot—"

"We'll keep him in, and we'll go out with him to make sure no one ever tries to throw him a piece of beef with arsenic or the like," Cary said. "He's a great dog. I am going to be much happier being here with Clover in the house."

"We can also rig the windows and doors, just in case someone does figure out where we are and can break into our alarm system," Jude said.

"I can start on that tomorrow. Right now, I'll head out to get Clover. Cary, they wanted to throw ideas, impressions, and thoughts around between us tonight, so—"

"Please! Go get Clover!" Vicky said. "I'm not doing anything until I shower and get clean clothing on!" she said.

"All right, then," Aidan said. "I will be awhile—it's a bit of a drive. But hey, I'm with law enforcement. Due to exigent circumstances I can speed a bit."

"Yeah, just don't go getting arrested!" Jude warned.

Aidan grinned and left them.

"You're going to love Clover!" Cary assured Vicky.

"I know I will," she said. "And—I'm off!"

Vicky disappeared down the hall toward her room.

He knew how she felt. He couldn't wait to change himself. Shower, of course, as if he could shower off wearing the clothing that had been with him when he'd rolled across pavement and dirt and gravel. Couldn't actually "shower" his clothing, but hell, it would be washed!

"Are you guys really all right?" Cary asked him anxiously. "When we heard about what happened, we were so worried!"

"We got out. Yeah, pavement on flesh hurts. But we survived, and we didn't even break any bones or get serious lacerations." He hesitated and shrugged. "I could feel it while driving. I don't know if I felt it in my mind, or if I could really hear or feel something change. Maybe it was just because of what happened to the judge. I don't know. But we were fine," he said.

Cary nodded. "She's cool."

"Vicky?"

Cary nodded. "Brave and determined. If I'd been in that car, they'd have had my resignation the next day!"

He smiled at that. "She's a perfect field agent."

"More than perfect. She knows what I'm talking about most of the time—she's savvy in cyber lingo and understands the uses of cryptology, how servers can be bounced about. She's like… seriously perfect. For this case—and probably tons of cases in the future. But we'll get you practically perfect by then, too!" she assured Jude.

He groaned and said, "Shower for me, too. We'll be out in a bit."

As he headed into the shower, he smiled a little grimly, thinking about Cary's one descriptive word.

Perfect.

And after perfect in his own mind came another thought.

So very perfect that…

He'd been around, he'd had his affairs that had meant something, and he'd had a few nights that hadn't really meant much more than a few drinks at a bar. He just hadn't found the person who understood what he did, who tapped into his mind and soul as well as his senses. He'd known, of course, from the time he'd seen her that she was an extremely attractive woman. But she could make him laugh while also holding her own in any situation. She…

…was perfect.

Technically, they weren't in the same department. FBI agents did have affairs, and he had friends who were with the Bureau who were married to other members of the Bureau, or those working in some capacity with the Bureau. And it could be amazing because of the hours, the secrecy, so much more to the job that had to be understood.

But…

He smiled to himself as he turned on the shower. He let the spray rush over him, lathered, let the water sweep away the long days—and all the dirt that might have adhered to his clothing and flesh.

He toweled dry and dressed while the perfection of Special Agent Victoria Tennant stayed on his mind.

She respected him as a partner. She had pushed for an understanding.

That didn't mean she found him appealing as a partner in any other way.

And under these circumstances…

"Under these circumstances…what?"

He'd been lost in his thoughts; he hadn't realized that they had both stepped into the hallway at the same time.

He laughed. "Sorry. Man, I was talking out loud, huh? Um, what else did I say?"

"Under these circumstances. That's all I heard."

He inhaled over clenched teeth, grimacing. "Well, our current circumstances. You know, trying to find someone who seems capable of killing at will by hacking computer systems."

"Oh, well, of course. So, I was thinking if I cooked, do you think you'd eat it?" she asked.

He laughed. "Just how bad are you?"

"Not horrible."

"Whatever you prepare, I will be glad to eat it," he assured her.

"I just don't feel like going out. It's already getting late. And I don't really want to have food delivered here anymore. I mean, we can't function if we get paranoid. I'd just rather go on common sense."

"Let me know what I can do," he said.

"I will—but it's not all that hard. Brown beef, throw in seasoning, and put mashed potatoes on it. Then we have canned veggies of some kind."

"Perfect," he said, wincing inwardly as the word left his mouth.

Well, dinner might as well be perfect, too!

She didn't really need much help. As she moved about competently on her own, Jude sat with Cary while she worked, explaining to him how the cryptogram they'd been given could be used to hunt down the site that had been removed.

She was talking to him, explaining a twist of letters, numbers and symbols when she suddenly let out a startled cry.

"What, what?"

Vicky rushed in from the kitchen to join them.

"I found it—I found the site that was taken down!" Cary

exclaimed. "Oh, and it's on here. First, there's the offer for 'anything you need, untraceable.' It doesn't exactly say 'murder for hire,' but here's one…it's on the yacht! And, of course, the email requesting the service won't exist anymore, but when you look long and hard enough… Well, that's the thing about the internet. Nothing is ever really deleted once it's been up. Look, look! Here's the order on the judge and…" She paused, looking from Jude to Vicky. "Here's the one that orders the hit on the car you had in Tennessee."

"What's the matter?" Jude asked her. "Why are you frowning?"

"I think I'm good at what I do. And we have another office on this, so maybe we'll find something eventually. But it disturbs me that I can't find any kind of an order for something to happen to Marci Warden. And it's frustrating, trying to follow emails and sites and servers that bounce across the world. But no matter where and how I look—no matter what I'm able to hack into—there's no announcement of any kind or a real name or traceable email. Easily traceable email, that is. And I haven't found how people are paying for the services, and I'm frustrated because, as I said, the only thing I can't find…"

"You can't find the order to kill Marci Warden," Vicky said.

"Right."

Vicky looked at Jude and Jude nodded in return.

"We need everything," Jude said, turning to Cary. "Okay, we know the Paul Sands has defended many very bad people, but on top of that, Aidan told us there was an association between the firm Marci worked for and the law firm Paul Sands works for. Something is slimy about that guy. He kept trying to defend a madman. And no matter how wild Carlos Rodriguez got, he kept defending him. We must find the connection. As far as working on the ground in the physical world, we're going to start tomorrow by pinning people down at the cemetery. If we keep at it, somebody will eventually give something up and give us a human clue to follow."

"I'm on it. I'm so sorry, I can't help that things take time," Cary said apologetically.

"Hey, of course!" Jude said. "And that's why we need to work in the field, too. Face-to-face conversations can still reveal things that a computer can't."

His phone rang. He looked at it and answered it quickly. It was Aidan.

"Just me, and I'm coming in with Clover," he said. "Under the circumstances, I thought I should warn everyone."

"Gotcha. And dinner is almost ready."

"Good. Clover will love it!" Aidan said.

The door opened a few seconds later. Aidan had returned with one of the biggest dogs Jude had ever seen. Clover barked and wagged his tail furiously as he entered.

"Clover, you know Cary. And that's Jude there and Vicky over there."

The dog seemed to have good sense. He rushed over to Vicky to let her pet him and talk to him, scratching his ears, welcoming him to the house.

The dog had amazing instincts; he turned to look at Jude as if apologizing for not coming to him first and knowing that Jude would understand.

The sad thing was that Jude did understand. He smiled to himself; he could understand the instinct to go right to her!

"It's okay, pup! She has that effect on people, too," he said.

His comment caused them all to laugh and Vicky to say, "Hey, thanks. But dogs are smart. They often have an amazing sense of when someone loves them!"

"Hey, I love dogs, too!" he said.

As if aware he might be causing a controversy, Clover ran over so that Jude, laughing, could give him some welcoming pets, too.

Then he hurried back to Vicky.

"Okay, dinner and theories and anything we've got!" he said.

Clover woofed in complete agreement.

And it was good. It was amazing what the presence of the dog could do. He could feel it. They were all just a bit more secure.

The massive pup had done that for them. And as they passed the food around the table, Aidan explained what he and Cary knew so far.

"Paul Sands represents not just Carlos Rodriguez, but a number of the big names when it comes to cartels and drug smuggling. Those deaths are usually more normal ones with bodies full of bullets in dark alleys, but without prints or DNA or usable forensics," Aidan told them.

"Yeah, I looked up his client list. Okay," Jude said. "So, the man has been a suspect in questionable homicides before. And Sands has kept him out of prison. But I don't think Sands was aware of Carlos Rodriguez's forays at the bar—drugging women to make sure they appreciate his godlike qualities. We lucked out in that Duncan Clark had been watching him and had him under surveillance."

"But," Vicky said, glancing at Jude, "we don't think Carlos Rodriguez is behind the AI murders—he was just a customer."

"And," Jude said, "it seems that Sands has been representing him all along. He's a criminal attorney. So, is the connection between the law firms between criminal attorneys?"

"We used facial recognition," Cary offered, "and as you know, we discovered that Carlos Rodriguez knew and probably did business with the captain of the *Lucky Sun*. Then we found out that the captain of the *Lucky Sun* did business with Marci's law firm—"

"In the criminal law division?" Jude asked.

But Aidan and Cary looked at each other, shaking their heads.

"Maritime law," Cary said.

"And it could mean nothing, but—"

"Facial recognition is pretty amazing," Aidan said. "Okay, so, we really don't know what the connection is, but in searching for Carlos Rodriguez through news reports, security cams, social media, and more, we found this... Let Cary just show you!"

Even while eating dinner, Cary had her computer at her side.

She hit a few keys and then twisted the computer so that they could see the image displayed on the screen.

And there they were.

Carlos Rodriguez, Paul Sands, and the captain of the *Lucky Sun*, all standing in front of Marci Warden's law firm, with the door being held open for the trio by Nathaniel Wharton, whose prestigious name headed the law firm of Wharton, Dixon, and Smith.

"See the connection?" Aidan asked.

"Visual, but loud and clear!" Jude assured him.

And in complete agreement, Clover let out an excited, "Woof."

NINE

"Tolomato Cemetery," Jude murmured. "Originally a settlement of Guale Native Americans who were being administered to by Franciscan friars. But as human beings, we've always been tribal, I guess. And different 'tribes' held the power here over the centuries. The Spaniards founded the city in 1565. Then the British took over in 1763, and being Protestants, burned the original church that the graveyard grew up around—but left the coquina shell bell, and of course the graves."

Vicky looked over at Jude. He had been thoughtful and quiet most of the morning, and she was surprised he was suddenly verbalizing the history of the cemetery.

That really had nothing to do with their case at the moment.

"And yes, I know a fair about this city, too. Tolomato Cemetery is incredibly old, very historical, tells the tale of years—the centuries—gone by. But it has nothing to do with today. It's not where Marci is being buried," she reminded him.

He nodded, glancing her way. "Yeah, I know where we're going."

"To the service at Marci's church, which is right by the

'new' graveyard, and we'll hang at the back. After all, we found Marci, but we didn't know her," Vicky reminded him. "We need to be tactful and careful because no matter what is really going on, most of the people we see today will have really cared about her."

"If they cared about her, they'll want us to do everything that we can for her—and for others who could be in danger if this thing continues. And no, we didn't know her. But we will fight for justice for her," he said.

He seemed to be contemplative—and aggravated about something that morning.

Vicky decided to push it. Even if he was going to get angry.

"You know you're being very weird today," she told him.

To her relief, he smiled at that and winced before glancing her way. "I thought I was always weird to you!"

"No, you just weren't up to date on the possibilities of AI. But hey, not to worry, most of the world, thankfully, isn't in the loop on extreme hacking. But you're tense—"

"Yeah," he said, grimacing. "Sorry, I hadn't mentioned it yet, but I got a call from Assistant Director Arnold today. It was nothing new—he was just warning me to be careful because we're dealing with a law firm. And whoever is doing this could press the right person to start up a dozen lawsuits against us and successfully cut us off from getting to the bottom of it before it gets ten times worse. So of course—"

"You went to law school."

He nodded. "So, I just don't like walking on eggshells. But I will do it, and I will not be such a jerk to you. I didn't mean to be."

"You weren't being a jerk. You were just—"

"Weird."

"When something gets at you, talk to me. I have my moments, too, you know."

He nodded. "Never expected this. You are an amazing partner."

"And you're weirdly wonderful," she assured him, smiling and drawing another smile from him.

But they had arrived, and their smiles soon faded.

Jude parked the car in one of the few remaining spots close to their destination, and Vicky looked at the beautiful church and the cemetery where Marci would receive her final services and be laid to rest.

"History," she murmured. "Only in this city could something that's a mere one hundred and fifty years old, approximately, be considered new."

Jude grinned and nodded. He looked at the sea of cars.

"We should get in."

"Yep. It's that time."

The church was beautiful inside as well with stained glass, pillars, and much more. But they hadn't come to look at the church. Or even to appreciate life, one's beliefs or sadly even to mourn for the woman they hadn't known. But maybe they had come to mourn as well, mourn the loss of a young life. But they had come for more, Vicky reminded herself.

They had come to seek justice.

"Hail, hail, the gang is all here," Jude murmured.

And they were. Thankfully, they had seen the pictures in the law office as well as images of many of the players online.

Wharton, Dixon, and Smith.

Vicky closed her eyes briefly. She remembered the display of pictures on the wall. The company dealt with corporate law, maritime law, personal injury, and criminal law. Wharton headed the corporate division; Lee Chan, maritime law; Barton Clay, personal injury; and Ms. A. Taylor, criminal law. And presumably Dixon and Smith kept an eye on all divisions and perhaps acted as the trouble chasers. They were all there along with many other people who would surely be on the list they would get from Celia Smith. They should have received it by now. But Celia Smith was evidently not fond of them or of having the law firm investigated in any way.

Apparently, Marci's work family had been her only family.

Others were those who worked in the various departments. Now thanks to what they'd learned about the meager threads of connection, they knew Nathaniel Wharton himself had to have met Paul Sands, and that Carlos Rodriguez had also known the *Lucky Sun*'s captain Ronald Quincy, and that Quincy had used the law firm of Wharton, Dixon, and Smith when he had filed a maritime claim.

"I'll take Wharton in the graveyard," Jude whispered when the service came to an end.

"Maritime law, that's... Lee Chan. He's in the third row right now with his wife, Gina," Vicky whispered in return.

"We'll be appropriate for the occasion, of course," Jude murmured.

The priest headed out the door and the others filed out as well. Celia Smith saw them as she walked out and frowned fiercely. With the crowd heading out, she was able to incline her head toward Vicky and whisper angrily, "This is entirely inappropriate!"

"Well, we're still waiting for your list!" Vicky said. "And we're here to honor Marci Warden in the best way possible."

Celia Smith walked on.

Wharton looked like a man who had been shedding tears. Dixon appeared duly distressed as well.

Vicky studied every face as they all filed out. Barton Clay's pretty blonde wife paused as she apparently knew who they were. Her attitude was entirely different from Celia's.

"Thank you for coming, thank you for caring!" she said, before heading on out.

Vicky recognized Barton Clay, of course, who paused just after his wife. "Belinda is truly distressed. She and Marci were friends. She insisted we all be here not just because Marci worked at our offices but because she knew Marci's family was all gone. So, thank you."

Vicky nodded and smiled, lowering her head. "Of course," she murmured.

They moved on out to the graveside services.

Like the church, the graveyard was beautiful. Handsomely sculpted angels sat here and there along with headstones, tombs, and mausoleums. The trees that shaded the paths cast sweeping shadows over the morning, adding to a strange and gentle feel.

Marci's coworkers gathered around as the graveside service progressed.

Wharton headed up by the casket to give a speech.

It was what one might have expected: a tribute to Marci's beautiful smile, her work ethic, and her family morals. While she'd had no remaining family of her own, she had made those at the firm her family, standing by others for every loss, remembering the birthdays of her friends, always ready to lend an ear or a hand.

Naturally she had been an amazing receptionist, making clients feel welcome and at home. She had put together so many of their important dinners, and their firm get-togethers as well.

He seemed sincere, incredibly sincere. Either the man should have gone into the movies instead of law or he was completely genuine, Vicky couldn't know. But something inside her believed him.

He was heartbroken by Marci's loss.

"Well, he has given me a great opening!" Jude murmured. As he finished speaking, the priest blessed the assembly and said they should all go in peace.

The crowd dispersed slowly. Many people had flowers to set upon the coffin before it could be lowered into the earth. That made it easier for Vicky to approach Lee Chan and his wife, Gina, when they turned to leave the grave site, having each cast down a rose.

Chan obviously knew who she was, or perhaps he just knew she didn't really belong here among his coworkers. And she was obviously approaching him.

"Mr. and Mrs. Chan, forgive me, but I'd like to speak with you for a few minutes."

Chan frowned briefly. He was a handsome man of about forty; his wife was an attractive woman of about the same age.

"Oh, okay, I know. You're one of the cops—"

"Agent, sir. Special Agent Victoria—Vicky—Tennant. Yes, law enforcement. And I do hate to stop you at this very sad occasion, but we've several people that we need to speak with—"

"Because you don't think what happened to Marci could have been an accident," he said. He shook his head. "I'm happy to talk to you at any time. We're a legal firm, and I like to think we all believe in law enforcement. We might specialize in defense, but that doesn't mean every one of us wouldn't want to track a killer who was running loose. But..." He glanced at his wife as if looking for words.

Gina Chan offered Vicky her hand. "Hi, I'm Gina. And I think Lee is so confused because we can't begin to think of anyone who would wish any harm whatsoever to Marci! Every word Mr. Wharton was saying here today is true. She was a sweetheart. She cared about everyone. She was kind. Oh, she could make you laugh, too, but...we loved her!"

"You knew her as well?" Vicky asked.

"Well, I didn't see her every day as Lee did, but we went shopping now and then, and a group of us from the firm went bowling sometimes, out to dinner...and...she was kind! She would open doors when she saw elderly people heading in or out somewhere, reach for things for shorter people when we shopped... Marci couldn't have had any enemies!"

"None known," Vicky said. "But as you may or may not have heard—"

"We heard," Chan said dryly. He looked out over the remaining crowd, as if guaranteeing that he wouldn't be heard by the wrong person. "Celia Smith sent us all emails, warning us we'd be 'bothered' by the police over what had happened because a boat also exploded. Of course, I knew about the boat because I was asked once to represent the guy who owned it, Captain Ronald Quincy."

"Oh, so you did know Captain Quincy," Vicky said.

"I knew him, but I never wound up working with him. He really had a personal injury suit, and it was settled out of court. I met him a few times," Chan said with a shrug. He winced. "I didn't really…"

"Yeah, and this guy we're talking to is an attorney!" Gina said lightly, smiling at Chan in a friendly manner, shaking her head. "I will be as blunt as possible—I'm not an attorney. The guy was a scumbag, and Chan didn't want anything to do with him. Celia Smith was aggravated until she read about the case and determined it could be easily settled. Personal injury is Barton's gig, but she swooped in and took over herself."

"Celia Smith and Mr. Dixon do that sometimes, when a case is complicated, when it's tricky, when there's anything that might cause a questionable relationship between a client and the firm. That's their job. Wharton started the agency twenty years ago, and he was always into corporate law. When he took Dixon and Smith on as partners, well I guess that was the agreement," Chan said. "But anyway, I'd help you in any way that I could. But I just don't see the correlation. Ronald Quincy was suspected of being a drug lord, a fantastic captain and tour guide, and a grade A asshole to anyone who wasn't giving him money. On the other hand, Marci was the best and sweetest human being known to man."

"She was so proud of that house," Gina murmured, shaking her head. "She loved it. She had us over for dinner one night so she could show us all the things the artificial intelligence in her house could do for me. And it can be amazing, of course. I was just reading that there's an AI piece of equipment that can detect cancer earlier than any other screening and certainly earlier than any human being. And we thought it was…fun. I never thought in a zillion years her house might go crazy and kill her."

Vicky nodded. "As you were saying, AI can be amazing. But AI is fed information and 'taught' by human beings, so…"

"But a house?" Gina said, shaking her head.

"And a boat and a car," Vicky said. "Oh, I'm okay at a computer, but I'm curious. Who at your company is the best with all that?"

"I would have said Marci just last week," Chan said. "I don't know… We can all manage our planners, accounts, even get into research when a case requires it—nothing illegal, I swear. We are a law firm. But… Oh, Celia Smith is good. And…" He shook his head. "Again, we all know a little." He lowered his voice again even though people had moved on, some still in the graveyard, talking in groups, some heading to their cars. "The worst? He needs help all the time! Mr. Wharton himself. Then again, he's a bit older and he didn't come through school in the age of computers. I think the man had typing classes if anything."

"Well, thank you! Thank you so much for speaking with me," Vicky said. "We will be talking to everyone at the firm at some point, and you made it very easy for me today."

Chan looked at the coffin and winced. "You're welcome. Feel free to call me any time."

He took his wife's hand and the two of them started away. But Gina pulled back.

"If someone did do this somehow, I hope to God that you

nail them! Marci was an amazing friend, and she deserved the best that life could give, not…this!"

Vicky nodded and told her softly, "Trust me. We are on this."

As she spoke, another couple came up to talk to Lee and Gina. Of course, she knew who they were from the portraits on the wall.

Barton and Belinda Clay. They were a handsome couple, he in his mid- to late thirties, tall and dignified, she a pretty, petite blonde who appeared to be several years younger.

"Wharton spoke well!" Belinda said to Lee and Gina. "He really cared!"

"He did," Gina agreed. "He brought tears to my eyes. Oh!" She realized Vicky was right behind her still, so she turned and quickly introduced Vicky to the others. "This lady is Special Agent Victoria Tennant and she's making sure that… Well, weird things have been happening."

Belinda Clay looked at Vicky with surprise. "It's wonderful that you're investigating, but… I mean, her house had a terrible, terrible glitch! Sadly, computers have problems. They're still just machines, but—"

"But," her husband said, shaking his head and letting out a sigh, "bad things happening that are a little too weird is a concept that has occurred to me, too. I assume it's not just the house. I mean, Captain Quincy's boat went all glitchy, too. I knew that man. I promise you—he wasn't suicidal."

"You're right. And Mr. Clay, we've wanted to speak with you, too, hoping that maybe you could help us, give us some insight on someone who might have hated him."

"I can give you something like the *Yellow Pages* on that!" Barton said. "Nothing against him was ever proven but he had a rep for being one hell of a…provider when it came to drugs. He started out by visiting our maritime law department, but he was hurt because of a broken board on a dock. He was wanting to sue the company responsible for the dock's upkeep. When

I heard he was going to be turned over to personal injury, I admit, I reacted badly—"

"You didn't react that badly!" his wife protested. She lowered her head.

"I didn't really have much say in the matter. Celia Smith stepped right in," he said. "Could someone want him dead? I would think so. But hating someone for being..."

"Slime?" Lee suggested.

Barton Clay shrugged. "He wasn't a nice guy. Of course, his accident—if it was an accident—happened before we...before we lost Marci. But—"

"I was already explaining to Special Agent Tennant that he and Marci were like night and day—Marci was loved. Adored!" Gina said.

"She was," Belinda said quietly. "We were all friends," she added for Vicky.

"Anyway, I'll be in the office the rest of the week, or you can call my home phone," Barton Clay told Vicky, handing her his card. "I... Well, we need to get on home."

"Thank you—all of you—for speaking with me," Vicky said. "We appreciate any help you can give us."

"The age of artificial intelligence is upon us!" Barton said. "And yet, intelligent men and women often disagree, so how intelligent is the intelligence?" he asked with a shrug.

"Think of the movies like *M3GAN*, about the killer doll!" Gina said. She shivered. "No dolls in our house after that!"

"Hey, *Chucky* was just as bad," her husband said. "And he was just a demon or something. Anyway..."

"Good night and thank you!" Vicky said.

The four walked toward their cars. She watched as they left and saw that Jude was by their Mustang.

He was in conversation with both Mr. Wharton and Mr. Dixon.

She still stood by the coffin and realized the cemetery employees were waiting for the mourners to leave so they could complete the burial. Nearby, shaded and in the background behind a group of beautiful trees, was a tractor outfitted with a backhoe, waiting to fill in the grave once the coffin had been lowered into the ground.

And it was time for her to join Jude.

But before she could walk away, Celia Smith came walking up to her.

"The funeral? You had to question people at the funeral?" she demanded.

"We knew that your people would be here," Vicky said pleasantly. "We had to get started since we're still waiting for your list, and oh! I really need to speak with you again. This is something that surely you had to have taken note of yourself since Captain Ronald Quincy was your client. Strange. His boat went haywire, and so did Marci's house."

"How dare you? Are you accusing me of something? I will have you in court—"

"I didn't accuse you of anything at all. I mentioned things that happened. Facts."

"Harassment—"

"I haven't harassed anyone, Ms. Smith. As a matter of fact, your people are anxious to help us in any way. They cared about Marci."

"Now you're insinuating I didn't!"

"I have no idea what your relationship was with Marci, Ms. Smith," Vicky said. She spoke flatly; there was no point trying to be diplomatic with this woman.

And if Celia Smith was the one who handled the case that Captain Quincy had brought to the agency, she was a step closer to being a suspect. Especially since they now knew Paul Sands, *Esquire*, had a relationship with the agency as well and represented Carlos Rodriguez, a known killer.

And thankfully, a narcissistic wild card.

"We are a family at the firm," Celia Smith told her. "And so help me, if you don't quit harassing us, there will be a lawsuit. You can count on it."

"That's all right. You can count on warrants from here on out," Vicky said, smiling dryly and walking past her. She was anxious to speak with Jude and stand by his side if his conversation with the men continued.

And she was anxious to get away from Celia Smith.

"Excuse me," she said to Celia, walking around her to go toward the cars.

As she walked by, she heard Celia speaking at the grave site to the earthly remains of Marci Warden.

"People don't understand, Marci. Just because I don't cry or laugh easily or run into someone's arms every time I meet them, it doesn't mean that I didn't care! But you know now, of course, that I cared about you, Marci, dear! You know."

Is the woman a twisted form of Jekyll and Hyde? Vicky wondered.

Had she cared?

She paused, hearing a very soft whirr.

Despite Celia still standing there, the workers had apparently determined there was more to be done that day.

They lowered the coffin down.

"Ma'am, step back, please!" one of the workers asked.

Celia ignored him.

It appeared that he was going to walk around to join her, perhaps set a hand on her arm and make a gentle attempt to remove her physically.

But the sound of a motor suddenly started up again, this one like a roar.

"David, stop!" the worker by the grave shouted.

Another man shouted back to him from a position near the earth-moving machine.

"It's not me! I'm not in the cab, and Jimmy isn't working the hoe!"

With a fluid spate of expletives, the worker by the grave walked toward the large machine.

But even as he did so, the machine started toward him, moving toward the grave as well and shaking the ground.

And Celia Smith suddenly let out a startled scream.

She was too close to the open grave. The earth's tremor caused her to slip.

And she disappeared into the earth.

"What the heck is going on?" Nathaniel Wharton demanded.

He and Donald Dixon had not had the least difficulty talking to Jude. While both thought that what had happened had to have been an awful accident, Wharton readily admitted Marci had been something of an expert when it came to artificial intelligence. And yes, it was weird that they had discovered the associations that they had—and yet, life was full of bizarre coincidences and sometimes it could be a very small world.

"Sad to say. Artificial intelligence helps us so much in our daily lives, but… I was trying to write a brief the other day about an accident that occurred by Tolomato Cemetery. My AI editorial program was determined that I had it wrong—that it had to be 'Tomato Cemetery.' AI is only as good as the information that goes in, but," he said and shrugged, "Marci might have gotten carried away while setting up her house. I mean, seriously, it sounded like a horrible, horrible accident—"

"Like the crashing of Captain Quincy's yacht?" Jude had asked him.

"It's far more likely that someone was after Quincy than Marci!" Dixon commented.

But that was as far as they got.

Celia Smith's scream rang out, and those who remained by the cars turned to try to ascertain what could have happened.

Celia had disappeared.

So had Vicky.

Jude ran. When he reached the grave, however, he saw Vicky was unhurt. She had apparently hopped down into the grave to help Celia.

"The backhoe apparently had a mind of its own!" Vicky announced. Jude saw that she had gotten Celia Smith to her feet and was holding the woman to steady her. He hunkered by the grave, reaching to slip his hands around the woman's midsection to lift her out of the grave.

She was shaking.

Maybe she would now believe that something was really wrong; maybe, just maybe, she'd quit being so damned nasty to them.

Wharton came up behind Jude, saying Celia's name with distress. Dixon was by his side, and they both started questioning her to try to ascertain if she was all right or if they needed to call an ambulance.

Jude looked at Vicky who shook her head and grimaced. He reached into the grave to lift her out as well, pulling her close for a minute. He told himself he hadn't panicked when he had heard the scream and hadn't seen her. He had rushed to the scene the same way he would have done with any partner.

That much was true.

But he might have held her then for just a moment longer than he might have held someone else.

It was okay. She smiled at him, and he nodded and turned around.

One of the cemetery workers had managed an extraordinary leap into the cab of the tractor; he'd manually turned it off, and his face still had a look of stunned disbelief.

"Sorry, guys, we're going to need a forensic crew out here," Jude said. "I'm not sure what else was planned for that equipment today, but it isn't going to happen."

As he spoke, he saw that Vicky was on the phone. A forensic

crew would be out momentarily; he imagined Aidan would want to be leading this one himself.

That made him glad again that Clover was with them; Cary would feel much better about being at their headquarters by herself with the dog by her side.

Celia was insisting she was fine.

Nathaniel Wharton, tall, lean, and weary, kept arguing she needed to allow EMTs, at the least, to check her out after the fall.

"Look, it wasn't that big a fall. I have a few scrapes and bruises!" Celia said. "Please, Nathaniel, I just want to go home." She paused, aware that Jude and Vicky were watching her.

"And you! You big federal know-it-alls! You find out who was responsible for leaving that tractor running. I will sue them on personal injury—"

"I don't know. We were all standing in the area, and that tractor was off, and the workers were waiting for you to get away from the grave site," Jude said, shrugging. "Amazing, isn't it? That tractor starting up all by itself?"

"No!" Celia raged. "These idiots left it running!"

"I was standing right here," Vicky pointed out. "That tractor wasn't running. It started up all by itself. Just like the way Marci's house came to life, the judge's car accelerated to ninety before crashing and exploding, Quincy's boat soared into the rocks…and, oh, yeah, the car assigned to us from the Nashville offices went crazy, too. So—"

"Whatever! The tractor is faulty equipment and the cemetery is responsible!" Celia raged.

"Celia, Celia!" Wharton said gently. "Please."

"Yes, please, just get checked out!" Dixon added.

"I want to see their so-called forensic experts—" Celia began.

But Nathaniel Wharton put his foot down. "Celia, I can call

an ambulance or Donald and I can drive you by the ER just to get checked out. I'm not suggesting, I'm ordering!"

"I'm a partner!" she protested. "You can't order me—"

"I made you a partner and I can unmake you a partner. I'm sure with your expertise you read all the contracts. Please, Celia, stop! Don't you see? Something is really wrong here—"

"Because these people say so?" Celia demanded. She sounded a little bit different. Almost as if she were pleading with them.

"Yes, because we people—and the director of the FBI—don't believe in this many consequences," Vicky told her. "And, oh, by the way, you're welcome. You could still be in that grave, you know."

Jude glanced at Vicky, willing himself not to smile.

So much for treading lightly.

Vicky had her gloves off.

"Let's go!" Wharton said firmly.

Celia lowered her head and shook it, but when Wharton put his arm around her shoulders to lead her toward the cars, she went along.

Even as they left, several cars from both the state and federal offices drove in.

He saw that, as he had expected, Aidan had come out himself.

He hurried over to the two of them and looked at Vicky, frowning; Jude realized that her hop into the grave had left a smudge of dirt on her face.

"Vicky just fished Celia Smith out of the grave," Jude told him, turning to wipe Vicky's cheek. She looked up at him with amusement as his fingers ran over her skin.

"I guess there's a lot of playing in the dirt on this one," she said. "Anyway, we've finally gotten in touch with a few of the people from the firm—all of whom are willing to talk. Except for Celia Smith. She's determined that we're after the firm on connections that mean nothing."

"Well, she is the one who fell in the grave, right? I mean, I guess she could have been really hurt, so…"

"So, if you want to look innocent, maybe getting hurt might be a way to do it?" Vicky suggested.

"I still say anything is possible at this point," Jude told her. "But—"

"Except it's somebody involved with that firm. So far, people have been helpful, they've wanted to find out the truth—except for Celia Smith."

Jude arched a brow at her, a dry half smile on his lips.

"Haven't we both learned that being nice doesn't make you innocent and being a jerk doesn't make you guilty, especially when it comes to murder?"

"We also know that Nathaniel Wharton is not supposed to have the expertise to have carried off something like this while most of the rest of the firm is pretty tech savvy. We need a connection. We need to know where the servers are that are being used—"

"And remember, that's a problem because they're being bounced around from all over the place," Vicky said. "But here is the good thing—if we can just get somewhere, nothing is ever really deleted."

Jude nodded, looking toward the offending truck.

Aidan had headed to the truck and hopped down a minute, walking over to them.

"Yes, even tractors and trucks have computers these days." He shook his head. "Cary and I were doing all kinds of research and there's been auto thefts across the nation because people can hack into phones pretty easily and lots of cars can be found—and started—by computers. It's like everything else in life. There's the good—amazing medical strides, for one—and there's the bad. People hacking into computers—and killing people."

"At least no one was killed," Jude said.

"Maybe that was the plan," Vicky said.

Jude looked at her. She might have something there, but…

"None of us likes her, but, again, we can't pin her as guilty because we don't like her," he said.

"Anyway, I'm getting crew out here to help with the equipment so that we can do our best to dive into the machinery on this thing."

Jude felt his phone chime. He glanced at it and saw that Assistant Director Arnold had just sent him a message.

He looked over at Aidan and nodded. "You're going to find out that someone hacked into the system. Whether it was supposed to look like Celia Smith was under attack when she fell into the hole or if she really happened to be at the wrong place at the wrong time is going to be hard to determine but if we can get to it, we'll be at the truth of the matter. Easier said than done. I think that at this point, we need to get an assistant district attorney involved. We have enough to get warrants to dig into the firm's entire computer system. And," he said, looking at Vicky, "we may have a break in the case. We need to head out now and get on the list that Wharton has promised me later."

She frowned at him. "What's the break?" she asked him.

"Samuel Hutchins is awake," he told her. "Out of his coma and the doctors have said that we can have ten minutes with him, no more."

"All right, let's go!" Vicky said. "If he knows that his ex-wife and child are safe—"

"He may talk. Or…"

"Or he may think that they can never be safe. Anyway, he's our best shot at this moment," Vicky said. "Ouch. Bad terminology—you know, considering the way he shot at us."

Aidan groaned and turned to head back to the tractor.

Jude just shook his head, smiling slightly and arching a brow.

"Let's move!" she said.

They headed to the cars together. By that time, the pathways through the graveyard were almost empty; management had apparently closed the gates for the day, or at least until they had their strange machinery problem solved.

Those who had attended Marci's funeral had been either gone before the tractor incident or ordered by Nathaniel Wharton after Celia Smith had fallen to get themselves the hell out of the place.

"Has anyone talked to Samuel Hutchins yet?" Vicky asked Jude.

"No. According to my message from Arnold, he's just coming out of it and his situation is still delicate so he decided that it would be best not to push the man, but to send us in because, obviously, he'll recognize us."

"What if he tries to kill himself again?" Vicky asked anxiously. "In his condition, it might not be so hard. I mean, has anyone told him—"

"That his ex-wife and child are safe? Yes," Jude assured her. "And, hopefully, that takes away the only reason the man might do something to himself. Anyway, he's only been conscious about an hour—hospital let Arnold know right away and Arnold texted me immediately."

"Let's go. And then, hopefully, by morning we'll have the warrant we need. And, of course, maybe our cyber sleuths will have found out more."

The drive to the hospital was short. Jude was glad to see that law enforcement from all angles were there, with two policemen in uniform in the hallway, a friend Jude knew from Florida Department of Law Enforcement seated in a nurse's coat behind the desk, and another friend from the Jacksonville office on duty in a cleaning uniform. He'd have liked to have spoken to those he knew, perhaps introduced them to Vicky, but besides the officers, they were undercover—not a time to chat.

Samuel Hutchins was being well-guarded.

The man's eyes were closed when they entered the room and Jude feared that he might have slipped back into a coma.

But he heard them, and he opened his eyes. He was still a young man and looked particularly young in his hospital bed. Young, lost, and miserable.

"Hey, Sam," Jude said.

The man winced, shaking his head. "You're the ones I was supposed to kill," he said miserably. Then he grew anxious. "They let one of the officers in. He said that my ex-wife and kids were fine. Please tell me that wasn't a lie! They said that if I failed..."

"I swear to you!" Vicky told him, sincerely. "They are fine! They are being carefully guarded. As you are. But you know that. I promise you. And you didn't kill us, you tried to kill yourself. And that was to protect your family."

"You don't know their power!" he whispered.

"And you don't know ours," Jude said, because they might be fighting and fighting hard, but he knew that they would keep going and going until the end—they and just about every other officer and agent out there, as well as Cary and Aidan and rooms full of cyber teams.

"We will find out what is going on," Vicky said. "But we need all the help we can get."

He almost laughed. "I would help you—if I could!"

"You can help us. Let me tell you what we're seeing so far," Jude said. "You were just a poor struggling dude on the streets, but somehow you crossed paths with our cyber killer. I'm not suggesting you ever met this person—they saw you somewhere. And they contacted you. Online."

Samuel nodded miserably.

"At first, I thought it was a joke."

"You were warned, but you didn't think about calling the police?" Jude asked.

He winced. "I opened an email. It was a picture of Jessy.

Below it was another picture—the same one but covered in blood. I'm supposing that it was created by using generative AI, but it was to show me just what could happen to her. I was to be on call when needed. I wasn't to go to the police. I was to obey when told. Naturally I wrote back that they should go to hell. But then the message ding on my phone went off. Right after I said they should go to hell. And it was a warning that they could kill anyone and that they would start with Jessy and then get to my kids. And if I didn't believe them… they'd prove it. I was on my way to the store for something and I was angry and I demanded how and…they took control of my car and almost crashed me into the side of a wall… I begged them not to hurt Jessy or the kids… They showed me more pictures, an exploded car, and said it could happen to me easily, which I should realize, and then they showed me a boat that had crashed and exploded and I knew about that, I'd seen it on the news. And I knew, I knew then that they were dead serious and I had to do what they wanted or…"

He shook his head.

"What about the gun? How did you get it?" Jude asked.

"A dumpster off Aviles. And they left me the pills attached to it, and warned that if I failed, I'd better not let the cops get me. Jessy would be fine if I failed and died, but if I didn't…"

"Jessy is fine. We'll find a way for you to see her and your kids soon," Vicky said quietly.

"Oh, my God, yes! I never stopped loving Jessy and I would do anything in the world—" Hutchins began.

"Including die, so we know you would do anything for them," Vicky interrupted, but her words weren't cutting. "Right now, we must keep all of you safe, so be patient, and believe that we will be working on it. All right, when we found you, you didn't have your phone or a wallet on you. Where is the phone? We have a technical crew that might be able to trace the calls and pictures."

He closed his eyes for a moment, his head sinking deeper into the pillow. He almost smiled.

"I did something right!" he whispered. "I mean, I can hope that they're still there. There's a loose stone in an old wall right across from Aviles Street. It's in a wall around an old building that houses a bunch of businesses, an airline office, a phone store…some other places. I put my phone and wallet in the earth beneath the stone. With any luck, you can find it there. Just…dig a little." He paused, shaking his head. "But I think they have a way of making things disappear. As if they are magicians!"

"We have people who are magicians, too. They can make things that have disappeared reappear," Jude assured him.

Jude nodded and Vicky nudged him; they had promised they wouldn't stay long, and they had something to go on—maybe everything that they might get from the man.

"All right," Jude said. "Jessy and the kids are at a safe house. When the doctors tell us that you're strong enough, we'll take you. We'll leave you now. Rest and get well. We're keeping the guards watching over you, even though we never let anyone know that you survived what you did to yourself. Rest and get well."

"So you can arrest me. But I deserve it," he said.

"We may not need to, not if the information you gave us helps us get to the people who really caused all this," Vicky told him. She squeezed his hand. "Rest. Get better."

Jude gave him a nod and caught Vicky's hand to draw her from the room.

She smiled and arched a brow at him.

"And now…" Vicky began.

"We're going on a hunt for buried treasure!" he told her.

TEN

"What are you thinking?" Jude asked, glancing Vicky's way as he drove.

"Well, I'm hoping we find our buried treasure," she said. "Other than that, I was putting together in my mind all that we know and, of course, it keeps leading back to Marci's law firm and the connections between the people who have died by manipulation—that we know of. We know for a fact that Carlos Rodriguez hired a killer through a site on the dark web. We have the site, but, of course, it was taken down. Now we know that they planned to take us out—or whoever as far as investigators went in case Maric's death wasn't being seen as an accident. We got lucky in Tennessee—someone knew that the team on the crash would be getting a car from the local offices, but they didn't see us, so they couldn't recognize who we were, therefore we were able to manipulate the situation. When we find Samuel Hutchins's phone, we'll have more for Aidan, Cary, and the cyber teams to go on and—"

"Burner phone," Jude said.

"Of course. Anyone sending that kind of message would

only do it on a burner. But our people may be able to find something. They can track the cell towers, maybe find out what kind of phone, where it might have been bought, who knows what they can discover! If we can discover the phone, that is!" she said.

"We will."

"Days have passed!" she reminded him.

"But we're good," he assured her.

She laughed at that. "We're as good as time and the elements allow us to be! Some kid might have found the wallet and phone—"

"Eh! We're almost there. Don't be a pessimist!"

"Not a pessimist. A realist!"

"All right. Let me be the optimistic realist, then!" he said lightly.

They arrived in the area and Jude found some parking just off Aviles Street. They exited the car. Vicky immediately saw the building that Samuel Hutchins had described. It was an old building—not dating back to the beginning of the settlement, but still architecture that had first gone up sometime in the early to mid-1800s.

The stone wall surrounding the property might have been there longer, guarding another property. Somewhere else, the old stone might have just appeared dirty and chipped.

Here, it seemed fitting.

It also ran the length of the street on two sides.

"Maybe we should have gotten the guy to be a bit more specific," Jude told her.

She laughed. "Divide and conquer?" she asked.

"It'll save time. Still..." His words trailed as he looked around. It was a typical late afternoon. Some people were getting off from work, others were tourists, some parents were simply out to dine or eat with their kids. It was busy enough.

"Are you suggesting that I be careful even though I'm going

to look certifiably crazy while I crawl around the ground looking for a loose stone?" she inquired.

"Something like that."

"I am always careful," she assured him, heading off in her own direction.

Buried treasure! Well, as it seemed as with the rest of the area, St. Augustine had dealt with an era of pirates. There was a wonderful venue, The Pirate's Museum, on Castillo Drive. She had a friend in Daytona who taught history and specialized in the pirate era, always frustrated about the fact pirates had become so romanticized and that every story had an X mark on a map and there was always buried treasure. Why would pirates bury their treasure? Wouldn't they want to use it? They did exist! They pillaged the coastline of Florida from the first settlements through the centuries. And when sanctioned by their governments, they were called privateers.

Today, however, she had to hope they could really come across the buried treasure they needed!

Passersby, be they tourists or locals, frowned, looked at her oddly and hurried around her as they saw that she was stopping every few feet to check the stones near the ground.

One man, middle-aged, gray-haired, and dignified in a gray-pinstripe suite stopped and said, "Excuse me, ma'am, you should know that it would be illegal for you to steal any of these stones. I realize it's a wall that's been here forever, but it's on private property and I believe it would also be considered a historic matter."

She winced inwardly and smiled at him. "Oh, don't worry, sir! I just lost a—a medallion near here and I'm hoping it got kicked into a wedge where the stone meets the earth."

"Oh, well then excuse me, I hope you find your medallion."

She wasn't at all sure he believed her, but he was moving on. She wondered then if they shouldn't have informed the local police about what they were doing because, of course, they did appear to be more than a little weird at the very least.

But it was as if the man had brought her good luck! The next stone she wedged sat on top of something that was leather. A wallet.

And beneath the wallet…

Yes!

Samuel Hutchins's phone!

She gathered her treasure and ran around the corner where it seemed that Jude was politely explaining himself to a pair of young women, one a young and attractive brunette and the other a young and attractive redhead. They looked to be little more than a year or two out of college and while she heard Jude explaining that he'd lost a ring, as she neared them she could see that the young women were grinning away, far more fascinated with Jude than with whatever he might be doing.

"Hey, darling!" she called.

She was glad to see that he looked at her with gratitude.

"Vicky!" he said. "Still looking for the ring. These young ladies wanted to help me once they realized what I was doing. Nancy, Madeleine…this is my…partner, Vicky. She helps me with everything. It's so nice of you, but really…"

"Oh, you're uh…" Nancy, the blonde began.

"Living together," Vicky interrupted quickly and sweetly. Well, that much was true! For the time, at least.

"Well, um," Madeleine, the redhead, said awkwardly, "I guess we'll get a move on. We're from Colorado," she told Vicky. "Here to see some fantastic old sights! And we're going to go and do that, right Nancy? Just needed to see if he needed some help."

"And, truthfully, to figure out just what the heck he was doing!" Nancy said.

"Nice to meet you and enjoy the city. The sights are fantastic. Take a few tours—the history remains the same, but the spin can be different."

The two walked off.

"Thank you!" Jude murmured quietly, watching them go.

Vicky laughed. "Can't help turning on the charm, huh?"

"Haha, so—"

"You're really going to thank me!" she informed him. "I have them!"

"The wallet and the cell phone?" he asked, his tone almost incredulous.

"Right, one of us was searching for buried treasure while the other was flirting."

"What? I wasn't flirting."

Vicky laughed. "You were looking a little bit desperate."

"I guess I did look a bit like a crazy person, digging around the base of the wall."

"And yet they were willing to take a chance!" Vicky teased. But then she told him, "I know, I got asked what I was doing, too. No one cute, though, just an older guy in a business suit. But then *I* went on to find the buried treasure!"

She produced the wallet and the phone for him to see and he smiled and nodded.

"Let's get them where they need to be!"

They returned to the car.

They drove to the main lab. Aidan was there with what had been recovered from the tractor at the graveyard.

"Obviously, it's not easy to pull information from any kind of hacked computer," he told them. "But it is possible to see that programs have been changed—that they have been hacked."

Jude shook his head. "How does this person—or these people—even know what computer needs to be hacked?"

"Well, this is scary, but information for law enforcement agencies is stored on computers, too. That's how they knew you would be following up in Tennessee," Aidan told them.

"They would have known your names, when you were arriving, and what car you were going to be given. They probably weren't counting on a man like Carlos Rodriguez going totally whacko on a power trip and giving up info on the old murder-for-hire site, but they might have planned to take it down and start over just because, whoever this is, they know that others can hack into things, too. Though this person—or persons—seems to be a little like Carlos Rodriguez. Certain of their own invincibility. Long and short of it is this—we know that every incident, including the out-of-control tractor causing Celia Smith to go into the grave today—has been caused by a hack."

"And the problem is that a hack can occur from just about anywhere—if there is a strong enough server," Aidan told them.

"And this person knows how to use an algorithm," Aidan said.

"Which is a set of rules that can be used to solve problems on a computer, right?" Jude asked.

"Technically, yes, the computer picks up on what is happening, be it a number, a specific search term…and through what it knows, it discovers more," Vicky said. "In other words, the computer knows that the person is interested in the crash in Tennessee, the boat explosion, the house explosion. And the person already has access to endless law enforcement sites—supposedly protected up the wazoo! But put them together and—"

"National security could definitely be at risk," Jude said.

"So far," Aidan said, "it seems to be murder for hire, murder by machine, nice and clean. The person ordering the murder can have an alibi that can't be disputed—dozens of people could have seen whoever wanted Marci, the judge, and people on the boat dead at the exact time that it was happening."

"Except that Carlos Rodriguez is so proud of his accomplishments and so certain he could get himself off that he admitted the deed," Jude said. "People!"

"We'll get what we can from the phone," Aidan said, frowning as he looked at it. "It's passcode-protected, however, it's easy enough to get into a phone through the manufacturer or provider. But—"

"Wait!" Vicky said, thinking about Samuel Hutchins. Aidan was still holding the phone. "We don't need any of that—Samuel Hutchins is cooperating with us. We can just call him, except that I'm willing to bet I know his passcode. We can try it now. 'Try *ChloeJustin*. Capitalize the *C* and the *J*."

"His kids' names, sure," Aidan murmured.

But when Aidan tried the password, it failed. He shook his head.

"Reverse them," Vicky said.

He did.

He looked at her, smiling. His smile faded after he looked back at the phone and brought up the man's messages.

"We're in," he said. "My God." He stared from the phone to Vicky and Jude. "Computer-enhanced, AI-generated images, but someone got a hold of real pictures of Jessy, Justin, and Chloe. You can see why the man was willing to kill himself rather than risk…this."

He handed the phone to Vicky and Jude looked over her shoulder as they both viewed the gruesome images that had been created. Whoever had this might have taken a cue from the murders of Carlos Rodriguez's daughter-in-law and her sister.

The images first showed Jessy trying to stop a masked figure in black with a machete from chopping at Justin. The next image was of Chloe on the floor in a pool of blood. And last, after witnessing the carnage of her children, was Jessy, eyes still open as her head lay on the floor in a pool of crimson next to her body.

"You must find out where those came from!" Vicky said passionately. "Obviously, AI, but…"

"We will," Aidan said solemnly. "And these aren't real, Vicky. Jessy is safe, the kids are safe. And the person who is behind all this didn't commit murders like this—Carlos Rodriguez did and thanks to you two, he won't get away with it now—even if the legal system is a machine all its own."

"Filled with computers," Jude noted.

But Aidan shook his head. "Rodriguez just made use of the site. The person behind this hasn't committed the violence themselves—they let the machine do it and they revel in what happens, something they did at a keyboard and not in person."

"I think you're right," Jude said.

"Well, go, get out of here. I'm on this. And Assistant Director Arnold is getting the necessary legal work done so that we can tear into the law firm's computers. You'll be bringing the warrant by tomorrow and interviewing everyone there to find out who has access to what computer and maybe, if the water is getting hot, someone will say something rather than boil."

"Right. We're gone," Aidan told him.

They said their goodbyes and headed out. Jude looked ahead for a moment as he drove but then glanced at her speculatively. "So, darling, where to now?" he teased in response to her earlier words.

She grinned and leaned back.

"Food."

"Yeah, that would be really good. Where? What kind?"

"The edible kind? Wait, I'm getting a real choice here? Dinner I don't need to cook, and we have the time to pick anywhere! Should I pick?" she asked.

"Yes, you should. I like all food. And we're not on again until the morning. We can pick any restaurant within driving distance—driving distance in a certain proximity, that is! We have time. I could take you to an elegant steakhouse—"

"Local food. Fun food. Delicious, fresh. I mean, I know of

a few places in the city. I did grow up not all that far south from here. But—"

"Crave," Jude told her.

She laughed. "Yes, let's see, funeral, hospital, digging under stones like crazy idiots, lab, and now, having skipped lunch, I'm craving food!"

"No. I think you'll like Crave. That's the name of the restaurant. Nice outdoor seating, smoothies, salads, wraps, popular with locals and tourists—"

"You drink smoothies?" she interrupted. She knew men, friends, in law enforcement, who wouldn't dream of touching something called a smoothie. Not all of them, of course. Just some. Which was maybe not fair—she had female friends who didn't like smoothies, either! And again, in their hurried lives, they were all prone to drinking their breakfast often enough, even when it was only coffee.

"Yep. Good ones, sure. And they make great ones," he told her, shrugging.

She laughed. "Then I'm craving dinner at Crave! And, of course, I'll need to try a smoothie."

Vicky looked forward for a minute as they drove. She lowered her head, smiling. *Jude*, she thought, *will always stand by the truth, even his own truth.*

As they drove, he told her that it had really become one of his favorite places.

"In this line of work, we become so involved, we often just don't eat. Then we grab whatever junk we can find. Came here with a friend once. Food was fresh, healthy, and fun. I decided that if I was going to live this life, when I could, I'd come to a place like this. You're going to love it. You'll get a kick out of the smoothie menu."

They parked and made their way to the restaurant.

She did. The place offered up mixes such as "First Date," "Funky Monkey," "So Matcha Love," and more.

"I may have to go with 'First Date,'" she told Jude.

"Well, it is, kind of, you know, darling!" he teased in turn. "So, smoothie and then—"

"Tuna wrap! I love everything in it!" she told him.

Jude opted for a shrimp bowl.

With food and smoothies, they sat outside. The early evening was beautiful, and Vicky loved being outside, so much foliage in her vision, and that night…

Just casual. Easy.

"And it's good?" he asked her. "At this point in the evening, I should have taken you for a giant scotch!"

"This is perfect. We'll get the giant scotch when we've gotten to the bottom of all this. Jude, it's nice just sitting here."

"I'm glad you like it."

"Love it." She sipped her smoothie and looked at him. "May I ask you a question?"

"That is a question. But, yes, you can ask me another question. I just don't guarantee the answers all the time," he told her.

"Okay. I know that even though it wasn't your fault, you blame yourself for what happened to your old partner. But that's not unusual. I know other agents who had their partners injured or killed in the line of duty and I guess there's no way out of a certain amount of second-guessing and guilt. But what made you want to get into law enforcement to start with?"

He leaned toward her, drumming his fingers on the table, partially looking very serious and partially holding back a grin. "I'll show you mine if you'll show me yours."

"That's very suggestive—*darling*," she teased.

"Not suggestive—flat out there," he said. But he leaned back and grinned. "My story is easy and probably a usual one. My dad was a cop, a detective with the state. I probably heard too much as a kid, but he and his friends were good guys, always working hard. They worked tough cases, but there was one that always stuck with me. A kidnapping/murder situation—the kid's babysitter was left for dead, and the kid was taken. The attempted murder was a last-minute thing—the killers had gone there to rob the place. The father was a diamond broker. Anyway, he and his team were gone for weeks—the guys responsible had hightailed it into the Glades north of Tamiami Trail. My dad found the boy in one of the old hunter's shacks that used to be common there. He'd been tied up and left. He would have been dead from dehydration, starvation—or a dozen other lethal things that can get you out there—if he hadn't been discovered when he was." Jude shrugged with a smile. "The kid grew up and he and his family keep in contact with my dad, though my dad retired years ago. Oh! The babysitter—who survived three good stab wounds—keeps in contact, too."

"What about the would-be robbers who were going to let a kid die out in a shack?" Vicky asked.

"They got them. They seemed to think they were the only people who knew their way through our great 'River of Grass,' but they underestimated Florida law enforcement. Oh, don't get me wrong—we know that people have gotten away with all kinds of illegal activities during the years because you can go deep, deep into the wilderness, but…"

"Still in prison?" she asked.

"One died in prison of cancer. The other will be there for life. The babysitter was in tears and had half the courtroom in tears as she testified about being terrified and nearly dead as she was repeatedly stabbed."

"Wow. So, horrible people made you want to go into law enforcement—"

"No," he interrupted. "The fact that the babysitter survived, the kid was found—and the men who did it went to prison and were off the streets before they could do something like that to anyone else—that's what made me know I wanted to be in law enforcement." He laughed. "Like I said, my dad was a cop. Adored him and still do. When I was a little kid playing cops and robbers with my friends, I was always a cop. That's it. Now. Your turn."

Vicky winced.

"Eh! I said, I'll show you mine if you show me yours!" he reminded her.

"It was bad. I was in college. We had a big room with a big bath—and four of us in it, dormitory style, I guess. Anyway, one of the girls didn't come home one night and her body was found a few days later in a canal—it had been weighed down with rocks. We were all devastated, of course, but I had known Casey better than the others—we had just clicked in our history classes and liked to roam the state together to find locations we learned about. Anyway, she had been seeing a guy, big man on campus, football player, the works. But she had suspected he'd been cheating on her and I heard the argument they had—they'd gone out in the hall but left the door ajar by accident, I guess. I suspected him. No one wanted to believe it—except for the homicide cop on the case. And he set me up with a wire and we found the right time and place and..."

"And?"

Vicky shrugged. "He tried to kill me—"

"They never should have put you in that position—"

"No, no, he didn't even get his hands on me. The cops were right there. He was hauled off to face murder charges, and I wasn't just fine, I was so relieved! This guy was kind of like Carlos Rodriguez—he thought he was too cool for anyone to touch. And my friend, Casey, embarrassed him, I guess, because she meant to leave him in the dirt. And, in his mind, girls did not break up with him. During the trial, a woman burst into tears and started shouting at him and demanding to know where her daughter was. Turned out he'd dated a young woman in high school who had mysteriously disappeared, and he laughed at her and claimed to know nothing about it. But the homicide cop on my friend's case started investigating and they found the other girl, decomposed after so many years, but with DNA and dental records they made the identification. And he'd been offered a chance to get the death penalty off the table if he gave the mother peace and let her find her child. He'd been so convinced no one would find the body—he'd used a fresh just-filled grave to get rid of her—that he wouldn't take any kind of a plea deal."

"What happened to him?"

"Death penalty. Honestly, I don't know how I feel about the death penalty," Vicky told him. "This guy was a monster and given the chance, he would have killed again. But I do always have it in the back of my mind that at some point the wrong man will be convicted as when Derek Bentley was hanged in England when it was his friend who did the shooting and his words, 'Let him have it, Chris,' which referred to the gun, were taken as a threat. I'd never want an innocent man or woman executed. All that philosophy aside—it's not up to me. I want to stop people doing horrible things to other people, bring them to justice, and let judges and juries decide the rest. Wow. Sorry. That's why I don't—"

"Get into lengthy discussions on the past?" he asked her.

She nodded. "Depressing, but—"

"But it gave the system an amazing investigator," he told her.

"Well, thanks. You, too. We'll be amazing if we get this done."

"We will. And I can tell you a good story, too," he said.

"Your story was a good one! Babysitter lived. Kid found!"

"Trust me, not all my dad's cases ended so well. But I wound up going with the Bureau—with my dad's blessing—because he was friends with an agent. We had a horrible hostage situation. Bank robbery gone bad. The FBI was in on it. A couple, a regular Bonnie and Clyde, were making demands and threatening to start shooting the customers and employees if they didn't get what they wanted right away. Anyway, when the bank was being surrounded, the Bonnie in the duo was shot and my dad's friend was able to go in, get the guy to allow a paramedic, and while the 'paramedic' was armed, the agent talked the guy into giving up so that she could live. Everyone walked out safely. Bonnie and Clyde both lived, they're doing time, but as model prisoners attending church services and both hoping that they'll eventually be pardoned and spend the rest of their lives in wedded bliss. Sometimes, talking the good talk is a more valuable weapon than a firearm."

"You've taken classes in negotiation?"

"Negotiation, profiling, and psychology. Hey, I like school, believe it or not."

Vicky laughed. "I like school, too, learning new things… profiling, of course. A few psychology classes and a special workshop on profiling at Quantico. And—"

"Lots of computer courses?"

"Yes."

He sighed. "Here's wishing I had more of those!"

They had finished eating. She sipped the last of her smoothie and let out a soft breath. It had been an interesting dinner. She didn't talk about the past that often herself. Maybe it hadn't been fair to ask him to talk, then again, fair in the end because they knew so much more about one another now—about everything that made them tick.

And while different events had occurred to them, the outcomes had brought them to a similar place in life.

"I guess we should head back," Vicky said.

"Bummer."

"Bummer?"

"First date," he teased. "We should have been hitting the town, staying out late!"

"Well, in truth, I loved this idea. My 'First Date' was delicious."

"Oh, you don't know the half!" he teased.

"I don't? I wonder what a 'Second Date' is like!" she responded, laughing.

"Now, wait a minute. This was *almost* like a first date."

"Only for weird people in law enforcement!"

"Now, hey, come on. We talked. Deeply. In a way, this was more than anyone usually discovers on a first date—"

"Because we've been almost glued to each other for the past few days?" she groaned.

"Because we talked. Really talked," he said, and for a minute, he was close and serious and she could feel as if his soul emanated from him, everything that she had come to care for and admire so very much.

And then, of course, he was simply physically attractive...

"So, honestly, would you go on a second date?" he asked her.

She couldn't tell if he was still teasing or not. She just knew that their knees brushed beneath the table, that their fingers almost touched on the table, that they were almost intimately close.

"Would you?" she countered quietly.

"A thousand more," he said, and she smiled as he rose, looking at her.

He meant it.

"And you?" he asked.

"I really love this restaurant, but I doubt we could come a thousand times!"

He grinned and offered her a hand to rise.

He kept her hand as they left the restaurant and returned to the car.

"It's still not that late. Ordinarily, I'd be a better date. I'd take you to a play or a movie, or, if you were into it, a sporting event—"

"I'm fine with sports. Basketball, football, and baseball, in that order. Basketball because, as my dad once told me, the game was often won or lost in the last ten minutes!"

He grinned and opened her car door.

"No basketball game tonight, I'm afraid," he said. "But then there's always… Well, you know that dating thing."

"Which dating thing? I'll be honest. I have dated, of course. But not a hell of a lot. It seems that all I do is work."

"Wow, we managed to work and have a first date!" he said lightly.

"Maybe not so bad. People like us…we may be the only ones who can really understand each other."

"And you are one good-looking partner!" he told her.

She laughed. "Hey, you got the girls trying to pick you up today. I just got one serious old business guy who was about to call the cops on me." She frowned. "What's that old dating thing that you're talking about?"

"A hotel room," he said. "Not that I'm suggesting—"

"If we didn't show up at the house, Cary and Aidan would have the cops out on us!" she said lightly.

"We do have rooms."

"In a house with other people!" Vicky said.

He'd opened the door for her. She was seated with her legs still out of the car. He hunkered down close to her.

"So…you would go to a hotel room with me?"

His eyes were so intently on hers. She loved his eyes, so green, sometimes as if they truly emitted the heat of an emerald fire…

She swallowed and he said, "You know, they do have their own rooms."

"But, um…"

"One of us can do the kid thing and sneak down the hall into the other's room," he suggested.

"Which one of us?"

"I'm willing to take the dare! Oh, of course," he said, still smiling but feigning worry, "I would want to make sure that you'd let me in."

His face was almost touching hers. And he managed to delve into the depths of her soul and make her laugh and…

She reached out, cupping his jaw, looking into the incredible green of his eyes, and leaning forward. Her fingers moved delicately over his flesh, and she found his lips with her own.

She'd meant a gentle kiss, a kiss that just said yes…

But it became deep, and he drew her up and into his arms and the kiss became heated and deep and intimate and it seemed to awaken a dozen senses and instincts within her, so often forgotten or shelved and it wasn't wrong because they were so very right for each other in so many ways and…

It was something she wanted.

But, of course, they both realized that though they were standing by a darker parking area and it wasn't exactly as if they were on stage, there *were* people out at night and they were probably becoming a little passionate for a public display.

They broke apart almost simultaneously.

"So, if I slip down the hall…"

"I will open the door. And then…?"

He grinned. "I told you. You show me yours, and I'll show you mine!"

She laughed and said, "Then I guess you'd better drive!"

ELEVEN

She lay at his side, dark hair spread over the sheets like shimmering sable, the softness of her flesh against his.

She lay sleeping, and Jude wished that he didn't need to wake her up, or, at the least, if he had to wake her up it was just to stay and play.

She was…magic.

He remembered their first meeting. His confusion about the entire situation. His own sense that she might be a beautiful young woman, but…

And Vicky, of course, despairing that he just wasn't seeing the real situation.

That made him smile. Well, in truth, he hadn't seen it—until he had understood everything that had happened. And while he could maneuver his way through files and life on a computer, manipulating algorithms, truly understanding the roles of servers and sites and more were beyond his expertise.

And still…

First, he had slowly fallen in love with her mind. The rest, wanting her…

That was nature, that was the chemistry that seemed to burn between them, more brightly every minute they spent together.

He didn't want to move. He wanted to watch her sleep, love the contours of her face, remember the feel of her flesh, the way she had moved against him…

He knew they'd both been deeply into their work through the years, that they hadn't had the time to give to relationships what others might, and if they had started out in relationships, often the demands—and ever the fears—of their jobs had made others leery, and thus…

Something waiting to end before it began.

He had at least sixty seconds, maybe even two minutes, before he had to wake her, creep back to his room, and take five minutes to shower and dress for the day.

In those moments he just looked at her, and remembered how he had slunk down the hall like an errant teenager, when they had hushed one another as they laughed, warning one another with fingers to their lips that they'd prefer their private lives be private.

He hadn't been seen.

She'd been so quickly in his arms. It hadn't been a parking lot; there were no observers. Maybe it was partially that the human being was an animal and sometimes, no matter how moral and ethical a man might hope to be, instinct kicked in, and thankfully…

Their instincts were shared.

He could look at her hair and still feel its silky softness beneath his fingers, see her naked shoulder and know the wonder of touching her. Laughter, passion, urgency, clothing strewn everywhere, those first moments, that first time together, then the shower and the feel of more heat cascading around them and every moment, touch, caress, kiss, intimacy that followed.

She stretched slightly in her sleep.

He eased himself from the bed, reaching for his clothing.

He trusted himself, he trusted them both, naked or dressed. They'd had so much of the night, and then when perhaps he should have slunk back to his room, there had been a silent determination that he would not, that the time together after was just as beautiful, holding one another, drifting to sleep at last...

Naw.

He might trust Vicky, but he didn't trust himself.

He slipped out of bed and hobbled quickly into his clothing.

Then he leaned over her, gently touching her shoulder, shaking her, feeling the brush of her hair.

"Vicky, Vicky, I'm so sorry. We've got to be out of here in ten, pick up the warrant, head to Wharton, Dixon, and Smith with it, start serious interrogation there."

She groaned softly.

Perplexed, he touched her shoulder with a little more force.

But she sprang to a sitting position, grinning. Her hair wild around her, her eyes bright, her very existence pure temptation to him.

"I'm aware of the time!" she said, laughing. "I need a two-second shower, clothing. I'll beat you to the kitchen!"

"Like hell you will!" he told her.

He grinned and hurried out.

And crashed right into Aidan.

"Not that I'm the fashion police, Jude, but..."

"Yeah, yeah, I'm going to clean up. Just had to make sure that Vicky was awake," he told Aidan.

"Oh," Aidan said. Jude wasn't sure if he meant it to be a question or an observation.

"Today, the law firm, and of course you're up and on this," Jude said.

"We're coming with you, you know—getting in there when you hand over the necessary papers," Aidan reminded him.

"Of course you are. You and Cary are king and queen of algorithms!" he said quickly, passing him and hurrying to his own room. "Oh! You're ready to go, then. Don't forget to feed the dog!" he called over his shoulder.

In his room he hopped in and out of an almost boiling shower, dressed, and hurried back out. On to work. Another day on the job, questioning, people, lies, stories, denial, same old, same old…

Okay, well, nothing on this job tended to be same old, same old. While some tricks were tried and known, criminals of any kind were adept at finding new tricks.

But that was work, and his work was a passion, something he embraced.

He just wasn't sure he'd ever be the same again. She was different from anyone with whom he'd ever been close or intimate before. For now…

Compartmentalize; that part of life had to go behind a closed door right now.

"As if I'd forget to feed a dog!" Aidan announced as Jude reached the kitchen. As promised, Vicky was already dressed and ready, already there; she grinned at him and handed him a to-go cup of coffee.

"Thanks," he told her.

She smiled sweetly and innocently. "My pleasure!"

He thought that he saw Aidan smirk. His imagination? Or had they—or just he—been far more obvious than he had thought?

But until last night…

Well, he'd intended total professionalism. And, of course, they could still be the ultimate professionals.

Maybe even better.

Cary was waiting with her own coffee near the door.

"As far as law enforcement goes, we're still scrambling into the computer age. There are limits on the time we can take… But here's the thing: everyone has a laptop these days. I have a feeling that what we're looking for is going to be on someone's private computer and they've been working all night to get all the warrants we're going to need," Cary said.

"Oh! The phone, Jude, Vicky," Aidan added. "We're hunting down the origin of the pictures on Samuel Hutchins's phone, but as expected, the phone was a burner—sold by dozens upon dozens in northern and central Florida. And still, we may discover where it was purchased. I doubt if a credit card was used, but a salesperson just might remember who bought it. And none of this means that it's a wash as far as giving us anything. While the team at headquarters is on it, most importantly, the last tower it pinged off is about a mile from the law firm. Your hunch may be right on the money. Anyway, Cary and I are all set to go. Ready when you are."

"Let's move," Jude said.

Clover whined, as if realizing his human companions were all leaving for the day.

"Guard, boy!" Aidan told the dog, and the animal instantly sat, and almost appeared to nod.

Even Clover knew that it was time to work.

As it happened, they didn't need to head in to get the warrants; a young agent from the field office arrived just as they were leaving, ready to hand them to the group. Jude knew him. He was Randy Jenkins, just six months out of the academy, assigned down in Florida, a good young cadet who was learning the local ropes as he moved along and, naturally, getting the "runner" jobs as he earned his way up the ranks.

Jude thanked him and introduced him to the others.

Randy was happy to greet them, and Jude quickly realized the young agent had done his homework on all of them. He welcomed Vicky "back home" and went on to tell Aidan and Cary how much he knew about their work and admired them.

It was a nice moment and Jude didn't rush it.

It was going to be a long day. But he knew, too, that the pressure wouldn't all be on them; Arnold was sending out a team.

They were heading to a law firm; the computers would be plentiful.

"Well, I'm just the runner today," Randy said, aware that they needed to move. "But I'm afraid that all the king's horses and all the king's men may not be enough. I mean, I think that whoever is doing this is smart—smart enough not to be using a computer at work."

"I'm sure that Arnold is working on warrants for personal computers as well. And the smartest person, not realizing that a warrant is on the way, might have a laptop on them," Vicky told him.

"Maybe, and anyway, I wish you luck!"

They waved goodbye to Randy and headed for the car they were using.

"Do you think that this is for money? Or do you think that something bigger is in store?" Cary asked, settling into the back seat.

"I don't know. But apparently that is something they're worried about at the top," Jude told her.

"Think any of them walk around with guns?" Aidan asked.

"Again, who knows?" Jude said. "But Vicky and I are armed, and I think I would bet that the entire place isn't in on it. Cybercrime is a different animal. Murder from a distance, as it's proving to be."

"We can bet that Marci Warden wasn't!" Vicky said.

"Right. But maybe the fact that she wouldn't get in on it was what got her killed," Aidan said.

"I do believe that will prove to be true," Jude said.

"I'm hoping that Arnold has a really, really big team arriving," Aidan said, studying his notes as he sat by Jude. "There are a lot of attorneys—and even more paralegals—in this firm. We have the big three—Wharton, Dixon, and Smith with Wharton being the head of their corporate law division. You've got Mr. Lee Chan heading up maritime law. They also specialize in personal injury, a division headed by Mr. Barton Clay. Last but never least, the division that deals with criminal law, A. Taylor, 'Ms.' A Taylor. Each division has a paralegal and at least two attorneys working under the head." He paused, shaking his head. "Wow. We are one litigious society! But hmm. The team should be there before we are—we're arriving a few minutes late. Traffic, not us!" he added.

"Not to worry too much—we're there," Jude said.

They exited the car. Vicky was staring at the building, frowning.

"What?" he asked her.

She shook her head, but a slight frown creased her brow.

"Attorneys and support staff are all supposed to be there today, right?" she asked. "And we've just received the warrants, but they knew we were seeking them, right?"

"What's wrong?" Aidan asked her. "This is going to be a long, long—long, long, long—day. We need to get started."

"I don't know. There's something about the building and the possibilities of sabotage if whoever is doing this is in there now has been forewarned we're coming."

"We're getting full cooperation from Nathaniel Wharton. But not even he knew for sure that we'd make it by this morning," Jude reminded her.

"All right, sorry, strange sense of foreboding," Vicky said. "But, Aidan! You're right. Long, long, long, even longer day. Ready to move!"

They headed for the building. Entering, they discovered that there was a cluster of people waiting for them, members of the local cyber division.

He knew most of them and introduced them to Vicky; they had all met Aidan and Cary before during various state endeavors and meetings.

They caught the elevators to the firm's floor. When they entered, the young woman who had taken Marci Warden's job was sitting at the reception desk, just as she had been the first time they had come.

"Hi, Nancy!" Vicky said cheerfully. She turned and announced pleasantly to everyone there, "Nancy Cole is new on the job. Naturally, the firm had to replace Marci quickly." She paused. "But, of course, Nancy's computer was Marci's computer, so…" she added softly, before trailing off.

As her voice trailed, the blonde woman stood, a look of combined horror and fury on her face.

"I don't know what you think you're doing, coming in like a football squad!" she announced. "But I'm going to inform Mr. Wharton—"

"Oh, Mr. Wharton knows we're coming," Jude informed her. "In fact, I'll just head in and find his office so that we can speak with him and supply him with the warrant papers."

"You got warrants!" the woman said. "That's impossible. That's illegal!"

"Look at that, will you?" Vicky said pleasantly. "She's the receptionist—and she thinks she knows the law. Oh, well, thankfully, there are real attorneys here. People who do understand the law—and what a warrant means!"

Nancy didn't need to reply to that; the door had opened. Barton Clay had just entered with his pretty wife at his side.

"Hey!" he greeted them. "My wife and were going to grab a meal together today. What's going on?" he asked.

"Sir," Jude said politely, "we have warrants for the firm's computers."

"Oh! Well, yeah, of course." He turned to his wife. "Honey, run back and get Nathaniel out here for these people, will you? I figured you'd be getting warrants. After we spoke, I've realized myself everything that's happened… Anyway, whoever wants my office, you're welcome to come along with me now."

Before anyone could move, Belinda Clay returned with Nathaniel Wharton.

The older man immediately nodded and Jude walked over to him to take his hand. "I knew you were coming, of course, I just wasn't sure when. I believe everyone is in and, Barton, you're even back from that settlement meeting. So, Special Agents! Please, make yourselves at home here, just tell our people what you need and we'll get going. Because, trust me, if anyone here is responsible in any way for Marci's death… I want them prosecuted to the full extent of the law!"

"Thank you, sir, we're also horrified that a young woman so needlessly lost her life," Jude assured him. "And, while our cyber crew works, we'd like to interview your people."

"You have the list. You may have my office and I'll get Dixon to give you his space, too. In fact, you can start with Dixon and me, and then Celia Smith."

"Celia is okay after her fall into the grave?" Vicky asked.

"She's fine," Wharton said dismissively. "But I warn you, she's a bit old-school and she thinks you're entirely crazy to believe that someone sabotaged Marci's house or that the other accidents were anything other than accidents."

"We know that the cars and the boat were hacked," Jude reminded him.

"I know that, and you know that. Celia is just behaving old-school." He lowered his voice and grinned. "She's a bit of a tyrant, that one. But you should see that woman in a courtroom! She is hell on wheels, the kind of attorney you want in your corner."

"All right, sir, thank you. Aidan has a list of the attorneys and their assistants. I believe that Cary is going to start right out here with what was Marci's computer and Aidan will get the other assignments going. Shall we?" Jude asked.

"We'll head to my office and if Special Agent Tennant comes along, I'll escort her to Dixon's office where they can talk, and then, Special Agent Tennant, he'll leave that space to you," Wharton told them.

"That's great. Thank you," Vicky said.

He nodded to Aidan who nodded in return, ready to divide his team of cyber sleuths and cover everything they knew about—and/or could discover—in the offices.

Yet even as they walked along the hallway, Wharton asked the question that was paramount for them as well.

"Say that someone here is involved in this—would they be using their desk computers here, or would they be using a laptop that isn't part of the firm's equipment?"

"Well, sir," Jude told him. "One of the reasons we were hoping to keep our arrival with the warrants unknown was so that anyone who has been using a private computer for hacking into other systems wouldn't know that they'd need to keep their personal property at home."

"Ah, but what if they have them hidden in cases, or—"

"Sir, read the warrants. We have the right to search the offices and persons here as well."

Wharton nodded. "Good. Now, I'm hoping, of course, that you find nothing. That no one in this firm is involved in any way. To be honest, I'm anxious to have that proven. And while I completely understand your educated suspicion that someone here must be involved, I'm praying that no one used this firm, and I would love to have my faith in my partners, my attorneys, and our support staff completely restored. Whatever it takes."

"Thank you, sir. But, of course, you realize that such a thing could happen. A communication with Paul Sands, say, could give us an idea of what was going on with him and his firm. The slightest cyber clue can go a long, long way, sir."

Vicky waved to him as she headed into Dixon's office.

Jude thought dryly that if they were just in the middle of a Sherlock Holmes mystery, the game would be afoot!

He spoke with Wharton for another ten minutes or so. Of course, it was always possible for the person in charge, apparently doing everything in their capacity to cooperate, could still be the power behind a crime. The criminal personality tended, throughout the cases he had worked, to veer in one of two directions—filled with charm and humor or so dark and evil that their every move seemed to be driven by hatred.

As in a man like Carlos Rodriguez.

And sometimes they did have to lean in on gut instinct and if he was any judge of human behavior at all, everything about Wharton was legitimate.

"If someone here is guilty of doing this, who would you think it might be?" Jude asked Wharton.

Nathaniel Wharton had insisted that Jude take his chair behind the desk. But he hadn't sat himself in one of the swivel business chairs facing it.

Hands folded behind his back, he paced for a minute until he stood before one of the windows that looked out over the city of St. Augustine.

"You know, this office…the views are exquisite. I can see the old fort—I can see Matanzas Bay. It was years ago and, of course, I had no idea how many high-rises would join this one, but I chose these offices so carefully. Anyone frustrated could look out on the beauty of the view and take a deep breath and maybe feel a little bit renewed. Now…you can see Old Town there, and even the outskirts and I think in that area you can even see what was Marci's home. Looking out far enough across the bay, you can see the opposite shoreline and, I believe, the jetty where Quincy's boat slammed and blew. Of course, you can't see all the way to Tennessee, and that was…"

"Different? But then, not," Jude said.

"But people can despise a judge. A man known to have sold drugs—out on a yacht with questionable people on board. Marci never hurt anyone in her life!" Wharton told him, shaking his head.

The man either beat the hell out of Brando as far as being

an actor went, or he cared deeply. Cared as much as a parent might about the loss of a child.

"Marci knew something. Something she shouldn't have known. And while whoever is doing this is brilliant with a computer, they may realize that others might put it together when that many accidents happened."

Nathaniel Wharton nodded gravely, shaking his head. "What can I answer for you? How can I help?"

"Well, you can tell me if you suspect anyone," Jude told him.

But the man shook his head again. "I personally interviewed everyone working here. I couldn't begin to point to someone who might do this."

Jude gave him a shrug and a rueful smile. "Perhaps you could send in Celia Smith."

"Right. Okay, Celia is...as we said. Fierce. But being fierce doesn't make one homicidal."

"I know that. We're interviewing everyone here," Jude assured him.

"Right, of course. And, if it's all right, I think I'm going to run downstairs for a coffee. Yes, we have a little kitchen here and a coffeepot. But the place downstairs does a mocha with an extra shot of espresso that is out of this world. Can I get you one?"

Jude laughed. He could use one.

But under the circumstances, he'd buy his own when the time was right. He shook his head and smiled, thanking the man.

Wharton headed into the hall.

Apparently Celia Smith was already there. She was arguing with Wharton, her voice hard and strident.

"I will not talk to that woman, Nathaniel! She pretends she's FBI, she pretends she knows things... Someone just picked her up off a runway or maybe even when she was working the streets, thinking she could be used to sway stupid men. I don't believe she's real for one minute—"

"Celia, you're wrong. I'm not an idiot. I researched the people investigating us. She was top of her class at Quantico and she's worked serious cases for several years now. But you don't need to speak with her. Special Agent Jude Mackenzie is in my office—you can speak with him."

"This whole thing is ridiculous, Nathaniel! That supposed cyber tech is in my office now, tearing apart my computer, looking into affairs that should be confidential! I've had it! I say we sue immediately. We have—"

"Celia, talk to the man for two minutes!" Wharton said. "The way you're behaving, you're making it look as if you're guilty as hell of something."

"Of being an attorney who represents her clients one hundred percent. Nathaniel, please, I can't believe that our people—"

Jude stepped out into the hall, arms crossed over his chest, a smile on his lips. "All right, Ms. Smith. Please. I have one question. If Barton Clay is head of the department that specializes in personal injury, why did you step in when the case involved Captain Quincy—and what is the relationship that this law firm has with Paul Sands, the man representing Carlos Rodriguez, the man who admittedly paid to have the judge killed, though he didn't mind bloodying his hands with his daughter-in-law and letting his son take the fall for it?"

Celia Smith stared at him, shook her head, and started walking away.

"Celia!" Wharton said.

"I'm going down for a good coffee, just like you were doing, Nathaniel. If Special Agent Mackenzie wants to wait, I'll be happy to explain my expertise!"

She headed down the hallway. Nathaniel looked at Jude and followed her.

Jude decided to follow them. What the hell? He wasn't that big on mocha but a large cup of coffee with two shots of espresso would be good.

The glass enclosed conference rooms seemed to be filled. People couldn't work at their computers while the cyber team was investigating them, and the majority didn't seem to care—they just took physical files with them into the other rooms.

They passed many of the firm's personnel as they traveled through the hallway to the reception area.

One door was open, and he could see that Barton Clay had remained in his office, watching as his computer was inspected, but apparently not very interested.

His wife was there, and he was telling her just to go home.

"I don't know, Barton!" Belinda was saying. "Maybe Celia Smith is right on all this. They're disrupting the entire day and if this gets a lot of publicity, it could hurt the entire firm. Don't get me wrong—I'd never side with Celia Smith. Her just deciding she was going to take a case from you was wrong! But..."

She broke off, aware that Jude had stopped in the hall.

"Oh!" she groaned, seeing Jude. "I'm sorry. I mean, I know you have your job to do, except... I mean, seriously? You think a lawyer might be doing this? Accidents do happen."

"That they do," Jude said. "But when they happen too often and they seem to be connected, well, I do apologize, but we must look into it."

Belinda gave him a smile.

Barton just shook his head.

"You are just doing your jobs and it's fine. And if word gets out, the word is going to be that we were cleared of any wrongdoing, so, in my mind, sir, you have at it!" Barton Clay told him.

"Thank you. I'm going to speak with Celia Smith after a major coffee run, and, after that, if you'd like to be next in line—" Jude began, speaking to Barton Clay.

"You bet. This fellow is welcome to my computer, and you're welcome to my mind!" Clay interrupted.

"I'm heading out," Belinda said. "Unless…lunch?" she asked her husband hopefully.

He grinned at her. "Sure. If Special Agent Mackenzie finishes with me, I won't mind stepping out for a few minutes. We'll be playing catch-up, of course, but I know what needs attention right now and I'll be on it!"

Belinda shrugged. "You're a big shot, my love. It will be fine if you step out and since you're happy to do so…hmm. I'll play phone games while I wait!" she said, grinning at Jude.

"Fun," Jude said lightly.

Phones. The place is filled with smartphones. All making use of AI and the internet.

"We'll move quickly," Jude promised Barton. He turned to hurry back down the hallway.

Once he reached reception, Jude couldn't help but notice the pictures of the main employees on the wall.

Would it need to be one of the major players doing all this?

Or just a brilliant paralegal? Someone not even in our sights as of yet?

Nancy Cole was at her desk and looked at him suspiciously. In her mind he was simply the enemy.

"They're heading down to that coffee place," she said. "But I guess you know that."

"Yeah, I'm going to join them. Can I bring you anything?" he asked politely.

She gave him an icy stare. No, of course, she wouldn't want him getting her anything.

She didn't bother an answer.

"Suit yourself," he said, heading on out the door.

Nathaniel and Celia were standing by the elevators.

Celia was still angry; Nathaniel was holding his own, but continuing to try to calm her.

He was going to approach the two, but decided he'd just

head down himself. He went to push the elevator call button, but it was already lit.

Well, at least they'd almost finished going down for their special coffees.

The elevator door slid silently open.

"Excuse me, it's here," he said.

As he spoke, Belinda Clay followed them from the direction of the offices. She grinned at Jude. "Coffee, why not? Nothing else to do while I wait around." She moved closer to him and said lightly, "I never went to law school. Most of these guys don't have two seconds for me or consider a word out of my mouth worth hearing! No, that's not true. Some of them are nice and, of course, my husband is an attorney, but," she grimaced with good humor, "sometimes I think even he considers himself a wee bit more intelligent!"

Jude smiled and shook his head. "Oh, I doubt that. A law degree isn't everything."

"Oh! It's here… Finally. You would think in a building like this the elevators would move a bit more quickly. Hey, Mr. Wharton, Ms. Smith! Come on! Elevator is here!" she called.

Celia turned sharply and, shaking her head, started toward the elevator.

The door was about to close.

Jude stepped forward but Belinda Barton had already caught it and held it politely open for the others.

With a sniff and a muttered, "Thanks," Celia Smith walked on in. Nathaniel started to follow her.

But as he did so, Vicky came bursting out into the hallway.

"Stop!" she cried.

"What?" Jude asked.

"Stop, stop, don't get in the elevator—" Vicky shouted. "Get off!"

Jude could reach Nathaniel; he jerked the man free from the car. Belinda Clay shouted, "Celia! Get off, come on, please!"

"Belinda!" Barton Clay called, shaking his head and hurrying for his wife.

But Belinda Clay reached for Celia, almost stepping into the car.

Celia Smith had moved to the back of the car; she just stared at them all furiously. "Stop it, stop it, just stop all this nonsense!" she shouted.

"No!" Vicky cried, making a wild run toward the elevator car. "No, no, something isn't right, there's something that's going to go wrong, please, get off—"

Too late.

The door closed with such vehemence that Jude, leaping forward to try to stop it with all his strength, almost lost an arm.

The elevator started downward…

They could hear the whoosh of the speed with which it was suddenly moving.

And they could hear the jolt and feel the vibration of the building as it slammed all the way down into the very foundation of the place.

Then, for a split second, dead silence reigned.

Then the screams began…

From Belinda, from offices throughout the building, and even from the street below.

TWELVE

Later, much later, they were back at their headquarters.

"You were there! A team of experts was there! How the hell did it happen?" Assistant Director Arnold was evidently more than disturbed by the chain of events.

Frankly, Vicky was surprised that he wasn't tearing into them all in person, but he was on speakerphone and she, Jude, Aidan, and Carly were there together, putting the events that had occurred so swiftly that morning into perspective.

And, of course, it was late, much later in the afternoon when he had a chance to ream them all out for what had happened.

She didn't want to remember the immediate aftermath of the elevator crash. She wished that she could wash the sight of Celia Smith's bloody body, entangled with metal and decorative wood paneling, from her mind forever.

Right now, of course, she could not.

Vicky took a deep breath, determined to speak in a clear and concise manner that could explain the fact that they'd had little control over what had happened—and that they had managed to get at least one person off the elevator before it shot Celia Smith down to her death.

"Sir. We just got the warrants. Every cyber tech there was working as thoroughly and quickly as they could. We couldn't have known that Nathaniel and Celia were going to determine that they just had to have special coffee from downstairs any more than we could know that someone was going to rig an elevator—"

"But you found the connection in Celia Smith's office!" Arnold said. "None of this makes sense!"

"Sir, the minute Aidan accessed deleted files and found that Celia Smith had visited the murder site that was taken down and that someone had been utilizing her computer to access building specifics, I ran like a rabbit, I swear it, sir, to stop people—"

"And, thanks to her speed, we did save Nathaniel Wharton," Jude put in flatly.

"And I'm sure he's grateful, though apparently his blood pressure soared and he's still in the hospital," Arnold said.

"We have people watching over him, right?"

Arnold was silent for a minute. "Apparently, Celia Smith was the one involved and Celia Smith is dead. I—"

"Sir!" Jude protested. "Someone accessed a site from her computer," Jude said. "Please, tell me that you can get someone over there—"

"All right! But if you don't believe that Celia Smith killed herself, aware that the game was over, you'd best have another explanation," Arnold said.

Clover let out a little whine. He must have known that "his" people were being laid out on the carpet and he wasn't happy. Of course, since Arnold's voice was coming over the phone, there was little he could do.

"All right, let's end this confusion. All this was found on Celia Smith's computer. She's the one who is dead. The woman apparently had a fit about the firm being investigated, about a cyber crew coming in," Arnold said.

"I just don't believe it for a second," Vicky told him.

"But, according to what I understand about her personality," Arnold said, "might she not have been the type to prefer death to being disgraced, to facing a trial and prison time? Wouldn't she see suicide as being much easier?"

"Suicide by crashed elevator?" Jude asked dryly. "Sir, the woman's death..."

"The best that can be said is that it had to have been quick," Aidan put in.

"Horrible, horrible, horrible!" Cary murmured.

"And, yet, as you said, Aidan, fast," Arnold told them. "But all right—"

"Wait, sir, please. I did a number on her computer, I swear. And I'm good at what I do and you know it, sir. Someone accessed the site—I didn't say that they'd created the site. The site was still created elsewhere."

"She could have created it on a private computer and accessed it at the office," Arnold reminded them.

"Yes. And anyone could have done so," Aidan said.

"All right. Good possibility," Arnold said.

"What?" Jude asked, looked at the others with a confused and quizzical frown.

"This situation remains far too serious. I wanted to make sure that you were still hotly in pursuit of the truth on this. Sure, Celia Smith might even have been in on it all along for some reason. But I don't think that she was running it all. And I agree with you that being smashed to death in an elevator doesn't seem to be a prime choice of method for suicide. The offices are closed tomorrow—all the businesses in that building are closed while the repairs are done. But that doesn't mean you can stop."

"Sir," Aidan said. "We haven't stopped once and even after

the incident, our cyber crews in the law offices kept working. But I'm afraid it's what we expected—office computers may have been utilized to sign on to certain sites, but also a personal computer has been used and—"

"Barton Clay. I think we need to pay the man a visit, Assistant Director Arnold. Under the circumstances, I believe we can acquire a warrant to tear into his home and every computer in his possession," Vicky said.

"And there's a reason you suspect that it's Barton Clay?" Arnold asked.

Vicky looked at Jude.

"Yes, sir," Jude said. "The connection between Paul Sands, Captain Quincy, and the firm had to do with Barton Clay. Apparently, for reasons we still don't really understand, Celia Smith took over on the personal injury case that Barton Clay's division would normally handle. There could be something there."

"Our teams are working on information regarding Sands as well," Arnold said. "Our latest reports from Tennessee suggest that Carlos Rodriguez has lost it completely—which means that he may be looking for an insanity plea. But since we're going to need warrants for individuals and for many people there—I don't believe the entire law firm is in on this—it is going to be a busy evening. So, get your thoughts together and get me the paperwork. Then go eat and sleep. Once again, I'll have you set for the morning. Clay should be at his house if you strike early enough—no one will be in the building as you know."

"Yes, sir!"

They all spoke at once. It was a solid chorus. Grinning at each other, they ended the call.

"Well, there's lasagna in the fridge. I'll get it heated and start back up, I guess," Cary murmured.

"Paperwork," Jude moaned. "I mean, might as well." He looked at Vicky.

She shrugged. "It always has to be done. Hey," she said, turning to Cary and Aidan. "Do you think that a site is back up or that the elevator—"

"Here's the thing," Aidan said. "We had warrants for everything in that place, but we had just gotten to the computers. Something people forget is that cell phones, our smartphones, are computers, too. I had started to collect a few of the phones when Celia slipped out of her office having one of her usual tirades and, Vicky, you and I stepped into it. What happened to Celia was certainly horrible, but Wharton and others might have been in that elevator, too, including Jude."

"We would have been in it—along with Barton Clay and his wife," Jude said thoughtfully. "Which leads me to wonder how one of them can be involved when they almost took the plunge."

"They almost took the plunge, but didn't," Vicky said.

Jude shrugged. "Doesn't matter, there's the connection. Anything that—"

"Dixon is in the clear. He was one of the first to give me his phone. I have a list of the paralegals and attorneys who turned theirs over as well," Aidan said.

"The elevator was hacked via someone's phone," Jude said. "Had to have been. There was someone at every computer."

"That we know about," Cary reminded him.

"I'm still saying phone," Jude told them.

"And you're quite possibly right. But finding that phone… burner, of course, is going to be like looking for a needle in a haystack," Aiden said. "Anyway…back at it. Oh, hmm, going to take Clover for a hike outside and make a call."

"Clover will appreciate that," Vicky assured him. "Okay, then…"

They sat at their computers. Cary was investigating sites, servers and more. Jude and Vicky filled out their forms. After his walk with Clover, Aidan soon joined them.

Cary looked engrossed and Vicky hated paperwork and filled it all out quickly—completely and thoroughly, despite her dislike of the desk work.

She could smell the lasagna heating.

And it smelled good.

"I'm on dinner," she murmured, getting up.

"I can help," Cary murmured. She was staring intensely at her computer, frowning.

"What is it?" Jude asked her.

"There was a site up that popped up in the last hour that's down already! And it looks like..."

"Like?" Vicky pressed.

"It...was created using an IP located somewhere near the law offices. Usually, these things are bounced around—I mean around the globe—so that they're hard to trace," she said. "It appears to have gone up and down in an hour, but the message..."

Aidan was up, standing behind her.

"Is confusing, or maybe...maybe it's innocent," Cary said, frowning.

"It's difficult to tell just what this site was selling," Vicky murmured.

"But those who are buying know what to look for," Jude murmured.

"Call Me for Your Personal Good Time?" Vicky said, reading from the site Cary had brought up.

"Right. And here are some of the replies that have been left on the site. 'Slaughter, yep, the gibbons, the gibbous gibbons, slaughter them all,' is one. There's a reply. 'Ah, got it, big money,'" Aidan murmured. "'Worth it."

"Gibbous gibbons?" Jude said.

"And now... Okay, I'm going to need to dig more to get to other deletions," Cary said.

"I'll get on it, too," Aidan assured her. "Except I'm starving. We can eat and work. Vicky, Jude—"

Jude laughed. "We're on it. Well, I should be on it. Vicky might be able to help you."

"We're good, just hungry," Aidan said.

"And I'm good, but nowhere near as good as they are," Vicky assured them all. "Lasagna it is!"

Jude shrugged and followed her to the kitchen. "If they get something—"

"We'll need to head back out tonight," she said. "I know. And it sounded like it was going to be a pleasant and easy evening. And one would think…"

"One would?"

"Well, I think that we're getting close. And you'd think whoever was doing this would settle down for a bit."

He shook his head, reaching for the plates. "Carlos Rodriguez," he said.

"The man might have been a mastermind criminal at some point, but I don't think he's acting and trying for insanity plea—though I'm sure one will be in the offering. I think he's stone-cold crazy. He can't be doing this—"

"I agree on all counts. But whoever is doing this is a Carlos Rodriguez. Someone so convinced now of their own brilliance that they're laughing while we run around."

"But—"

"We'll get them," Jude said with flat determination.

"Jude, I just hope it's soon. Yes, Celia Smith could be hard on everyone but no one should have died so horribly. Maybe she was on to something, suspected someone—"

"Barton Clay. Maybe that's why she took his case."

"But he had other cases," Vicky argued. "So, maybe she was involved in this whole murder-by-AI thing and she was protecting her own knowledge or suspicions…"

"Her computer accessed the site," Jude reminded her.

"But anyone in those offices could have snuck in and used her computer. I mean, seriously, if you were looking at something illegal, you wouldn't want to use your own!"

"True," Jude agreed. "Lasagna," he reminded her.

"I know, I know. I just believe that, sadly, as law enforcement, we're always a step behind because we need to do things—by the law. By tomorrow, any burner phone that was used could be in a million pieces and thrown out into Matanzas Bay!"

"That's true. But if we turn into crooks or murderers, we're no better than they are."

"But what could be the endgame?" she asked, frowning and shaking her head. "I am sorry! I'm just frustrated."

"Arnold and the crews that are on twenty-four seven will be on everything, Vicky. Try to take a deep breath. Dinner!"

She nodded. "Dinner and then..."

They were in the kitchen alone. He set his hands on her shoulders, looking down into her eyes.

"Then, recreation and pleasure when we can get it! Your room or mine? Or, wow, am I being too presumptive? I mean, maybe that was rude..."

She started to laugh. She realized that was one of the things about him she loved so much. He woke her senses in a way she had never known, but he completely respected her mind and abilities, and when things were the hardest, the most taxing...he could make her laugh.

"I guess mine. I mean, we could try out new things—ooh, such as actually getting dinner out for our hard-working cyber partners!" she said.

"Right!"

"Wait, Jude!"

"What?"

"Do you think that they...um, wonder about us? Oh! Or maybe the two of them—"

He burst into laughter on that. "No, no two of them. They're both happily married to other people. I was lucky enough to get to Aidan's wedding."

"But they're here together constantly. Don't their partners—"

"Happily married to other people. Spouses who trust them, oh, and are also in the biz, in a way. Aidan's wife is an amazing forensic artist and Cary is married to an undercover cop. Their only problem, she's told me, is determining when they can have children. He's gone a lot, too."

"Oh, but then—"

"Sure. They both suspect that something is going on between us. And I'm sure they smile about it and make jokes when we're out. But I'm also sure that they think it's great. They like us both. And they may be cyber cops—but they're not after us!"

"They're not worried that our relationship could be dangerous to our work—"

"No. Because we're both dedicated professionals and they know it. And..." He hesitated a minute and then shrugged. "And because any two people who work as partners long enough grow to consider the lives of one another paramount—we are expected to preserve life first, always. Including our own lives."

He arched his brows to her, grinned, and headed out with plates.

Aidan and Cary were preoccupied; the two of them really could maintain total concentration on a task and consume a meal at the same time.

To make life easier for the two of them, Jude and Vicky were quiet as well.

And when the meal was over, the two of them cleaned up. In the kitchen, Jude slipped his arms around Vicky and said, "We never know what the future will bring! But we do have a wee bit of time this evening, and..."

She smiled at him, ready for the night. A shower. Hours

spent in the heat of his body, to feel the searing touch of his fingers, his lips, the two of them, when such a relationship was so very rare in the life she had chosen for herself.

But then she heard Cary, reporting in to others, discussing the words on the site that had gone up—and then down—so quickly.

"'Call Me for your Personal Good Time,' I've sent encryptions for our work but, using that search term, yes, you can find it. And then almost a joke, 'Slaughter, yep, the gibbons, the gibbous gibbons, slaughter them all.' Then 'Expensive.' And lastly, 'Worth it.'"

She was speaking with a superior in the department, Vicky knew.

But the words suddenly seemed to also be just for her.

"Jude! Slaughter!"

"Right, the rascals, like a kid—"

"No, no, Jude. *Slaughter.* Like Slaughter—or Matanzas—Bay or Matanzas River!"

"You think that something is going to go down in the bay tonight? Another boat?"

"Something. Jude, come on, the site went up and down. That's all that Cary could get so far. Gibbous gibbons? Jude, it's a *gibbous* moon tonight! And people from here…they'd know what it meant. We need to get people out there—we need to get out there. Oh! Not in anything with a computer. A simple motor vehicle!" she said.

She didn't need to convince him. Whether she was way off or not, her argument made enough sense that he agreed it needed to be investigated.

"I'm on the phone while we walk, alerting all the powers that be, getting us a boat—with no computer. Tell Aidan and Cary what we're doing," Jude said.

He was on the phone instantly, and she explained briefly to Aidan and Cary and they were out the door.

To their old computerless car.

Jude turned to her as he finished his calls. "All right, Arnold is on it. Every law enforcement group in the area knows what we're fearing. They'll be setting up blocks, stopping any of the pleasure cruises. But if someone wants a bunch of 'rascals' killed, I don't think that it's going to be a tourist pirate ship or the like. I think we're looking for another drug runner."

"A drug-running boat to hack. But..."

"But what?"

"Wouldn't that blow up the drugs?"

He nodded. "But it sounds as if someone is supposed to be eliminated. True, if someone was into drug money, blowing up the drugs isn't a great idea. But you've got the Castillo San Marcos in one area, Fort Matanzas and, of course, technically, the bay is part of the river and leads out to the Atlantic. Something could be going in and something could be going out and..."

"You have pleasure boats out there and tour boats and... it's sheer luck that no one else was hurt when Quincy's boat wrecked and exploded," Vicky said.

"All right, I've talked to Arnold. The police are aware, the coast guard is aware..."

"Wait! Jude. Their boats—I think—have computers, sonar devices, communication devices... We need to be out there in a pack of things that can't be hacked. What if the 'gibbous gibbons' are those watching out for the law and not the drug dealers at all?"

He nodded. "That's highly possible. I'm going to contact Arnold again. Someone in power might have thought about that already, so..."

They reached the port. A local agent was there, another man Jude knew and introduced to Vicky as Mickey Tucker. He was ready with their boat, a little speedboat with a motor—and nothing more.

"We've notified everyone through a few of our people in power that were already on it after that incident with Quincy's yacht. Anyway, others will be out there in similar vessels. One of our people thinks that he found a hack on a coast guard vessel, so extreme care is being taken. Anyway, here." He handed them a walkie-talkie. "Captain Damon and his crews are on the receiving end. If you see anything...get a call through."

"Damon is going to be out here?" Jude asked.

"He's already on the water in a small boat like this and he had two more teams out here, same mode."

Vicky grimaced. "I hope I haven't put people to tremendous trouble for nothing."

"I think we're actually all hoping that it stays quiet!" Mickey Tucker said. "Trust me, we're all aware that we're more or less sitting ducks until this is solved. The old adage is true: better safe than sorry!"

"I'm glad you feel that way!" Vicky said.

"Hey. I don't want to be afraid to get in my car every day. Of course, until the judge, I'd only heard about a lot of cats being stolen through phones! Crazy. Anyway, I'll let you get going."

They thanked him and headed to the boat.

Vicky looked up at the sky. Tonight, it was cloudless, something unusual in her experience in her home state. And the gibbous moon, curved, more than half shining, the other part in shadow, was beautiful and high in the sky.

"I might be reaching," she murmured.

"It *is* a gibbous moon," Jude said.

"But it will be tomorrow night, too," she said.

"So, if nothing else, we've taken a nice boat trip at night. And the young agent just informed us that a hack on a vessel was caught."

"You're right, of course." She smiled at him. "It is beautiful out here at night." Looking to the shorelines, seeing the ancient structures: Fort Matanzas guarding the bay; Castillo de

San Marcos, an iconic landmark, against the shore. In the city tourists were headed out on the pub tours, tasting brews and being fascinated by St. Augustine's history.

"Be ready for anything," Jude warned.

"Of course," she murmured.

"If something is coming in, it will be from the Atlantic."

"Seems far north in the state. I always thought most illegal drugs came into the Keys or the Miami area—though, of course, I know the state is one big coastline."

"Yep. Florida has tons of coastline, and a giant 'River of Grass' or wilderness in the middle. As beaches and Everglades, I love it, but…"

"Okay, so…that looks like one of the pirate cruises over there, a guy coming in from fishing, I think—even at night you can see there's not much room for anything else in that boat," Vicky murmured.

Jude revved the motor, and they moved closer to the stretch of water leading out to the Atlantic. He cut the motor again, and they drifted silently in the night, the gentle lap of the water the only sound around them for a moment.

"It is *really* beautiful out here," Vicky murmured. "I remember being a kid, coming out to go on sunset cruises, dolphin-watching excursions…and all kids love a pirate boat!"

He nodded. "I still love coming out here. There's nothing like being out on the water to feel… I don't know. Feel the beauty of nature."

"And," Vicky added dryly, "sometimes the mosquitos."

"Well, that, too, sometimes!" He looked out across the water. The half-moon, the stars, and the city lights made visibility possible.

He looked at her. "I've always known things could be hacked. Bank accounts, emails, all those kinds of things. And I know our cybercrime division is one of the biggest now. But

I never thought that the crimes would turn so deadly. And if one person—or a few persons—have managed this…"

"Jude!"

"What?"

"That boat is coming in slowly…and it's dark. I mean, this sounds ridiculous, but if it was a person, I'd say that it was slinking in!"

He looked where she pointed.

"You're right." He reached into a compartment by the helm and produced a pair of binoculars. "And there's a second boat, bigger. Looks like they're transferring something from one to the other and…hmm, looks like they're armed as well. And they're holding there…as if they're waiting for something to happen."

"You think a coast guard vessel was supposed to go crazy, attract any attention, and let the smaller boat slip through?" Vicky asked.

"Maybe. There are…four on the smaller boat. They have a bunch of fishing rods, too, just good old boys out for the night. Four, all armed."

"We have our Glocks, but we're just two."

"Ah, but we have friends out here, remember?"

Jude pulled out the walkie-talkie that Mickey Tucker had given him. He pushed a button, and they heard a voice on the other end.

"Damon here."

"Sir, we're seeing two boats just in from the Atlantic. They're transferring strange crates from one vessel to the other and we believe that they're well-armed."

"Hold position until we reach you," Damon told him.

But it turned out that wouldn't be possible. They should have looked like a pair of young lovers, just out for a romantic spin on the bay.

But they were seen.

"Down!" Jude shouted.

She was already down, aware that someone was shouting, "They're watching us! They just ditched the patrol boats, they're after us!"

Bullets were flying across the water.

Thankfully, while the men might have been armed, they weren't crack shots. In the hail that came toward their direction, only one shot connected with the bow of the boat.

"Throw down your weapons! Federal authorities and the locals are on their way, too!" Jude shouted.

Someone fired wildly again.

But along with the chaos surrounding them, there was a new sound, that of several small speedboats coming upon their position.

Warning shots were fired from those boats, and Vicky heard another shout of authority, warning the shooters to throw down their weapons.

She wasn't happy with the situation; in the near darkness it was impossible to tell if someone was holding a weapon, ready to draw it quickly when the boats came closer.

But someone from what they assumed to be a drug-hauling vessel cried out. "Guns are down, guns are down!"

The local authorities moved in quickly and Vicky couldn't help but be glad.

No one was going to die tonight.

Their walkie-talkie rang, and Jude picked it up quickly.

"Damon here. We've got them. You're free to head in if you like. We can manage this."

"But we want to talk to them," Vicky said. "And find out—"

"Tomorrow, after the warrants," Jude said quietly. "Let these guys process them. If they learn anything, they'll let us know right away. Vicky, you and your 'gibbous' moon and 'slaughter' have done it for tonight. Let them get this all started. We'll work it tomorrow. Whatever the plan was tonight, you beat artificial intelligence."

"No, not really. I mean, tonight they were human beings, not AI, and we had help!" She knew, too, that this was bigger than any two people could handle and that they had to work with the rest of law enforcement. And she was grateful.

"We'll head in," Jude said quietly. "Thanks!" he told Damon.

"Feel free to share all long shots!" Damon said.

"Will do!" Jude promised.

He revved the motor and turned their craft around. In a few minutes, they were back at the dock. Jude hopped out quickly and turned to give Vicky a hand.

"You okay?" he asked her.

"Yeah. Really. I just feel as if..."

"As if we left something unfinished?" he asked her.

"I guess. But, of course, I know that it takes a whole village, so I'm okay. And you know what? It's getting late now. Long day, long day tomorrow. And..."

"Hmm, okay, it is unfinished. I have the keys to this thing—"

"And there's your friend, Mickey Tucker!" she told him, seeing the agent at the end of the dock.

He grinned. "Home," he said. "Um, you may not feel like a visitor—"

She laughed suddenly. "Maybe I've never felt more like one!"

"That will work for me," he said.

When they reached the house, they discovered Aidan and Cary had cracked a bottle of champagne.

"Did you hear?" Cary asked excitedly. "One of the coast guard vessels had been hacked—but they found it because of us! They don't know if it was just supposed to go speeding out into the Atlantic, creating a distress situation, or... Well, the way it was rigged, the motor could have exploded. We saved the day!"

"We saved the day," Vicky agreed.

"You know, I've cracked all kinds of financial scams, but tonight… I feel as…as if…as if I really mattered! Okay, well, Vicky, I'm sorry—you're the one who figured out 'slaughter' and 'gibbous,' but without digging into the cyber world—"

"Without you, tonight couldn't have been," Vicky assured her.

"Champagne?" Aidan asked. "I got permission from Arnold. Actually, the man suggested it!"

Vicky laughed. "A quick glass."

They all raised their glasses. Sometimes Cary was right. What they did mattered. And they would know more about the situation the next day.

A few agents, she knew, couldn't police the world or handle every situation.

"Well! Good night. Early morning again," she said, careful not to look at Jude.

"Good night!" Cary and Aidan chorused.

She gave Clover a pat good-night and headed to her room. Once there she shed her clothing quickly and headed into the shower.

She heard her door open and close. A moment later Jude was behind her.

She smiled. She forgot the trauma of the day, the crashing elevator, the rapid gunfire when they were on the boat.

She turned into his arms and immersed herself in the intimacy of another human being, one with whom she was…

Falling in love with his mind and soul?

And inwardly she laughed at herself because she was also falling a little bit in love with the hard heat of his body and his touch against her, his fingers and lips upon her…

Ironically, an incredibly good ending…

To an incredibly horrid day.

THIRTEEN

Coffee.

At six in the morning, it seemed to be the very stuff of life. He had friends—even friends in the agency—who didn't drink the brew. And that was great—for them. For him, it was an amazing eye-opener, a way to shake off sleep and, unfortunately, the sweetness of the last hours.

But it was morning. And he was on his second cup of coffee.

Cary was at her computer again, as was Aidan. But he knew that Aidan was studying records that had already been drawn up, rather than seeking the deep unknown at the moment.

Vicky was also seated at the table, coffee in hand, reading from her computer.

She looked up at him. "This is interesting. CEOs and founders of many tech companies—creators of AI—are asking for moratoriums. They're afraid that AI is now making itself so intelligent that it's becoming seriously dangerous. One of Google's top scientists quit—to warn the world!" she said.

"But we believe that a person—or persons—are responsible for what's happening. AI isn't to the point where it can create its own murder sites," Aidan said.

"Right. I know," Vicky assured him. "I was just looking at various articles. And, apparently, anyone with the right knowledge to access an elevator's control system could have caused yesterday's accident. And I've discovered, nationwide, self-driving cars and those with computer systems that are accessible through phones and other devices are being stolen right and left. I'm liking our old guy—the car—out there better and better all the time," she said. She shook her head. "I've always loved computer sciences and what we can do with them. Now..."

"Ah, don't hate computers. I've managed to access a slew of truly interesting files here—because it's also amazing what you can learn on a computer," Aidan said.

Jude laughed. "Everything is learned on a computer these days—even drivers' ed is on a computer many places. And all kinds of stuff that isn't true at all is learned on computers!" he reminded them.

"People need to learn to verify the source of information, check out legitimate sites," Aidan said. "And in this case, dig around and you can find a great deal that is in public documents. Well, my suspicions aren't in the public documents, but lots of facts are. Take our good friend Mr. Barton Clay—Esquire, of course. He's leading the personal injury division where they also take on cases of wrongful death and heirs fighting for their inheritances. Seems he's excellent at both wrongful deaths—and digging through red tape and possible holdups on those deaths that have been considered natural but may be suspicious to the heirs who then need a good lawyer to get them the money the dearly departed left behind. And it's truly amazing how many of his clients, suing someone or a business entity for wrongful death, had marital or family problems before their passing. In many cases, the plots thicken! The deaths very conveniently left those family members who were on the outs with the deceased the heirs due to collect their personal fortunes. Most of them were able to quickly settle out of court with Clay's help." He paused, shaking his head as he looked at them all. "Take this case. Anton Ripley had spoken to his attorney about a divorce. He hadn't yet filed papers. Then, he died suddenly of a heart attack—he had a prenup with a much younger wife and if he'd followed through with the divorce, she'd have gotten nothing. With his sudden and untimely death the young woman became a millionaire and Barton Clay apparently collected a nice fee—a very nice fee—and I'm thinking maybe a little extra under the table."

"But a heart attack?" Jude asked.

"The man was forty-four and his would-have-been-divorced wife was a lovely young thing of twenty-five," Aidan supplied.

"Still, if a medical examiner ruled natural causes..." Jude murmured.

"Oh, come on, Jude! We all know that there are many ways to bring on an entirely natural-looking heart attack!" Aidan said.

Jude grimaced. "I'm just being the opposition here. Slimy. Almost as slimy as Paul Sands in Tennessee."

"Well, here's hoping he didn't hide everything beyond the possibility of finding—the warrants allow us to search the house, garages, cars...you name it," Aidan said.

"Well, it's time to get those warrants on the man, his wife, his cars, his home, and everything that he touches," Jude said.

"Already delivered," Cary said, looking up. "They're on the table by the door. I believe that a new site will go up on the dark web today. If I can only find something when it first goes up..." Her words trailed and she shook her head again. "There has to be a way to catch this at the source!"

"There is, and we will find it," Aidan assured her. "Jude and Vicky may be off to find it today. And, hey, maybe the two of them will find another Carlos Rodriguez who just decides to blurt out their cleverness about how they can manipulate anything!"

"Yeah, maybe," Jude said dryly.

"Oh, we have information on Carlos Rodriguez, just by and by," Aidan said. "And, yes, as someone suggested, apparently he's now going for an insanity plea. And that's a little scary. From what I'm reading, his attorneys are painting a picture of a man raised in a society where he would have been worthy of death himself if he hadn't behaved in a way that maintained his son's honor. Then, because his son was humiliated, the only decent thing for him to do for his son was allow him to take the blame. And, from a news conference, Paul Sands was saying he believed his client belongs in a mental health facility, and the one he's mentioned has the weakest security system on record."

"I don't believe any judge and jury will buy all that!" Vicky said.

"Then again," Jude murmured, shaking his head. "We've all seen stranger things happen. Well, we aren't judge and jury. We just need to stop people from dying. Maybe one day the AI will make itself so smart it can take over. But right now there is a human being—or human beings—behind this. We need to discover who is doing all the manipulating—someone very much flesh and blood. Vicky, shall we?"

"We shall," she said.

Jude looked at Aidan. "You and Cary are coming to the Clay house, right? Starting up there?"

"We were told to let you get there—and a team of both FDLE and FBI are coming right behind you, a group of eight, to search every nook and cranny of the place. We'll be along in another thirty minutes. We're going to be taking their personal computers. The kind of searching we need to do can't be done in a matter of minutes. Digging into the cyber and AI world can take time." He smiled a little grimly. "Actually, I would love to see the man's reaction when he discovers the scope of the warrants you'll be serving him with, but…"

"I'm sure Barton Clay will threaten to sue us," Vicky said. "He was all helpful at Marci's funeral and at the office, but…"

"Now Celia's dead, and we're after him. Yeah, that will make a difference," Jude said. "Anyway, we're going to head on out." With a wave he headed toward the door, stopping to pat Clover on the head.

"Strange, isn't it?" Vicky murmured, when they were out and in the car.

"What? Life in general? AI?" he asked.

She grinned. "I was thinking about Clover. I mean, supposedly, this location and us being in it as a dedicated headquarters is top secret, only known by the heads of heads. But someone who can hack cars, boats, and houses could surely break into the most encrypted files. So, it's strange that I'm counting on a dog more than anything else to keep us safe."

He smiled. "Nothing beats a good dog!" he agreed. "Seriously, since Aidan is out when it calls for a forensics expert and Cary is alone, it's great that we have Clover. And, of course, the security systems for that house are state of the art."

"I know. I've felt safe enough." She grinned at him. "Especially knowing that we both wake up at the drop of a hat!"

He nodded. "The things this job will do for you!"

She smiled. Surprisingly, for once, the "job" had done something very good for her—put her with Jude Mackenzie. She'd spent so much time working she hadn't given much thought to her personal life.

Then again, she hadn't met anyone before who made her wish she didn't work so much.

But…

He was assigned, by choice, she understood, to the offices here. She lived in Northern Virginia and worked out of the main offices. Not that, per regulations, they could be full-time partners and full-time…partners.

But the future was just that—in the future. Now they had to deal with what was going on in the present.

"Nice place!" Vicky said as Jude pulled up in front of the Clay house. The front wasn't gated but they could see that the two-story Victorian did have a handsome wooden fence around the back.

But it was easy enough to exit the car and walk up the steps to the porch with its handsome pillars and ring the doorbell.

"Nice house," Vicky murmured.

"Ah, but we're in St. Augustine, not New York or Los Angeles or even Miami. The house seems appropriate for an attorney with as prestigious a firm as Wharton, Dixon, and Smith," Jude told her.

"If he's making money under the table—"

"If he's making it in cash and hiding it in a mattress, there wouldn't be a paper trail," he reminded her. "But I believe most of the money he makes is legitimate—on paper. I don't know if his clients have been helping wealthy family members meet their early deaths or not but representing people in their quests to secure large inheritances…well, that can give a man a good income."

The door opened.

Of course, it wasn't opened by either Barton Clay or his wife.

The young woman who opened the door was an attractive young brunette in a black-and-white maid's uniform.

"May I help you?" she inquired.

"Yes," Jude told her. "We need to speak with Barton Clay."

"I'm afraid he's not available to speak with right now," the woman told him.

"May we speak with Mrs. Clay?" Vicky asked.

"She's not available now, either," the maid said flatly.

"Are they here, at home?" Jude asked, adding, "It's a felony to lie to a federal officer." He flashed his badge.

"What?" the maid asked.

Jude inhaled a deep breath. "I'm asking you if either of them are in the house and if so, you need to please let them know we're here. And I'm letting you know that it's a felony to lie to a federal officer."

"Wait!" she snapped.

She turned and left them standing there, the door just ajar. Vicky looked at Jude, arching a brow.

"I guess they are here," he said.

"And don't want to be bothered," Vicky agreed.

A minute later the young maid was back down. "I'm sorry. Mr. Clay is very busy and asks that you return later."

"What about Mrs. Clay?" Vicky asked. "I'm sorry, I don't know your name—"

"Darla. I'm Darla. And I'm so sorry. Mrs. Clay is occupied as well," the young woman said. "If you care to leave a card and state your business, I'll be happy to relay your desire to speak with the family and I know they'll get back to you as soon as possible."

Jude smiled—very pleasantly, he hoped. "No, I'm afraid that if we can't speak with them, we'll need to speak with you. We are federal investigators and other are coming. We have search warrants, and if you'd like, you're welcome to wait outside while we see that everything is processed. We'll be needing you to stay out of the way."

She stared at them then as if they were aliens who had come down from outer space.

"Miss?" Vicky said.

As she spoke, Jude turned to see that several cars were arriving.

On the one hand he was surprised that Arnold had managed to get warrants that were so inclusive. What they had on

Barton Clay was circumstantial, but his association with Celia Smith and the firm's association with Marci Warden, Captain Quincy, and even Carlos Rodriguez via Paul Sands must have proven enough to influence a judge.

Not to mention the fact that Celia Smith was dead.

None of it, however, was nearly enough to put the man behind bars. Not unless they could discover something today.

"Wait here!" the maid announced furiously.

They waited, with little choice. She had slammed and locked the door in their faces.

"Just what we didn't need," Vicky murmured.

"A door in our faces?" he asked.

She shook her head. "They already know we're here. Now she's telling them we won't go away. That's more time for her bosses to take care of anything they don't want us to find. Look at this place, Jude! It's old. It's surely been repaired, renovated, many times. There could be little hidey-holes anywhere."

"There could be, and we may still find what we're looking for," Jude said.

"Okay. I'll be more optimistic—"

"And if they don't let us in soon, we'll get some of the team to break the door down," he assured her. "You know, it's just a wooden door, I could prove my prowess and kick it open, but this thing looks like it's several inches thick, so…"

"Well, I could try to help!" she said lightly.

But the door opened.

And it was Barton Clay himself who stood there, looking confused.

"All right, I'm not at all sure what's going on. I understand that you searched the firm, and given what happened to Celia yesterday… Well, I guess someone might well know something or perhaps someone even rigged that elevator as you obviously believe, but…my house? My home?" he asked.

"Yes, sir," Jude said politely.

"You honestly think that I…"

"Sir, it's not a matter of thinking. It's a process of elimination. If we can prove that you aren't involved in any way, you'll be completely exonerated," Jude assured him.

"Come on in," Barton said and, indicating the legal papers Jude held, he added, "Of course, I will take those."

"Of course."

Jude handed him the papers.

Vicky gave him a similar speech to what she had given the maid, informing him that he could stay or step out, but he couldn't impede the search.

"You don't think I know my legal rights, young lady?" he asked.

"I'm sure you do. We're still required—" Vicky began.

"Right, right. We wouldn't want anything tossed out of court now, would we?" he asked dryly. "Seriously, go ahead. Be thorough." He shook his head and let out a sigh. "You may not believe it, but… I was writing a eulogy for Celia. Nathaniel was closer to her, but he's asked me to do it and with this being the second death in the firm in a very short time…" He broke off, shaking his head. "Do you care if I continue working on it—longhand, of course."

"Not at all. Except I'd like to ask you a few questions," Jude told the man.

"Oh?"

"I'd really like to understand the firm's connection to Paul Sands," Jude told him.

"No real connection. Sands represented Captain Quincy for some business in Tennessee. We represented him—well, Celia wound up representing him—here. Sands came to St. Augustine to see Captain Quincy and Sands knew there was another suit going on and he came in to speak with Celia." He frowned and shook his head. "Even with what happened, if something has gone on that concerns the firm, Celia…"

He stopped speaking.

"You didn't care much for her," Vicky said.

"No, I think you misunderstand the way we all dealt with Celia. She was hell on wheels, yes. But she made us all better attorneys. I didn't hate Celia. And I sure as hell would have never wished anything on her like what happened. But damn! You two were both there. Well, Special Agent Tennant, you were the one who came running out but my wife and I and Special Agent Mackenzie were almost on that elevator, too, along with Nathaniel Wharton."

"You could have been on the elevator, but you weren't," Vicky said.

She could feel the chill as Barton Clay stared at her angrily. "Oh, my God, you've got to be kidding me! Come on, lady. We heard people talking. Whatever you found came out of Celia's office. I still have a hard time thinking that Celia could manipulate so much using a computer—she grew up in a different age. I guess she is, though, fairly good. First-graders have tablets now but Celia…she went to school in the dark ages! Then again, she's a smart woman and anything can be learned online these days!"

"Well, that may be true," Jude told him. "But you've had some interesting cases."

"Nothing that had to do with hacking!" he said. "What? Yeah! I got a man's money for his wife when he'd intended to divorce her. Sue me!" he said dryly. "Look, his family hated the poor woman. But she was married to him when he died."

"Died young," Jude commented.

"Sadly, many people die young. And you do realize, don't you, that you're prejudiced toward defense attorneys or those of us who fight for people you may not believe deserve it. But that's just it—everyone is entitled to a defense. Law and order and judges and a jury system are things that define us as Americans. You must read people their rights sometimes—or,

I guess agents do as well as cops. The thing is, you may not like what I do, but everyone out there deserves the best representation possible."

"Or that money can buy," Jude said, glancing at Vicky.

She knew his look. They weren't getting anywhere; they needed to lighten it up.

And the team had gathered just outside the door.

"All right, sir," Vicky said. "Thank you for speaking with us. And, yes, of course, you may continue working on Celia's eulogy longhand. Just be aware that—"

"They can tear the place apart," he told them. "My computer will be easy to find. My home desktop and my laptop are in my office, and, hey, they can go through every nook and cranny in the house—they are welcome to do their jobs."

"We're going to need your wife's laptop and phone, too, sir," Vicky said.

"Fine. Everything is at your disposal," Clay told them.

"Everything of yours, and everything of your wife's as well," Jude said.

"Whatever you want. I'll get Belinda and let her know what's going on," Barton said. "She's up in her office."

"She has an office, too?" Vicky asked. "Nice. What does she do?"

"On paper?" Barton said dryly. "She stays home and takes care of the house and our lives. In truth, she helps out at the firm a lot. And it's nice when she does happen to be there, meeting me for a meal, whatever reason. She could smooth things over between Celia and others. She may not have gone to college, but she's got a better heart than most therapists out there. Despite what you think of my law practice, we also give to a lot of charities—she works with them. She makes good use of her office."

"That's wonderful," Vicky said. "Well," she turned to the

doorway, nodding to the forensic investigators who had arrived, "they'll get started."

"I'll get my pen and paper," Barton said. "Belinda will be down to say hello to the two of you."

Before he could head up the mahogany staircase, Belinda Clay came hurrying down. She appeared to be confused but not dismayed.

"Hi!" she said, greeting them pleasantly. "What are you all doing here? Sorry, nice to see you. I didn't mean to be rude, but… Oh, I'm still so distraught over everything. I thought that—well, this is so horrible, but I thought that whatever was going on, Celia…" She broke off with a wince, but then continued with, "Celia wasn't terrible. She was fierce. She taught the people around her. She was just amazing to watch in court! And not a bad person, really! But…"

She paused again, looking at her husband and then sighing and saying, "I thought that she had done whatever the firm was supposed to have done and that's why when it seemed you all knew that she…she did what she did yesterday."

"We don't know that Celia did anything, and we're skeptical that she—or anyone—would commit suicide via being crushed to death in an elevator," Jude said.

"Then you suspect Barton?" Belinda said, staring at her husband in absolute bewilderment and disbelief.

"The powers that be will probably be checking out everyone at the firm—" Vicky began tactfully.

"To this extent?" Barton queried dryly.

"You know, we're just the foot soldiers," Jude told him.

"Right, right. Belinda, I've told them to do their jobs," Barton said to his wife. "So, they're going after all computers, tablets—and, oh, our phones."

"Convenient! Mine is here, in my pocket. I can hand it right over," Belinda said. She was wearing a casual blue pantsuit with pockets, and she reached into the left side and produced her cell phone. "Here you go! Oh, what are we going to call people on?" she asked. She laughed. "Wow. Hmm, life is sad, huh? Can't imagine going all day without my phone!"

"The team will provide you with phones until we return yours," Jude assured her. "We're not out to hurt anyone here. And we're truly sorry for this invasion of your privacy."

"I understand. I don't think… I cared about Celia. But I loved Marci. I still have trouble believing anyone could set a house to attack someone, but…" She laughed and glanced at her husband. "What do I know? I haven't got a law degree. Oh, I don't even have a college degree—I wanted to get out of high school and fly the friendly skies!"

"You were a flight attendant?" Vicky asked her.

"I was. Luckily, I was working first class when Barton was headed to the Big Apple and… Well, we chatted during the flight, and the rest is history!" She linked an arm through his and grinned. He grinned in return and smoothed back her hair.

"So," he said. "I'm going to keep working on the eulogy."

He looked at the people who were now moving into different rooms. Then he shook his head again as if trying to clear away incredible confusion and disbelief. He arched his brows and looked at Jude and Vicky with a grimace. "Ah, make yourselves at home! Well, I guess you will."

Aidan and Cary came in then, nodding gravely as they saw that Vicky and Jude were speaking with Barton and Belinda Clay.

"Ah, that's your prime team, right?" Barton said quietly.

"They're good at what they do," Vicky said.

"The best? And your best hasn't managed to solve this yet?" Belinda asked, sounding a little sad and desperate. She turned to her husband and asked quietly, "Barton, what will this do to the practice? Poor Nathaniel—he really is such a good man!"

"I don't think Nathaniel Wharton will have much to worry about. His reputation is spotless, and while something may have been going on under him as the head of the law firm, AI taking over is such a new concept that I don't believe he'll be blamed. We will get to the truth," Jude informed her. "So, we'll get started, and I promise, we'll do our best to keep your home as is."

"Okay, follow me. I'll show you the offices and you can start ripping everything up!" Barton said.

He headed for the stairs. Vicky, Jude, Aidan, and Cary followed.

The rest of the team was moving downstairs, dividing to work in different rooms.

An hour later Vicky was still going through the clothing and bins in the extensive double walk-in closet in the bedroom that Barton and Belinda shared.

Jude was going through drawers.

"Anything?" he called.

"Belinda really likes shoes!" she returned. "You?"

"Bathing suits. They must truly enjoy their pool."

Aidan walked into the room.

"Did you find something?" Jude asked him.

He shook his head. "Of course, real digging takes time and we'll be taking the computers and phones to work on. So far, nothing. But we've collected every computer, tablet, and phone—so Cary and I are going to head back to the house, connect with the teams working at the main offices, and keep trying to dig."

"All right. Has anyone started on the cars yet?" Vicky asked.

"Yep. Team went through them both. If Barton and Belinda are hiding anything, they're doing it very well," Aidan said.

"Ah, but if you're good enough to do everything that's being done, you're smart enough to see that anything that could incriminate you is gone, gone, gone," Aidan said.

"But," Vicky reminded him, "they didn't know we'd be showing up this morning."

"Now that's true," Aidan agreed. "Anyway, I wanted to let you know that Cary and I are out of here and that we'll be at the house."

"Thanks. I have no idea when we'll see you!" Jude told him.

Aidan left them.

There were still dozens of pockets in outfits for Vicky to search since a burner phone might easily be hidden in a pocket of a blazer or even a pantsuit—Belinda had already shown them she liked to carry her phone in a pocket. If she had another...

But Vicky had to sit for a minute.

She walked out and plopped down at the foot of the bed.

"Ah, come on! We've hours to go," Jude said lightly.

She smiled at him and shook her head. "It's all so... I don't know. I mean, we've had extremely clever criminals through the ages, and we've had machines since man first figured out how to use tools and looked for ways to make them better. The industrial age came and machines became king, but..."

"A computer is a machine," Jude said.

"Well, a computer runs on electricity. Machines may run on gas or another form of fuel," Vicky murmured.

"I know that. I looked it up, too. But AI started with everything being fed into it—and it is true that many top technicians now worry about what AI can teach itself. And that's for people far more brilliant than me to figure out. We need to remember—right now, someone is manipulating AI. Someone who could crack into the building's system and access the elevator controls."

"But what we found did come from Celia Smith's computer," Vicky reminded him.

"And Celia is conveniently dead," Jude said.

Vicky nodded and stood. "Back to Mrs. Clay's extensive wardrobe," she said.

She returned to the closet. And she went through everything.

It took hours for them to finish in the bedroom, but they

didn't find a hidden tablet, phone, computer, or anything else that might implicate the couple in anything illegal.

By early evening the house, garage, and Barton's and Belinda's cars had been systematically searched. Vicky knew the teams from the Bureau and the FDLE were good and that they'd been thorough.

Careful not to destroy the home or leave it in a dismantled condition, but still thorough.

Nothing.

And it was time to give it up.

Except, of course, the computers and phones that had been taken were still being searched and it was possible Aidan, Cary, or the cyber sleuths working diligently from afar just might find something.

Still…

Barton and Belinda, appearing almost amused instead of indignant, walked them out.

"I told you," Barton said. "While I find it almost impossible to believe, I guess that Celia had to have been involved in some way and, of course, I'm horrified that the firm is liable in any way. Not even I know what this will mean in the future, but! I told you—I had nothing to do with any of it."

Belinda smiled, linking her arm through her husband's.

"I told you!" she said, "And I could swear it on a thousand bibles! Barton has nothing to do with this!"

"My practice may be a little on what you see as the smarmy side," Barton said dryly. "But I'm an attorney. I do my best to make the law work for my clients. That's not a crime."

"Well, of course, we thank you for your cooperation," Jude said. "And we'll get out of your hair now!"

The forensic search teams exited ahead of Vicky and Jude, letting them do the talking.

It wasn't until they were in the car on the way home that

her phone began to ring and Vicky looked down to see it was Aidan calling them.

She answered the call, telling Aidan, "I've got you on speaker. Did you find something?"

"Not what we were looking for, but… I won't be surprised if you don't get a secret call from Mr. Barton Clay," Aidan said.

"A secret call?" Vicky asked, puzzled.

"You know, a call asking you not to share anything that we've discovered with his wife."

"Oh?" Jude asked.

Aidan's phone was set on speaker mode, too, because they heard Cary's voice next.

"He's going to ask you to keep personal information secret," she said. "You know the sweet young receptionist who was hired immediately after Marci Warden's death? Nancy Cole?"

"Yes, of course. She hopped right into protective mode when it came to Celia Smith and the firm," Vicky said.

"Well, she slept her way into the job," Aidan said. "There are calls and texts between Barton and Nancy. They were having an affair, and she needed a job—he got her one."

"He knows you'd find all that," Jude said.

"And it might prove motive," Vicky murmured, glancing at Jude. "Belinda is little Miss Perfect housewife, adoring and protective. What if Barton Clay got nervous—frightened first that Marci knew what he was doing. That she'd caught him somehow. And Marci was friends with Belinda, from what I understand. So…"

"Kill Marci. But why the rest?" Jude asked.

"Maybe Nancy was brought in to help with a project that was already ongoing—murder for hire, the judge, Captain Quincy…" Vicky wondered aloud.

"Well, she's due for a deeper investigation, that's for sure," Jude said. "Anyway…we're heading on home."

Aidan didn't answer.

They suddenly heard Clover barking furiously over the phone line.

"Hurry!" Aidan said. "Electric is out. Something is going on right here I think. You can hear Clover."

"We're just a few blocks away. The backup generators should kick in any minute," Jude said.

"Aidan!" they heard Cary calling to her coworker over the line. "Aidan, the stove is starting to burn up!"

Jude glanced at Cary.

Whoever the hell was calling the shots had figured out where they were living!

"Get out!" they shouted in unison.

Then the phone line went dead.

FOURTEEN

They were just a few blocks away and Jude sped through those few blocks, heedless of his speed, watching only for living beings in his way. As he drove, Vicky put through a call, asking for immediate backup.

When they arrived, he barely jerked the car into Park before Vicky jumped out, Glock in her hand, ready for anything they might come across.

He moved like a bullet himself, but he had a feeling the danger they'd be facing wasn't flesh and blood—not here, at any rate.

If I'm going to need to shoot anything, he thought dryly, *it would need to be the appliances.*

But as they burst into the yard, they discovered Aidan and Cary had gotten out of the house safely along with Clover. The dog was tense, making a sound that was half whine and half growl, ever wary of everything around him. He was there to protect his people.

Aidan also had his Glock out as he looked warily around their environment.

But it appeared nothing else had been disturbed or disrupted near them; streetlights had come on as the day had turned to dusk and they appeared to be burning just fine.

Aidan looked relieved to see them arrive.

"Well, I guess we shouldn't be too shocked. Strange. Dogs do have some kind of instinct. Clover started that funny wary sound of his just seconds before the lights went out. I thought there might be someone out here—"

"Thank God you're both all right!" Vicky cried, rushing to hug Cary and then Aidan.

By then, sirens filled the street. Local backup had come. Jude tried to explain the situation to the officers rushing out of the car. Listening to him with confusion, and frowning, they stared at the house, not sure what to do, and waiting for the senior officer in the group to take the lead.

"All right, the lights went out and the stove burst into flames? Forgive me. I don't understand the emergency. Did you check the fuse box? Did you leave something on the stove? Do you believe that armed intruders are in the house?"

His officers were heading up to the door.

"No!" Vicky cried.

The man who appeared to be in charge stopped, looking at her as if she was either crazy—or someone who should be arrested for creating unnecessary problems for the police. He was an officer in his late forties or early fifties, tall and solid in his build, a formidable man.

"LaRue, Detective LaRue, and I'm sorry," he said flatly, "but you called for help—"

Jude broke in then, saying, "Detective, I've been trying to explain to the officers. I didn't know how much danger our coworkers might be in when we called for backup. I know you must have heard about the AI in a smart home going crazy and killing a woman. It was in all the papers and the news—and it's been shared with police, FDLE, agents, and even the coast guard. We don't think it was an accident, or that events with boats and cars have been accidents… No one can go in that house until we're sure the systems are cleared of whatever the hacker set up."

"What?" LaRue said. "Lights went out and a stove caught on fire. These were just electric lights—"

He stopped speaking and they were all silent. Because suddenly the lights on the street and in the nearby houses started blinking on and off. Darkness had come in full, and the flickering could have caused serious damage to someone with epilepsy or other health issues.

"Detective LaRue, we do need vigilant help now because we don't know what is going on. I need to get to a computer with good power and we don't know if ours were hacked into when all this happened," Aidan said.

"Wait! I have my laptop in the car. It wasn't here, and…it's my personal computer, fairly new, so I doubt anyone has been into it. It's charged and ready to go and I believe you'll discover it's up to getting this all straightened out," Vicky told him.

"Let me have it!" Aidan said.

She hurried to the car with Aidan on her heels. Cary followed him, along with Jude and LaRue.

Detective LaRue still didn't seem to understand at all. "This house is controlled by AI, too?"

"Someone has hacked the electrical server. No, the house isn't controlled by AI, but the alarm system has probably been compromised and maybe the water systems—let them work on this and make sure the house itself isn't going to attack the officers when they go in. Aidan and Cary are experts—they'll fix this. The area will appreciate the electric being straightened out."

"I'll get Arnold to get whoever is in management at the electric company right now," Vicky said.

Aidan went to work; Vicky made the connections.

Jude realized Clover had followed Cary every step she had taken, and he was glad once again that they'd brought the dog to the house.

Clover saw Cary as the one to protect. And that was great. She had s often been the one alone at the house. And dogs had something AI didn't—the instinct of a living creature. It sounded as if Clover had known before anyone else that something was wrong.

It was probably safe to go in the house; they hadn't been using an AI system to run the house, turn lights on and off, start any of their appliances. The stove catching fire might have been managed through the electric system. Tampering with the electricity and the alarm system—both attached to other systems—was about the extent of what could be done there.

But, of course, it didn't matter. They'd need to leave their comfortable headquarters now.

Because someone knew where they were—information only available to law enforcement—which meant someone had hacked into FBI files.

He frowned, looking down the street. People were out of their houses, some alarmed and many angry. Some were hurrying toward them, anxious to speak with the police officers, to find out what was going on.

There was one person, though, who didn't seem alarmed or angry.

Just curious. No, fascinated. And wearing a sweatshirt and a baseball cap pulled down low.

And Jude thought that he'd been looking at the house, watching them and not the spectacle of the lights.

"Vicky," he murmured.

But she didn't hear him; her concentration was on Aidan and her computer.

Just my imagination? Is the person watching the house just because the police cars drew up there, or is he waiting to see what happens…

Because the house locks did work with the alarm system. Were they hoping Aidan and Cary would be locked in the house, and it would be set ablaze and they would die in the smoke and flames?

He started across the street. The man saw him coming and turned, walking away at first, glancing back and realizing that Jude was crossing the street and coming after him.

He began to run, slamming into a woman who fell into the grass.

Jude shouted back that time, yelling for someone to help the fallen woman.

A car was moving quickly through the street; he barely managed to elude it, using a hand on the hood and a leap across the vehicle when the driver tried to stop.

Naturally he could hear the driver swearing as he tore on.

But the fellow he was trying to stop was pushing forward, heading toward Aviles.

By then Jude realized his shout had been heard. While the man he was pursuing was pushing others out of his way, officers were hurrying behind.

They reached a main crossroad and Jude drew his gun, shouting, "Federal agent! Stop!"

The fellow stopped.

He pulled out his own weapon and fired.

Jude saw it coming and leaped low, rolling across the pavement to take aim himself.

Not to kill.

We need the man alive.

He was a good shot. He caught the man in the lower left calf, probably breaking the fellow's leg, but stopping him in a nonlethal manner.

And while the man let out a scream of agony and fell, he was still clutching his weapon. While screaming and grasping at his leg, he fired again, but the shot went wild, blowing apart a mailbox in the form of a dolphin.

He couldn't fire again; Jude had reached him and stamped a foot down on the hand grasping the gun.

He let it go, shrieking hysterically.

"You don't understand! They'll kill my kids, they'll kill my kids!"

Same old story—the perpetrator using AI, generating fake photographs to scare people into doing what they needed to be done.

Without risking themselves!

"Well, that's where you're wrong," Jude said. "I do understand. Perfectly. I need to know where your kids are right now, and anyone else you fear may be in danger, and we'll see that they're protected."

LaRue was behind him then, trying to comprehend the situation but more lost by it than Jude had ever been himself.

"I don't understand," he muttered, "this man was shooting at you—"

"Detective, we'll make you understand," Jude assured him. "I need an ambulance for this man. And I want to travel to the hospital with him. But this is all important." He hunkered down by the sobbing man who was clutching his leg.

Again, the fellow chosen to scope out the situation was young, maybe thirty, tops. Somone easily caught off guard, shown pictures of a child being horribly tortured.

"Where's your family, where are your kids?" Jude asked again. "The detective will get people right to them. They'll be in protective custody."

"Fast, please, fast!" the man said, giving them an address off Ponce de Leon Boulevard.

By then Vicky had run up behind LaRue. And as she did so, the lights came back on.

Strongly. They didn't flicker. The neighborhood was softly aglow with the streetlights and those streaming from homes.

It seemed they were going to stay on.

"Vicky," Jude began.

"I heard," Vicky said. "Ambulance is on the way. Detective, we need to go. Now. This is no joke—this man's family needs protection! And I will do my best to explain everything as we drive."

She turned and LaRue nodded, hurrying to follow her.

"The pictures…you had to have seen the pictures. They knew my address—they knew where my daughter was in school, and her little brother was in day care. I was supposed to make sure that the house burned down. To watch and see if anyone got out."

"Where's your phone? Where are the pictures?" Jude asked.

"Dumpster by the hot dog place near my house," the man told him, groaning with pain. There were tears in his eyes, perhaps from pain, perhaps from the situation, as he looked at Jude. "I was told to get rid of it before I came to see if the house burned. I was told to…to shoot you. Or myself. I didn't want to kill you, man. I didn't want to hurt anyone. I just didn't want… The pictures of what they'd do to my kids…"

"I understand," Jude assured him. "Right now, we've got to get you to the hospital, get you there safely and get you patched up."

"My family!" he moaned. "I need to know—"

"My partner is heading to your house. She's the best, and she's with a hell of a senior detective. They will get to your family before anything can happen and they'll be okay."

"How can you be sure!" he moaned. "This…all this…the lights, gone! Whoever this is can do everything that they threaten they can do!"

"Not when we know," Jude told him. "Not when we know. Trust me, I'd say that even before we get to the hospital, I'm going to get a call and it's going to be my partner telling me everything is going to be okay. What's your name?" he asked the man.

"Ted. Ted Lansing. My wife is Celeste, and my kids are Gordy and Eva."

"Great," Jude murmured.

All the officers who had first answered his backup call might not have ever gone in the house—but they were proving their worth now, keeping the crowds away from him and the fallen man, making way for the ambulance and the EMTs when they arrived. Despite the utter chaos that had come to the night, they saw to it that the EMTs could get a stretcher to Ted Lansing and he and Jude could get into the ambulance. Jude was careful to keep his distance, even in the confines of the ambulance, letting the EMTs take the necessary procedures to care for Lansing.

The ambulance's siren ripped through the night. Despite the noise, he first called Vicky. She was just arriving at the address, and he could tell her Ted's name and his wife's and kids' names, too. An easier intro when she tried to explain what was happening. Then he put through a call to Arnold, having him make sure that the garbage by the hot dog stand was searched.

Aidan and Cary were going to be busy, he knew, trying to trace the source of the hack.

Then he sat back, knowing he was going to be considered obnoxious at the hospital, but he couldn't leave the man alone.

Not for a minute.

Houses, cars, boats, schools, government files. Whoever was doing this could hack just about anything, no matter the firewalls and encryptions that might be used.

That meant they could hack a hospital, too.

And the question remained…

Was it all about money? Or just what the hell was this person trying to prove?

LaRue wasn't a bad guy, Vicky determined. He just had a difficult time understanding just how far artificial intelligence had come in the world.

They talked as they drove. His given name was Jeff, and

he admitted that he'd thought it fun that he could talk to his watch—and that his watch would talk back.

"Years ago, when I was a kid, I saw a Dick Tracy movie. My friends and I all thought that Dick Tracy had the coolest gadgets ever. Now, I ask my watch about the weather, the time… all kinds of things. And it answers me. So far, it hasn't lied. But, then again, Kyle Laker, one of the techs at my precinct, was talking about some kind of 'chat box' thing that came out with a statement saying that guns were safe for kids! Now that doesn't seem all that intelligent to me!"

"The problem is that AI systems go off what they're fed and create algorithms to create the answers or statements that are requested. If it was fed misinformation or confusing information, it can provide strange answers—such as the one your friend was talking about," Vicky explained. "Oh, trust me, I'm not good enough to do anything like the things that have been done, but it's like any tool. Any tool can be used for good—and for bad."

"A gun is a dangerous tool that belongs only in the hands of someone sane and moral who knows when it's necessary to use," Jeff LaRue said firmly. "So!" He looked at her and grinned. "Do I need to be worried about being replaced by a robot cop?"

She laughed. "Well, some of our security systems are close!" she said.

"I admit to being confused. From what you've told me, the attack on the electric system was an attack on your tech and forensic folks in the house. But, then the electric grid started dancing across the entire neighborhood, so I don't get it. What was the point?"

"Cary and Aidan aren't the kind to panic. I wasn't there, but I'm assuming that they got the fire under control quickly and got the hell out of the house, too. I believe that the plan might have been for them to be stuck in the house and with the electric system going haywire, a real blaze could have started up, killing them through smoke inhalation or burning them alive," Vicky told him.

"Dear God!"

"And…we're here!" Vicky said, noting the address.

It was just past dinnertime so she hoped that Celeste and the two children were home—and that they were going to believe her when they explained they had to be taken into protective custody.

Celeste Lansing wasn't a fool. When they knocked at the door, she didn't just open it.

"Who is it?" she asked politely after a moment.

LaRue glanced at Vicky, and she said, "Mrs. Lansing, my name is Victoria Tennant. I'm with the FBI and I'm here with Detective LaRue of the local police."

The door had a peephole; the woman, Vicky knew, was looking at the two of them.

She produced her badge and LaRue did likewise.

The door opened. Celeste was a petite woman in her late twenties with sandy hair artfully cut around her face. She looked completely confused, and then horrified.

"Oh, no, oh, no…my husband, oh, my God, is he—"

"Wounded, Mrs. Lansing, not dead, and he's going to be all right," Vicky said with certainty. He was going to have a hell of a time walking for a while, but she believed the man would be fine.

Jude would see to that.

"Oh… I need to see him. I must get a sitter, but I need to see him right away! What happened? Was there an automobile accident?" she asked, bewildered.

"No, Mrs. Lansing," Vicky told her. "I'm afraid that—in his desire to keep you and the children safe—your husband became embroiled in a serious crime. But—"

"What? No, never! He's the most honest man in the world, a

hard worker, a good husband, an even better dad. He's a good man!" she protested, staring at them, her eyes darting from Vicky to LaRue and back again. "No, no, no!" she begged. "Then…an attorney! His doctor—"

"Mrs. Lansing, the most important thing at the moment is to get you and the children out of here and to safety," Vicky told her.

"What?"

Vicky glanced at LaRue, wanting to make sure she used the right words.

But he took over.

And, to her surprise, he did so well.

"Mrs. Lansing, your husband didn't intend to do anything illegal, but he was desperately worried about you and your children. He was threatened by someone who has proven their power to hurt others, and he wound up in a bad position because of it. Now, we swore to him that we'd get you and the kids to safety—that was his prime objective and remains his only desire. Special Agent Tennant and I will be here with you while you get yourself and the kids packed and we'll be taking you to a safe house where you'll be guarded until this mess is brought to closure."

"How long will that be? I have work, there is school…"

How long would it be? Vicky wished to hell that she knew!

"Hopefully, not long," LaRue said.

"Dozens of people are working the case," Vicky assured her. "But, please, we need to get you to safety. You don't want your husband to worry more than necessary," she added softly.

"This is real?" Celeste Lansing whispered.

"I'm afraid so," Vicky told her.

"All right, all right. But the kids just went to bed. It will take me a minute. My little girl can help but she's just seven and my son is four! I'll hurry. I'll do my best!"

"Wait for one second," Vicky said. "Do you have any kind

of control of your house through your phone or any other gadget?"

Celeste looked at her blankly.

"It's okay, go ahead," Vicky said, offering her a smile.

But she remembered just how upset Lansing had been and she quickly dialed Jude.

"We've got Celeste and the kids," she told him.

"Great. He's about to go into surgery. I'm going to hand him the phone so he can have a quick word with his wife, so that they know they're okay. Quick. Are you getting out of there?"

"ASAP!" Vicky assured him.

She handed the phone to Celeste. Tears filled the woman's eyes as she begged her husband to tell her that he was okay, as she assured him that she was.

Vicky took the phone back.

"Okay, hurry, now. You're okay. Let's keep it that way. I'll help you pack a few things, but, please, let's move," Vicky said.

They did.

Jeff LaRue kept guard in the parlor of the home, looking out the window—and occasionally checking the door.

The lock and bolt on the Lansing door were, thankfully, manual.

LaRue checked them now and then. He also went through to the kitchen to check the back door and walked around, assuring himself that the downstairs windows were closed and locked.

But Vicky realized she wasn't worried about the house—she was, however, anxious to get the woman and her children out of it.

The person doing this believed when their blackmailed minions failed, they'd have the sense to do themselves in. And if they didn't…

Unless another minion was in reserve, they were all right getting out of there.

And they were.

The children were adorable, so sleepy that they barely woke up to get out to LaRue's car. They were confused, of course, but if their mother said they were going on vacation, then they were.

LaRue, without her suggestion, drove around for a while before heading into a small complex. He explained quietly that it belonged to FDLE, that they held the entire building and it was the location his captain had said they were to use.

Arrangements were being made, however, to share the man-hours—and the costs of 24/7 guards—with federal and state agencies.

The family was quickly ushered into the house; they met with the first two officers who would be on guard duty and then, at last, LaRue looked at Vicky and asked where he should take her.

"Your safe house isn't so safe anymore," he reminded her.

She nodded. "I think my partner is still at the hospital."

"I will drop you there."

Twenty minutes later she thanked him as she got out of the car, called Jude, and found out where he was.

Lansing was already through surgery; Jude was in the man's room—on the same floor where Samuel Hutchins would remain just another day or so before he could be reunited with his own family.

It all made good use of the officers and agents on guard duty there.

"There's a little waiting room—" Jude told her.

"I know where it is. I'm coming."

"The wife and kids are good?"

"Define good!" Vicky said. "They've had their lives uprooted in the blink of an eye, and they're confused and scared… but alive and well. See you soon!"

She hurried to the elevators and up to Jude.

He had coffee waiting for her. She smiled and accepted the cup.

"Where do we go from here?" she asked him, sitting wearily at his side.

"We're setting up in the building you just left. Aidan and Cary are working with local folk to do whatever needs to be done to the security systems there to make sure that someone hasn't been into them already."

She laughed. "That's good to know. We'll need to grab our bags. I'll only need a minute—I pretty much live out of my bag when I'm on assignment."

"That's taken care of—Arnold sent agents in. We're out completely. When we leave here, we can just go and get some sleep."

She nodded. "Good. But that's not what I meant. In our sights, we had Celia Smith. She's dead. Then we were starting to think that Barton Clay had to be involved, but so far, all we've discovered is that he was cheating on his wife. So, where do we go from here?"

He was quiet for a long minute.

Then he let out a sigh.

"I still don't like Barton Clay."

"Jude, we were there, or we had just left there, when all this started tonight. But here's something I've been thinking. Our person doing this might be brilliant when it comes to artificial intelligence. But when it comes to the dirty work, they trick others into acting."

"Oh, Lansing's phone is with our cyber people now, too," Jude told her. "They sent me the pictures on it. You want to see them?"

She shook her head. "I know what they're going to look like. And I just saw those kids. No, I'll take your word that they're horrendous and gruesome, that they might make a man willing to do just about anything. I'm also willing to bet that they were sent from a burner phone." She sighed. "One day, the entity doing this is going to pick on the wrong person, though. Someone who will head straight to the police."

"Whoever it is, they're picking on people who have children. A man—or woman—might be willing to take a spouse to the police, but when it comes to kids, I imagine that it is terrifying. Especially to the average Joe who isn't a cop, a hunter, or someone familiar with self-defense. Also, the news is out there. Some people haven't paid much attention—or believed it—but some of the stories about the events—the deaths—have talked about AI. People are scared. First off, they believe that there are people out there willing to chop them to pieces. But even so—how do you fight an enemy you can't see?" Jude asked.

She shook her head.

"Aidan and Cary?" she asked.

He smiled. "At the new headquarters. Setting up. Our offices here, FDLE, the local police—everyone has helped to get the transition moving smoothly. Hey, finish your coffee. If all is well for the night—or as well as we can make it—I'll introduce you to Lansing. He wants to thank you for making sure his wife and kids were all right."

Vicky smiled and nodded, motioning to her coffee cup. "And this was good and needed!" she told him, swallowing the last of it.

"It's horrible coffee out of that machine."

"It's still coffee and what is it now..." She glanced at her watch and groaned. "Midnight!"

"Yep. Another long day. But Aidan and Cary are fine. We're fine. And Lansing and his family are fine. And tomorrow..."

"What? Are you about to channel Scarlett O'Hara? Tomorrow is another day?" Vicky asked.

"I was going to say that it was going to be another hell of a long day again," Jude said dryly.

"We've a plan?" she asked. "They have someone else at the

firm that they believe might be doing all this—or might, at the least, be involved?"

"We're going to start with the lovely Nancy Cole who managed to get her job the day after Marci Warden was killed."

"Right, but… Barton Clay got her the job and we had just left Barton and his wife when all this happened," Vicky said. "Wait. We had *just left*. The whole investigating crew was gone. They were alone. And still…"

"I don't care how thoroughly we all searched. One of them might have had something stashed somewhere that wasn't found. Also, Aidan told me some of the things that happened could have been timed—like the whole thing hacking into the electrical grid. Why bother to make lights blink on and off when it isn't dark? And, if you plunge a neighborhood into darkness, dozens of people will be out on the streets, making it easy for one to watch the events to report on them, and simply look like they were part of the crowd."

"Hmm. I wonder…" Vicky murmured.

"What?"

"This was another failure," she said.

He frowned. "Aidan and Cary—and Clover—are all fine. So, if they were meant to have gone up in flames, it didn't happen. In the last situation, as far as anyone knows, Sam Hutchins is dead. But this time…"

"You think that they'll try to reach Lansing?"

"I don't know. But I think it's time that I go talk to him, let him thank me. And see what he has to say about the way he was supposed to report back!" He nodded.

"What?" Vicky asked when he frowned.

"Barton Clay," he told her.

"You just don't like the man."

He laughed, shaking his head. "What's not to like? Guy cheats, might be guilty of murder or conspiracy to commit murder previously with clients who made a windfall when a loved one died, and might be behind all this."

"He didn't seem in the least disturbed that the warrants meant we could tear everything that he owns apart," Vicky commented.

"Which is a way he might behave if he knows he has himself covered."

"True, and still... Do we go to another funeral?" she asked.

"Not tomorrow. Tomorrow, we pay a visit to Nancy Cole, the darling, sweet receptionist who was alarmed when we wanted to talk with Celia Smith from the get-go. The lovely young thing who got her job the minute Marci Warden was dead. But for now..."

"What room is Mr. Lansing in?" she asked.

"Right down the hall."

Jude led the way, nodding to the officers on guard duty and opening the door for Vicky.

Ted Lansing was awake. He was staring miserably at the ceiling. His leg was bandaged beneath the covers but not in any kind of sling or stabilizing apparatus.

"Hey, I'm a good shot," Jude whispered to her. "He'll be out of here in no time."

Seeing Jude enter with Vicky, he sat up, wincing as he did so.

"I'm on some painkillers, but I don't like extremes!" he said, as if in explanation for his discomfort. "You're Special Agent Tennant. And you were with my wife and kids and you let me talk to her and... Thank you!"

"We're all incredibly grateful that they're fine and you're going to be okay," Vicky told him. "But, Mr. Lansing, I have a question for you."

"If my wife and kids are safe, I will tell you anything. Do anything!"

"What exactly was your assignment?" Vicky asked.

"To make sure that the house burned down," he said.

"But what if it didn't? How were you supposed to convey the information if it didn't—especially since it didn't? Were you given a number to call—"

"No, no. I was told that I'd hear from the writer again—everything was in text messages. They found my phone, right?" he asked, looking at Jude.

Jude nodded. "They found it. I've seen the pictures. I know how terrified you were."

"Read the messages. I received a few of the pictures first, then images of the things that have happened, then instructions on where to be when and… It's all in the phone."

Vicky looked at Jude. They'd gotten away from the scene that night without reporters being around.

It was possible that the perpetrator might not know that Ted Lansing had been shot and taken to a hospital—and that his family had been swept up.

That is…

If the threats could have really been carried out.

"Thank you," Vicky told him.

"What's going to happen when I don't respond?" Lansing asked anxiously.

"Oh, you're going to respond!" Jude assured him. "But don't worry about that. Get well and we'll get you to your wife and kids as soon as we can."

"Good night," Vicky told him.

"But wait! I mean, you're going to arrest me, right? I have a permit for that gun, but I fired it in a crowd. He'll kill me in jail, you know!"

"I'm not arresting you," Jude told him. "Get better!"

He urged Vicky to the door and out.

"Let's get something of a night's sleep," he told her. "We've got to get to the new place, get settled in…"

"And find out just how far away my place is from yours?" she asked lightly.

"Yeah, something like that," he told her. "Tomorrow—"

"Is another hell of a long day!" she said. "It's time we nail someone!"

"Vicky, this has just been intense. It hasn't been that long—"

"In the world of artificial intelligence? Way too long!" she said. "But that's tomorrow. Oh, wait, it is tomorrow. See, it's already being a hell of a long day!"

FIFTEEN

The arrangements by local authorities were extensive, well-planned, and excellent, Jude knew, and while St. Augustine itself was a historically significant and popular tourist destination, it might have been surprising, since it did not have the population of a Miami or Ft. Lauderdale. But it was just south of Jacksonville, a major player in size, home of federal offices, and a FDLE regional office.

When they arrived at their new destination, it appeared they might be walking into any apartment complex, neither poor nor ritzy, but one the average working man or woman could afford.

But the door opened into a large living area where in this instance, there were desks, tables, computers, scanners and printers, anything that might be needed or desired for a work environment, especially in the cyber world. To the left was a large kitchen with a dining table, divided from the central room by a broad archway. From the living room a long hallway stretched toward the rear of the "apartment."

And, of course, when they entered, Cary and Aidan were at their computers.

"You're back at last!" Aidan said.

"And you're still working," Vicky noted.

Aidan glanced at Cary and sat back, letting out a deep sigh. "AI," he said. "The most wonderful stuff in the world—and the most terrifying. I've been looking at some of the dangers facing us now—foreign powers accessing huge grids that control water, electricity, and communications. All they need is one inside person at many a facility and we are in serious trouble. Someone accessing our armaments—ships with serious capabilities and weapons. I have been worrying. This person is good. We believe that they do have access to the law firm especially because of the connections and, of course, the elevator situation. What if it's not just a murder machine? What if all this is just practice for a major hack on national systems? All right, sorry. That's something I'm sure we've all worried about. Cary and I have spent the last few hours working with the team in DC to see that our own systems have been revamped, new firewalls, encryptions, you name it. Because someone got into something to discover where we were before. But..."

"We're so grateful that you and Cary are okay!" Jude said.

"Which makes me think!" Vicky said, walking around to take a seat at the giant worktable by Aidan's side. "The electric grid was like a sideshow or something. Perhaps a way of showing that they can do what they want. The electricity at the house, causing the stove fire...that was a mistake."

Aidan frowned. "You mean they didn't mean to do it?"

"I mean they messed up. They were successful with Marci's house, but that's because everything in it was set up to be managed by AI. Not the place we were in. The man sent to check out the finale told us that it was supposed to burst into flames and burn to the ground, taking whoever was in it with it. But you put out the fire. Miscalculation."

"One that makes me very glad!" Cary said lightly. "And, grateful that Aidan was with Clover and me and knew right where to find the fire extinguisher and how to use it quickly. And, of course, we all ran out immediately, too, as you said. But hmm, true. I guess that the house was supposed to burn down—with us in it."

"Someone brilliant with AI, but not so brilliant when it comes to physical realities," Jude said thoughtfully.

"And so I wonder," Vicky murmured, "if we need to be as worried about a coordinated strike on national security as we need to be concerned about this whole thing taking flight on its own."

"AI becoming far smarter than any of us is something that troubles the minds of our greatest techs out there," Aidan said. "There have been so many amazing minds leaving companies and warning the world, but…we just don't know right now what the hell is going on, and our theories are theories, except that I do believe we're on the right path."

"Barton Clay," Jude said.

"You have him stuck in your mind," Vickie warned.

"Well, we'll stay on him, on his finances, on his work record, we'll just keep looking and looking," Aidan promised.

"Yeah, we are about to call it quits for the night," Cary said. "Oh, and we put your things in the back. King bed, the works."

"Um, whose things?" Jude asked.

Cary and Aidan looked at one another and burst out laughing.

"Both of your things, of course! And don't worry, we only know what's going on because we're all here together. We see you two as nothing but perfectly professional at all times and in every situation!" Cary said, laughing.

"Hey, guys, go for it!" Aidan told them. "This is a rough world we live in. You risk your lives daily. Make moments count."

Vicky groaned, lowered her head, and laughed softly.

"Cool. You guys gave us the best room. Thanks!"

"Just the best for two people," Cary said. "I took the single with the whirlpool bath!"

"Yeah, I got just a regular room," Aidan said. "What I won't sacrifice for friends!"

"Okay, then, it is tomorrow, so…"

"All right," Aidan said. "I'll start. Good night!"

He headed down the hall and Cary hit a few keys and rose as well. She waved and headed off to her own bed.

Vicky looked at Jude and said, "Well, let's go see our room."

He nodded and grinned, and they walked down the length of the hall together.

Aidan and Cary were right; the room was nice. It offered a king bed, walk-in closet, and a private bath.

"Well, since the gig is up," Vicky murmured. She turned to him and grinned. "I must take a shower. It has been…"

"A long, long, long day again. Let's go for it."

She grinned. It was almost a pity the room was so neat—their clothing went flying everywhere, laughter rose softly between them, and the feel of the water was nearly as sweet as that of his hands. But the shower was swift. And still, they were new enough to being lovers that the shower led to intimacy that was almost as quick that night, but urgent, searing, ending with them curled together, still in one another's arms, the feeling of just being there, touching, holding…

"What are we going to do?" he whispered.

"Interview everyone at that flipping firm!"

He smoothed the silk of her hair from her face. "About us!" he said softly. "Because I don't think that I can let you go."

She lay against his chest, and he felt her lips curl into a smile.

"Thank you!" she whispered.

"Oh?"

"I was worried about that myself. Logically, we have known each other such a short time. And yet I feel as if I've been waiting for you all my life. I know. I'm crazy. You're crazy. Some might say we're just both desperate because we don't really have lives outside of work, but…maybe it's true, too, that there are people who seek things in others that are like a list of needs and suddenly, you find… Never mind, I'm getting crazier." She started to laugh. "Wait! We may be crazy, but not as crazy as reality TV, so I guess—"

"Wait," he teased, "you think that reality TV is real? We may need to rethink this!"

They both laughed. He smoothed her hair back. They didn't need to talk, then; it was a perfect ending and the reality of their lives was that the light of the already long day would be coming soon enough.

The intimacy of body and souls was a sweet segue into sleep for what they had remaining of the night.

And, as always, the alarm rang too soon. Cyber sleuths had been working through the night at the main offices, but there were no new directives.

"Coffee, coffee, coffee," Vicky said.

As they headed to the kitchen, Clover—who had, of course, moved to the new headquarters with them—sat up and went into attention mode. He began to bark, racing toward the door.

Jude glanced at Vicky, and they drew their weapons, heading toward the door.

"Stop!" Aidan called from the hallway. "I have an app that shows me who is at the door and near the complex, but this place is all cops, so…hmm. No one at the door. But there were people walking by down below, and Clover didn't like something about someone. There are cops all over this building, though, someone up at some time…"

"Clover, heel," Jude said. He didn't need a leash for the dog; Clover would obey him. He was the perfect law enforcement officer, just a retired one.

"I'm going to reroll the footage from the past minutes," Aidan said.

"You can do that?" Vicky said, surprised. "The app shows me the front door, but—"

"There *are* some things I know that you don't," Aidan said, smiling.

"Call when you've got something. Whoever it is may be long gone."

Jude headed out the door with Vicky right behind them. They walked out onto the street.

There were only a few people up and about, but one of them, leaning casually against a car as if waiting for someone, was a cop Jude knew, Steven Knight.

"Hey, did you see anyone around here who shouldn't have been, who was acting suspiciously in any way?" Jude asked him.

"Hard to say what is suspicious these days. Saw a kid—sorry, not really a kid, maybe a young man, eighteen or so—walking by and dropping papers on the street. I would have given him hell and told him to pick them up, but I don't leave my post. I pay attention when people head toward the building," Steven Knight told him.

"Just dropping trash," Jude murmured.

Clover growled softly.

"Dog has great instincts," Vicky murmured. She frowned, looking toward the sidewalk where the papers had been discarded. She shrugged and walked over to retrieve them, Clover protectively at her side. She looked back at Jude and then reached into her pockets for a pair of gloves.

The papers were probably nothing.

But they might have been something.

There were three sheets of paper. She picked them up and shrugged as she looked at the first two. But at the last she turned back to Jude.

"Clover does have great instincts," she said.

"That kid was someone doing something wrong besides littering?" Steven said, surprised and straightening with a frown.

"Well, I think this is a message intended for us," Vicky said.

"What does it say?" Jude asked her.

She looked at him, shaking her head and reading, "'You ain't seen nothin' yet.'"

"And the others?" he asked.

"Blank," she told him.

Jude turned to the officer. "This was about ten minutes ago now?" he asked.

"Just about," Steven told him. "Hey, I never thought—"

"It's all right, you did what you're supposed to do, kept your eyes on the building," Jude said. "What did the kid—or young man—look like?" he asked.

"About five-eleven or six feet even," Steven said. "Almost shoulder-length, reddish hair, messy-looking, but the way boys or young men that age wear it. He had on a sweatshirt that advertised a band, a new group, the Claymores, jeans, and sneakers."

"Clover, let's go. Toward the west?" Jude asked.

Steven nodded. And with the dog, Jude and Vicky quickly hurried off in the same direction.

"He could be in a car by now or he could have grabbed an Uber or slid into a house or be almost anywhere. He could have started running once he was past the house," Vicky said as they hurried along.

"Clover is on the trail," Jude said. "Yes," he added, looking over at her. "I'm going to be optimistic!"

"Clover seems optimistic enough," she agreed.

And she was telling the truth. The dog was on the scent, nose to the ground. He moved along swiftly, and they had to move themselves to keep up with his pace.

Luckily, it was still early. The school and workday hadn't begun and they could follow Clover without knocking others over.

Clover got excited by a doughnut shop, stopping in front of

it, wagging his tail and barking. Jude looked inside the plate-glass window.

There was a young man standing in front of the counter; his jacket advertised the band that Steven had mentioned, his hair was long and reddish and shaggy.

"Clover's optimism paid off!" Jude informed Vicky.

She rolled her eyes at him. "He doesn't have a service tag so Clover needs to stay out here. I'll be on dog duty. You go get the litterer!"

"On it," Jude said. "Oh, should I get some doughnuts?"

"Knock yourself out," she said. "Large coffee with a shot of espresso!" she added.

He grinned. It was unlikely he'd be able to get anything—depending on the mood and nature of the young red-haired man.

He walked in. The fellow had gotten his doughnuts and coffee and moved to one of the cocktail-style tables by the front of the shop.

There was a free chair across from the man. Jude sat in it, startling the man who looked up from his cell phone.

"Um, hi," he said.

"Hi, yourself. My name is Jude Mackenzie. Special Agent Jude Mackenzie."

The redhead frowned. "What does that mean?" he asked.

"It means that I'm with the FBI. And I'm going to start off by warning you that it's a felony to lie to a federal officer."

"You're just messing with me, right?" the man asked. "Who put you up to this?"

"One more time," Jude said, cautioning himself against impatience. He produced his badge and credentials. "My name is Jude Mackenzie. Special Agent Jude Mackenzie. My partner is outside with the trained police dog who tracked you down for us."

"Why?"

"Start off with your name."

"Linc," he said, and then seemed to give himself a little shake. "Sorry. Lincoln Adison. And I don't know why—wait! The FBI. You're going to arrest me for—for littering? No, man, it wasn't anything like that, really. The dude in the car said that his friend was coming out to get the papers, that it was a game they were playing, but that he had to be cool because cops watched the area. It was just a game!"

"A game. Two blank pieces of paper and a warning? 'You ain't seen nothin' yet?'" Jude asked.

"Yeah. I guess they play tricks on each other or something," Linc said.

"Who plays tricks on each other?"

"The two guys."

"Okay. Two guys. So. Who was the 'dude' in the car? And who was the friend who was supposed to come out and get the papers?"

"I, uh, I don't know," Linc said, wincing and looking down.

"You don't know? You were dropping papers from one dude to another but...you don't know the other guy, either?"

"No. I... I just got laid off from my job! I was working at the pool for the hotel down the street, but they've had it closed now for a month because one of the chains just bought the hotel. I'm a lifeguard, a good one, I swear it. But I haven't found a new place to work—a lot of people are scrambling. I'm supposed to go to the university in Gainesville in the fall. I even have a scholarship but not enough if I don't supplement my income."

"So, you did this because someone paid you," Jude said.

"Yeah, I was shocked. Figured rich people can afford to screw around big-time, but...he gave me a hundred bucks just to drop three pieces of paper! What idiot would say no to that?" Linc asked, sounding desperate as he studied Jude's face.

"All right. So, you don't know his name—"

"No, I'm not even sure it was a 'him.'"

"Start at the beginning and explain that statement."

"I love to come here for coffee and doughnuts—I can walk from my place, which is down another few blocks. So, I'm walking, and a car pulls up and someone calls out to me. I almost ran. There was only one person in the car, the driver, and I thought it was some kind of a freak or a murderer or a whacko at the very least, but they started laughing and saying, 'Hey, wait! I'm not going to hurt you. I just need to see if you'd like a quickie job for good money.'"

"What made you think that the person was a freak or murderer or whacko?" Jude asked.

"The mask!"

"This person was wearing a mask?"

"Yeah, like one of those things from the movies. The one worn by the killer every time he stabs someone to death."

"Okay, a person driving down the street in a theatrical mask called out to you. You thought you should run, but you were offered big money?"

Linc nodded solemnly. "I told you. I need money."

"All right. What kind of a car?"

"A black one."

Patience! Jude reminded himself.

"What kind of a black one?"

"I didn't notice the make or model."

"Okay, a van, a sedan, a truck, SUV?"

"Like a little SUV, I guess."

"If I were to show you vehicles, could you pick out the kind, at least?"

"Um, yeah. Probably. I mean, when someone is wearing a mask like that while showing you a hundred-dollar bill, you're just not paying that much attention to the car!"

"Speaking of which, you still got the hundred-dollar bill?"

"Um, no. I just bought coffee and doughnuts with it. Mr.

Bellini is a really nice guy. He says no one buys doughnuts with a bill like that, but for me, he'd dig out the change. And if it will get me out of trouble, I can give you the change!"

"I don't want the change, and you're not really in trouble—unless you want to give me a hard time now," Jude said pleasantly. "I'd like you to come back to that building with me. I'm going to pull up pictures of cars and you're going to try to give me a better description of this 'dude.' Give me a minute."

"May I finish my doughnut?" Linc asked hopefully.

"You may."

"Oh, man, Mr. Bellini is a good guy. I don't want to get him into anything bad—"

"Don't worry. I'll give him a hundred for the hundred, okay?"

"Cool. Thank you. Look, I swear, I never imagined that I was doing anything bad, really. I mean, rich people, you know, they don't mind spending a fortune on a trick."

"You're not in trouble. The littering fine for that kind of trash is a hundred dollars, but no one is going to charge you for the littering—as long as you help. Finish your doughnut."

Jude looked out the window. Naturally Vicky was looking in. She stood by Clover, her hand set gently on the top of his head. She arched a brow to him.

He gave her a sign that he'd be just a minute and she nodded, turning her attention to Linc, who was finishing his doughnut.

He walked up to the middle-aged man behind the register, smiled, and tried not to be intimidating in any way as he flashed his badge.

"That kid just paid you with a hundred. Do you still have it?"

The man, Mr. Bellini, according to Linc, frowned. "Was it stolen?" he asked. He seemed completely stunned and confused that that might be the case.

"No, no, nothing like that. I'm assuming you do still have

it. I'll trade you a hundred for the hundred if I may. And no, that fellow didn't do anything wrong," he assured Belliini.

Linc was watching them, worried, chewing as he did so, but managing an anxious expression in spite of that.

"Yes, of course, I have it!" Bellini said. "I mean, who the hell tries to use a hundred? No one even uses cash much anymore!"

Jude dug in his wallet for the money, produced it, and then remembered to say, "Hey, can I also buy a large coffee with a shot of espresso?"

"Uh, sure, of course. No, no more money. It's on me. I have a feeling that you could have confiscated that bill as evidence or the like, but…never mind. I don't want to know!"

He produced the bill.

Jude realized he'd need to send Aidan or Cary back to get the man's fingerprints for elimination, because he didn't have any equipment on him. He used a napkin from the counter to accept the bill and slipped it into an evidence bag as he returned to the table.

With the bill.

And Vicky's coffee.

"Let's go."

Outside, he introduced Linc to Vicky and Clover.

Clover was suspicious at first, but Linc evidently liked dogs and made that apparent to the shepherd/mastiff mix.

Clover decided to accept his presence and they started back, Jude explaining the conversation they'd had in the doughnut shop to Vicky.

"So, wait! You don't even know if it was a man or a woman?" Vicky said incredulously.

"The mask thing—it made the person's voice all weird. It was almost as if…"

Vicky looked at Jude. "A voice changer incorporated in the mask. I'm going to go out on a limb here and suggest then that it was someone who would be recognized, someone we'd know if we were able to get a description," she said.

"What is going on? What did I do?" Linc asked, perplexed.

"There's been a lot going on," Jude told him. He hesitated, glancing at Vicky. "Someone has been using the internet to kill people."

"What?"

Linc stopped walking, his expression horrified.

"Oh, my God!" he gasped out. "Then…man, am I mixed up in this, too, now? Is this scary dude going to try to kill me now?"

"Scary dude has no idea that we found you along with the papers. In fact, we would not have found you if it hadn't been for an observant cop and Clover," Vicky said. She glanced at Jude. "If you're worried—"

"Worried? I'm terrified!" he said.

"We can keep you safe," Jude said. "At least you won't need to miss any work right now," he added dryly. "Come on, we're going to need to get to Aidan. With any luck, we may be able to pull fingerprints off the bill. We need to try, anyway."

"And there's something else," Vicky said quietly.

"What's that?" Jude asked.

"They know about this place, the police building. And if they know about it…"

"Let's get in," Jude said. "Come on!"

They hurried back. In their apartment, they found Aidan and Cary tensely glued to their computers.

Aidan looked up, frowning as he saw that they'd brought a guest, but intense as he told them, "There was a cyberattack on this place. We managed to get in to subvert it, but we're working with others, desperately changing codes and so on. If there's anything else…"

"No. Keep at what you're doing. Vicky, I want to show Linc cars."

"The room, head to our room, out of the way of these guys, and I'll open my laptop and then we can get Linc parked in front of a television or something—" Vicky said.

"Stay here? I should stay here?" he asked.

Aidan looked up, a question in his eyes.

"Ah, no, Vicky. We'll take him with us. I'll get to the lab to get help on the bill. All right, we'll get out of your hair," Jude said.

"Leave the dog!" Cary begged.

"Of course," Jude assured her.

"I'll still grab my laptop. I can sit in back with Linc and get on the car pictures," Vicky said. "And Aidan, Cary, if anything seems to threaten you—"

"No, there's no AI that can get us, we've seen to that. And a SWAT crew is going to be outside on the street. We're fine, just go!" Aidan said.

They did. As they left, Jude could see that the building would be well guarded. There wasn't just a police presence on the street.

There was a visible police presence.

Jude drove. As he did so, he listened as Vicky brought up pictures of cars.

"There!" Linc said suddenly. "That's it. I mean, I think. They all look a lot alike. You know, I mean, in the shape of the body of the car. But, hey, I think I saw that logo thing on it, too."

"Okay, I'm calling it in, along with a few other models," Vicky said for Jude to hear.

"Got it. Good. Get a crew to the local PD station, too. We'll get the bill there, between them, they can get someone out to the doughnut shop and start on the fingerprints. And we can..." He hesitated. "And we can leave Linc there, safe at the station."

"You want me to just sit in a police station?" Linc said.

"They have a break room. Play phone games," Jude told him.

"Hey. You're the one who is scared," Vicky reminded him.

"Yeah, but… Uh, never mind! I'll play phone games!" Linc said.

They arrived at the station; a crew from the Jacksonville office was on the way down. Jude handed over the bill. A search would go on for the car.

They were informed as well that the building that housed the law firm would be reopened for the businesses it housed the following day. If they were going to interview Nancy Cole, they would need to find her at home. With the address in hand, Jude and Vicky were ready to head out.

But before they could leave, the desk sergeant stopped them.

"This car you're looking for—the black SUV?"

"Yes, you found something?" Jude asked.

"I just got a report in. A car matching that description was just found abandoned in a grocery store parking lot. Seems it was stolen yesterday. Guy was missing his phone—which had an app to find and start his car. Phone and car missing. Phone still missing. Car found," he said.

"Great. We need a forensic team on the car, see if anything at all can be learned from it," Vicky said.

"Copy that!"

They left the station at last.

In the car Vicky murmured, "That was a stupid and senseless prank. Risk stealing a phone and a car, dressing up in a mask, and just grabbing a guy off the street. For what? To taunt us?"

"I thought for the longest time that it was a money thing," Jude told her. "Now…"

"Now?"

"I'm beginning to think that it's something different. That someone has something to prove."

"And that's why they taunted us?"

"Possibly. Dennis Rader, the 'BTK' or Bind, Torture, Kill murderer, loved to write letters to the police. Berkowitz, the

'Son of Sam,' sent a letter to the daughter of one of the detectives on his case, promising to kill her. Then, never caught, Jack the Ripper. That just names a few. Twisted minds cause a person to do twisted things."

"And as you said, Jack the Ripper, never caught. BTK—eluded police for what, a decade? We can't let that happen now, Jude. We can't!"

"We won't."

"You still think that it might be Barton Clay?" she asked.

"I can't help it. I do. When you put all the pieces we have together, he always seems to come out in the center of them all."

"But nothing other than the fact he's a cheating slimeball has come out of everything we've researched," Vicky reminded him.

"True. But we haven't found anything else that implicates anyone else—except for Celia Smith and she's dead. Via an elevator system that went haywire. Hmm. Hacked," Jude said.

"Well, we'll see what Nancy Cole has to say," Vicky told him. "There. That little house is hers—we're here!"

Jude parked the car.

"What if she doesn't answer?" Vicky asked. "With all this going on, I'm not so sure I'd answer my door!"

"I'm not so sure I'd feel safe in my house. We'll identify ourselves, of course. And if she doesn't answer, we'll spend some quality time alone with Mr. Barton Clay a bit early." He smiled. "We'd need a reason to break down the door."

"What if we heard screaming?" Vicky asked.

"You'd lie about that?"

"No. What if we really heard screaming?"

"Then we'd break down the door," he assured her.

They knocked at the door and rang the bell. Nothing. Jude looked at Vicky.

"Nancy! Special Agents Tennant and Mackenzie!" she

shouted. "We need to speak with you. Please, come to the door. We will just keep coming back!"

A second later the door opened a crack. Nancy Cole, in a casual housecoat, looked out at them trepidatiously. "What?"

"May we come in? Please," Vicky said.

Nancy Cole unhappily opened the door farther. They walked into her small, but pleasant, living room. The house was more of cottage—reasonable living, Jude knew. A group of these bungalow-type places had been built in the 1920s for workers doing repair work on some of the aging buildings and road systems in the city.

"Um, sit, I guess," Nancy said.

They took the sofa; she sat in one of the armchairs by its side.

She looked miserable. No help for it.

"Nancy, we understand that you've been having an affair with Barton Clay," Jude said flatly.

It appeared that every ounce of blood drained from her face.

"We know it to be true," Vicky said gently. "It may not be particularly moral, sleeping with a married man, but it's not illegal."

"Oh, my God! You didn't...you didn't...tell her, did you?" Nancy whispered.

"No. It's not our business to destroy or repair marriages," Jude told her. "But murder is illegal. And Marci Warden was murdered. The next day, you were in her chair."

"You think that I—that I killed Marci Warden?" she asked horrified.

"Did you?" Vicky asked.

"No! No! She was gone. They needed a receptionist. I'd met Celia Smith before and I'd even met Nathaniel—"

"Through Barton Clay?" Vicky asked.

"Um, yes. He suggested that I go in and fill out an application. I—I don't have a college degree. I'm not...well, I never did well in school. But I know how to be polite, and I like people and he thought that there might be a position for an assistant somewhere in the future and… I never wanted anyone to die so that I could have a job! I swear it!" She hesitated. "Oh! And I barely know how to use social media, anyone can tell you that! She was killed by her house and you think that someone rigged the house—that person couldn't possibly have been me!" Nancy swore.

"What about Barton?" Vicky asked.

Jude thought that Nancy was silent just a second too long.

But she shook her head vehemently. "No, no, he and Marci were friends. He certainly didn't hate her! That's just it—no one hated Marci. All right, he was frustrated with her, talking about her frowning about him taking some kind of action with a client—"

"What client?" Vicky asked.

"I don't know! We, uh, didn't talk a lot about his business because…"

"Because," Vicky pressed.

"Because we were usually busy doing other things!" Nancy spat out. "But Barton… No, no, no! He didn't kill anyone. He sure as hell didn't kill her to get me a position at the firm because Celia had already talked about taking me on as one of her assistants!"

"You have no idea what the argument was about, or which client might have been involved?" Jude asked.

"I swear I don't!" Nancy vowed. "But…"

"But?" Vicky pressed.

"He didn't do it! I know that Barton didn't do it! He couldn't have. He was… He had snuck out for a few hours. He was… sleeping with me the evening she was killed!"

SIXTEEN

"The question is," Vicky said thoughtfully when they were back in the car, "do we believe her?"

"She wasn't pleased that we knew about the affair," Jude said. "And since she wasn't so thrilled, why would she lie about being with him when Marci's house went bonkers?"

"Well, there's another question," Vicky told him.

"What's that?"

"We're still talking about doing things through the internet, AI, and not having to be physically present to get something done. Two possibilities if she was telling the truth. Barton Clay is guilty—and he managed to get online while he was with her and A, she's guilty, too, or B, she's oblivious, and he managed to hit a few keys while she wasn't watching."

"Those are the two possibilities?" Jude asked.

"No, that's one possibility, assuming that Nancy Cole is telling the truth. The second possibility is that he's still guilty—he planned it all with a timer set for the hack and used her as an alibi if we were to get this close."

"It's time to talk to him again, anyway. And I know he's

been my concentration, but Arnold has had the cyber sleuths on everyone else at that law firm—he's had people talking to people. And we're just not coming up with anything else."

"And we're not coming up with anything solid against Barton Clay," Vicky reminded him.

Jude stared ahead as he drove, slightly shaking his head. "Okay, that's true. But there's something that's not right. Just something that we're missing. And if we skewer him long enough, we're going to get him."

"Well, we can try again. And even if other agents and officers have spoken with the rest of the attorneys, paralegals, and everyone else at the firm, we may need to take a better look at them. I'm going to agree on one thing. Unless I'm the most horrible person known to man when it comes to reading other human beings, I think that Nathaniel Wharton is innocent, horrified and broken by the losses of Marci and Celia Smith. We haven't spent much time with Dixon, or the other heads of the departments."

"Okay. But you'll humor me on this trip out to see Barton Clay, right?" he asked, glancing her way.

"Hey, we're headed that way," Vicky told him. "Except..."

"Except?"

"Except I wish we had something, anything!"

Their phones started ringing simultaneously.

"Aidan," Vicky said worriedly, grabbing her phone. "He and Cary were working on the hack that was attempted at the property! I hope nothing else—" She broke off, answering the phone. "Aidan! Are you all right?"

"Fine, and Cary and I are good, new firewalls, codes, you name it. We're good. And I'm proud to say that as good as this hacker might be, in some ways Cary and I are better."

"No surprise and thank God!" Vicky said. "Anyway, Aidan, we saw Nancy Cole who swears to innocence and says that

Barton Clay was with her when Marci's house went haywire. Jude is driving. I'm putting you on speaker."

"Well, forensics are finally paying off," Aidan said.

"You found the source?" she asked.

"No, no, sorry, not that good! But we did discover something. Cyanide."

Vicky glanced at Jude.

"Cyanide?" they said together.

"So, here's the thing. You can't walk into a drugstore and buy cyanide capsules in the aspirin aisle. Most cyanide poisoning is something slow and there are four different kinds. For one, people can get cyanide poisoning from a burning house and say exposure to contaminated ground or air or food. So, someone having a cyanide capsule like Samuel Hutchins? It was designed for him before being left where he could find it if he erred and wanted to save his family."

"Okay, where are we going with this?" Vicky asked.

"The capsules—and I'm assuming there are more—were made. And I believe that they came from a certain rodenticide, or rat poison. And I do have something for you—the fact that Barton Clay purchased a large supply approximately three months ago. Also, since the house didn't give up anything when our crews went through, Cary and I decided to do some deep, deep dives. We discovered that Barton Clay had an uncle who died last year. He owned a house in the woods near Ocala National Forest. The house should have gone to the uncle's daughter, Barton's cousin, but she's been living in France for the last ten years and has no desire to go rough it. She asked Barton just to keep the property in the family, check on it now and then. It's a wooden shack that sits on a few acres of land. If you were going to practice some chemistry, making little capsules out of rat poison, it would be a great place to do it."

"Head there now—"

"There's a team on the way," Aidan said. "But I wanted to

let you know right away because we knew that you and Cary were going to eventually be off to talk to the man again. At the very least, we know he purchased the poison."

"And it's something to work with!" Jude said. Vicky glanced his way; he was looking at her. "Ask and ye shall receive!"

"What?" Aidan asked over the phone line.

"Sorry!" Jude said. "We were just wishing we had something more to go in with. You delivered in a timely manner."

"Oh, well, great. I'll let you know as soon as we know more. Should be soon. A chopper is taking them down there. The distance isn't that great, but still, much faster by air."

"Great. Keep us advised. We're on the way to the Clay house now."

They ended the call.

"Occam's razor," Jude said.

"What?"

He laughed. "Philosophy. Solve a problem using the smallest set of variables, or, to put it another way, the simplest answer is usually the right one."

"Back to Barton Clay! Jude, come on now, think about it. You are obsessed!" Vicky said, "And then again, you may be right. Except that one might think that with all his prowess and money—slimy as it may be—*one would think* that he would have fled somewhere by now. Physically, that is. Think about it. Only poor souls who were broke or panicked that horrible things could happen to their loved ones did anything that needed a physical presence. And those failed, miserably. The things that have been successful have been done online using AI. Barton Clay could do things on the internet from just about anywhere in the world, so, why take a chance on prison here?"

Jude was thoughtful for a minute. "There's just something about the way everything seems to come back to him. Why not his confidence? He's like a Carlos Rodriguez, so sure of himself that nothing matters. He's just certain that he'll beat it all."

"Well, we're here now, so let's try this new tactic," Vicky told him.

"We are here," he agreed, setting the car in Park. "Time to find out about rat poison!"

They headed to the door and rang the bell.

The maid answered and sighed wearily. "I will tell them you are here," she said, clearly aggravated they had come again.

But a minute later Barton Clay came hurrying down the stairs. He looked at them, frowning. "All right, well, I thought you knew everything about me, including all the things that you don't like, so, what else can I do for you?" he asked.

"Tell us about poison," Jude said.

Vicky wondered if they shouldn't have tried to get the man to let them in first. They didn't have him yet—if he was guilty.

But the man stared at them, frowning, as if he truly had no idea what they were talking about.

"Poison," Barton said. "Celia Smith died when the elevator went down. Captain Quincy died when his boat crashed and exploded. Marci was killed by her house—whether there was or wasn't someone behind the glitches in her system. And I know you're investigating the car death of the judge who condemned Carlos Rodriguez's son in Tennessee, but…none of them died by poison!"

"I'm sorry, but we need an explanation," Jude told him politely. "We can talk here, or we can head to the local police station."

"We can talk here. Come in," the man said.

As they entered, Belinda came hurrying down the stairs, appearing as confused as her husband that they should be there again.

"Your uncle, Desmond Clay, passed away, leaving you a house," Jude said as he nodded to Belinda but spoke to Barton.

"What? Now you think I killed my uncle?" Barton asked, shaking his head.

"No, sir," Vicky said. "We just need to know why you ordered so much rat poison to his house."

"Rat poison!" Barton said. Again, he appeared to be truly astonished. "I didn't order any rat poison. There may be rats there, I don't know. But I don't care. I promised my cousin I'd see to it that nothing on the property would be a code violation, but…it's in an unincorporated area in the woods. There isn't much she could do that would attract anyone and I personally hate the place. I hate the Everglades, mosquitoes, snakes, and alligators, and that property gets them all."

"Rat poison was ordered on your credit card and sent to that destination," Jude said. "I'm afraid that there are records to prove it."

"What credit card? I watch my cards! There was no rat poison charged on them!" he said indignantly.

Belinda stood by her husband's side, her arm slipped through his protectively.

"He isn't lying!" she cried vehemently. "We never go out there. The wilderness is just not… Well, I mean, I know it's there, but a vacation for us is a great hotel on the beach with waiters running around with piña coladas…and a spa!"

"This hacker has stolen my identity!" Barton said. "Whoever is doing this is trying to frame me. You know, I've made mistakes in my past. I've twisted the law and I've represented some questionable people. But I didn't do this! Marci was my friend. And Celia was a bear—but she was our bear! I would never have hurt either of them. And I don't understand. No one was poisoned."

"No, but people hired to ensure that some of the deeds were done were supplied with capsules or pills—laced with cyanide. They were to die rather than give anything away," Jude told him.

"Get your people on it. Please, get your best people on it," Barton said, shaking his head, his denial adamant. "I'm telling you, I didn't kill anyone. I'm a victim myself! I check my cards. Some are business, some are private. I didn't charge any kind of poison, rat poison, any poison, I swear it!" He paused. "Am I under arrest? Am I being charged with buying rat poison?"

"Not now, but there has been a warrant issued and they are searching that property now, as we speak," Jude informed him.

"They won't find anything. And now, unless you are going to arrest me, leave!" Barton said.

"As you wish," Jude said pleasantly.

He looked at Vicky. She nodded. As they left, they could hear Belinda's soft voice, whispering, "Oh, my darling, why are they persecuting you in this horrible manner! You must sue them. I mean, Nathaniel will know how to sue the federal government and those horrible people individually!"

"Well, that went pleasantly!" Vicky murmured as they left the house. "Too bad we can't arrest people for absolute nastiness!"

Jude smiled at that. "At first, he seemed stunned. I'm hoping that there is a way for our cyber people to tell if Barton Clay's identity was stolen or not. I had been thinking he was a lot like Carlos Rodriguez, so sure of himself that he'd dare us to prove he'd done anything just because he'd bought rat poison. And just buying it doesn't make him guilty of anything."

"A curse and a blessing," Vicky said.

"The internet."

"Yep!"

"One way or another, it has changed the world. Now I have friends who are telling me that their kids want to grow up to be 'influencers.'" He laughed softly. "That wasn't an option when I was a kid!"

"Ah, well, I don't think it would have changed anything for either of us," she told him.

They had only driven two blocks from the Clay house when Vicky's phone began to ring.

"Aidan," she said, answering it quickly. "On speaker, of course!"

"Then you're not still with Barton Clay?" Aidan asked.

"No," Vicky said. "We just left. He swears he didn't buy the poison, that his identity was stolen, that he checks his credit card, and no credit card that he has purchased poison."

"Well, that's odd," Aidan said. "Because they found the poison, all kinds of chemistry paraphernalia and pills in the house by the national forest. You can go back and bring him in. Thank God our people were prepared. The place is a hazardous waste dump!"

"We're on it," Jude said.

"And we're charging him with—"

"Attempted murder," Jude said. "If we can't prove he's been manipulating AI and killing people through it, we can prove he was creating deadly 'weapons' and with Samuel Hutchins's testimony, brilliant attorney that he is, Barton may not be able to beat the rap."

"He'll be out on bail tomorrow," Vicky said.

"Maybe," Jude murmured. "But we're bringing him in."

He turned the car around and they headed back to the Clay house. This time Jude banged on the door.

And, of course, the maid answered.

"They don't wish to see you. Unless you have another warrant," she told them.

"We need Mr. Barton Clay. Now!" Jude snapped.

"I'm sorry, he's out," the maid informed them.

"His car is still in the driveway," Jude said.

"Jude!" Vicky murmured. She was looking through the open door. There was an archway from the living room or parlor to the dining room and kitchen. The rear of the house had been modernized with a solarium that offered wall-to-wall glass windows and a sliding door.

The sliding glass door was ajar as if someone had just left—and not closed it completely as they had done so.

"He's gone through the back," Vicky said.

"I've got him, hold here. He might double back once he thinks we've gone!" Jude told her. He caught her by the shoulders, leaning close so that the maid, who had stepped back, couldn't hear. "Talk to the wife, see if she knows about the affair. She might get angry and give us something!"

"On it," Vicky murmured.

Ignoring the maid's attempt to close the front door of the house, Jude pushed his way in, shoving her aside and allowing Vicky a chance to enter.

"Where is Mrs. Clay?" she demanded as Jude hurried out the back.

The maid stared at her angrily. "This is illegal!"

Vicky let out a sigh. "Reminding you once again that lying to a federal agent is a felony!"

"Breaking and entering is a crime!"

"We didn't break and enter anything!" Vicky told her. "You opened the door to us. Now, where is Mrs. Clay?"

"What's going on?"

The maid didn't need to tell Vicky anything. Belinda Clay strode in from the kitchen.

"What is going on?" she demanded.

"The other one burst through the house, Mrs. Clay," the maid said. "I'm so sorry, I couldn't stop him, he's…big!"

"And where is Barton now?" Belinda asked.

"Um…um…" the maid stuttered.

"He ran out the back. And Special Agent Mackenzie went after him," Vicky said.

"He ran out?" Belinda said.

"Mrs. Clay, I'm very sorry to tell you this now, but your husband *is* under arrest," Vicky said.

"But why? For what?" Belinda asked, big blue eyes open wide. "He's an attorney. He said that you couldn't arrest him for buying poison—the poison he didn't buy, by the way—

and you have nothing on him, nothing that would allow you to bring him in!"

"Mrs. Clay, we need to talk," Vicky told her. "Seriously. I'm afraid there are things you don't know and I'm afraid they're damning for your husband."

"I don't know how to get her out," the maid said.

"Darla, don't worry about it," Belinda said. She was staring at Vicky, and now she had a slightly sick look in her eyes. "Special Agent Tennant, I was just making coffee. Will you join me in the kitchen, please?"

"Yes, thank you," Vicky said. "That would be a good idea. We need to talk."

Vicky followed Belinda Clay through the house to the kitchen. The maid, Darla, watched them go before heading toward the back.

Did she intend to run out into the back, through the alley there, perhaps into the empty forested lots behind the house or maybe through the neighborhood to the nearby park, seeking to reach her employer first?

"I just… I can't believe any of this about Barton!" Belinda said. "Oh, don't worry, she's like his loyal dog. Darla, I mean. She's just trying to warn him, I guess. Though, if he took off, he must have been worried about something."

They moved into the kitchen. It was large and sunny and offered a circular breakfast table in the center.

"Please, sit. I brew a great cup of coffee!" Belinda said. Then she sighed. "I just can't believe…"

"Can't? Or you don't want to?" Vicky asked quietly, taking a seat at the table.

"He is a brilliant man!" Belinda said. "He attended the best colleges. He was asked by dozens of firms to join them! He liked Wharton and Dixon and even Celia. He said it was great to have a bear around so long as it was your bear, and… I just can't believe this. As I said, he's just brilliant! And he married me, little old me, high school education—everything else, anything else, self-taught!"

"Mrs. Clay, education can be important, but a person can be very bright even if they don't have years of college and law school behind them," Vicky said. "I'm sure that you're very bright yourself and that's why… Well, it's why we need to talk. You're certain that Barton and Marci were friends, and—" she paused, partially feigning her regret at going on "—that he was also very good friends with Nancy Cole, the young woman who came in to take her place?"

Belinda worked by the coffeepot, her back to Vicky so that Vicky couldn't see her face to read her expression at that question.

"Cream, sugar?" she asked Vicky.

"Black is fine, thank you," Vicky told her. She thought she'd lighten up for a minute. "I used to love cream and sugar in coffee, but since a lot of offices wind up with curdling cream and no sugar, I learned to love it black!" she told Belinda.

Belinda brought the two cups to the table and set them down, taking a seat at the table opposite Vicky.

"I love it black, too! Strong coffee. You're going to like mine—I seriously brew a great cup of coffee. Maybe that's why Barton married me!" she said.

"He married you because he loves you, I'm sure, because you're bright and beautiful," Vicky said pleasantly. "But sometimes men like your husband…"

Belinda took a sip of her coffee. Vicky did the same. The coffee was strong. As much as Vicky liked strong coffee, this was a little too bitter.

She pretended to enjoy drinking it, barely letting it touch her lips.

"Men like my husband, who went to the best college, top of his class in law school—I know what you're going to say—such men start to believe they're a bit above the rest of the world and that they can do whatever they want." She took a deep breath. "You're about to tell me he's been having a long-time affair with Nancy Cole. And you think that Marci might have died because of that—so that Barton could get her a job at the firm. But she was going to get a job there, anyway."

Vicky asked carefully, "You've known, or suspected, that he was having an affair with Nancy Cole?"

"Oh, I'm pretty sure he was having an affair with Marci Warden, too," Belinda said. "But, I've liked being the wife of such an important man. They come and go. I stay." She laughed suddenly. "I assure you, though, he wasn't having an affair with Celia Smith!"

"But, Belinda, maybe he felt that Marci needed to be out of the way. And… I am sorry, because unless it's proven that his identity was stolen and someone else broke into the house he was watching for his cousin, he'll…"

Belinda suddenly smiled. "No, no, no. You mustn't worry on my account. You see, from early on, I realized Barton saw me as eye candy. He has never thought I was bright enough to figure anything out. But, hey, you'd be amazed by what you can learn these days if you master the web! Did you realize you can learn just about anything in the world online these days? You can learn how to make bombs! How to make poison pills, how to manipulate electronics, and even how to manipulate AI?"

Vicky stared at the woman, ready to draw her Glock.

Was this what we've been missing all along?

"That's right, Special Agent Tennant. You see, everyone in the world underestimated me! And so, I had to prove I was the brains of the operation. But, of course, I've done it all very carefully. Barton will go to prison—he'll be right where he deserves to be after cheating on me year after year after year! You've wondered, surely, why he hasn't fled the country. Because he is innocent! But that isn't going to matter. Because it's all working out brilliantly. When your partner comes back, he's going to find you dead. And I'll be screaming and crying that Barton came back and shot you." She smiled sweetly. "Because Barton will come back—he will come back before Jude gets here. He'll slip through the garage door. And I may need to shoot him, but I plan on only wounding him because I want him to rot in prison. Then, well, I have tons of money. And a plan to escape the country myself. AI! I just fell in love with it and then I discovered I could make a ton of money by killing that judge… Marci just had to go. And Celia was suspecting that I had used her computer when she wasn't in her office, so… I really preferred making money. Oh, of course, I was paid well to see that Captain Quincy died, too."

The coffee. There's something in the coffee. She had barely sipped it, but she could barely move!

Belinda rose, heading for a cabinet. She returned with a little Smith & Wesson while Vicky struggled to reach her bag, furious with herself that they had been so blind.

They hadn't seen the *power* behind Barton Clay. They'd been right, of course. It had all come from his house, it all related to him…

It's just that he wasn't a killer.

He had married one.

Though impacted, she managed to reach her Glock. She produced it, aiming at Belinda Clay as she aimed back at her.

"Ah!" Belinda said. "You didn't really drink much coffee! But I'm willing to bet that you drank enough, that I can squeeze a trigger before you can!"

It wasn't difficult to catch up with Barton Clay. The man wasn't old, and he wasn't in bad shape, but apparently he didn't spend much time on physical fitness.

He barely made it to the end of the alley where he was about to hop a little wall to get into the empty forested lots behind the house; it appeared he intended to double back to his house.

Why?

Maybe his wife was prepared to help him escape in some secret fashion.

Jude was able to quickly draw his weapon and warn the man, "Stop! Federal agent, and you're under arrest. Damn it, man, don't make me shoot you!"

Barton stopped and crawled back down, his hands in the air.

He turned and looked at Jude. "I didn't do it! I swear I didn't do it!"

"Clay, they just found a whole chemistry lab at your place in the woods—the creation of suicide pills for the minions you tried to rule," Jude told him.

The man still shook his head. "I didn't do it! Yes, I did bad things. I cheat on my wife. I represent people who might have done very bad things—that's the way it is. Even crooks get the best representation they can afford. But, please, man… I didn't do this!"

Suddenly, someone shouted from behind Jude.

"Drop it! Leave him alone!"

He turned. The Clays' pretty young maid was standing behind him. She was armed; she had both hands on her weapon, but her hands were shaking.

"No! Darla, no, thank you, but—" Barton began.

Jude groaned. "Ah, man, you're sleeping with your maid, too?" he demanded.

She's shaking hard. She doesn't know how to use the weapon she's carrying.

"Lady, you drop it. Now!" Jude commanded. "I really, really do not want to shoot you!"

"Darla," Barton added. "Please, don't make this worse. Drop the gun. I'm innocent and I will prove it in court!"

Darla looked confused but she lowered the weapon.

“Where did you get that, anyway?” Barton demanded, looking at Darla with a frown.

“From the pit,” Darla said.

“The pit?” Barton asked her.

“The pit, the cache…the place behind the wall where Belinda keeps her things!” Darla said.

Clay truly looked astounded.

And it was then that Jude knew. He’d been wrong. The man was innocent. Innocent of everything except for arrogance and stupidity!

“She’s expecting you back, right? Belinda. You were supposed to double back, and she’d have supplies ready for you to find some place to hide out or a way to leave the country. Except, you fool, she doesn’t intend to help you, she intends to kill you and pretend that she had to!” Jude told the man.

“My God!” Barton breathed. “No, I… No!”

He almost wailed the word. But it was as if a blindfold had been lifted.

“She could have done it so easily, gotten a credit card in my name—she has the keys to the place in the woods. She…she’s always, always on her computer!” he wailed.

Jude didn’t wait; it was all so very crystal clear now.

Belinda Clay. Just a dumb blonde. Needing to prove something? So bitter against her husband and his continuous affairs that he had to pay and it didn’t matter who else was in on it. Or was there more, was she planning more…?

The forensic crew had found nothing except what they were supposed to find. Her computer and guns and money weren’t even kept on the property; they were buried in a covered wooden pit in the empty lot behind the house and the wall.

She’d had this planned out. Barton fleeing, him going after Barton, her alone with Vicky. Belinda Clay, a woman who had created cyanide suicide pills and God alone knew what else…

He ran. And he was fast. Belinda might have been ready to

shoot Barton the minute he entered, and then she'd wait for Jude to return and she'd cry her eyes out, telling him Barton had been guilty, how she'd had to shoot him after he'd killed Vicky…

He slipped through the side door as silently as he could. And he headed to the kitchen.

And they were there. Vicky at the table, struggling to hold her Glock. Belinda, laughing as she made fun of the way Vicky was holding her gun.

"Drop it!" Jude roared.

But Belinda didn't. She spun around, ready to shoot him.

But Vicky's gun went off even as he gave the command.

Belinda's shot went wild.

Because Vicky had caught her right in the back.

She went down—so did Vicky, slipping from the chair, falling in a curl on the floor by her chair.

Pulling out his phone, he called for an ambulance as he hurried first to stoop down by Belinda. To his amazement, she half opened her eyes.

She managed a smile. "You ain't seen nothin' yet!" she told him.

Her eyes closed.

He felt for a pulse. Weak, but there. He hurried over to Vicky. She was already struggling up. "The coffee. I was an idiot," she murmured. "Belinda. Is she…alive?"

"Yes, EMTs on the way. They'll get her to the hospital. And you. You must go to the hospital, too."

"I'm going to be all right. I didn't drink that much of the coffee. I barely brought it to my lips."

"Thank God!" he whispered.

Sirens blared. Barton Clay burst through the back door, followed by Darla. "She was trying to set me up! Oh, my God, she was the friggin' wicked witch. I'm going to kill her—"

Jude caught hold of Barton, stopping him. The EMTs arrived

in record time. Belinda was swept away, and despite her protests, Vicky was taken, too.

"We must know what she gave you!" Jude told her. "I'll be right there. As soon as cops or agents get here, I'll be there."

"But I heard her!" Vicky cried. "Warn Aidan and Cary and the others! She'd done something else!"

And she was right. Jude swiftly put through another call.

"We're on it, but I think we were already on it. The hacker used an AI tool, broke through government firewalls. They almost accessed a ship with missiles, ready to make them strike New York City, but we've got it, Jude, we're on it and we've got it."

"Hospital, I'm on the way to the hospital as soon as—"

Other agents burst in, and Jude quickly briefed them before hurrying out. Barton Clay might have been innocent in it all, but both he and Darla were going to have a lot of questions to answer. He doubted the prosecutor would be charging them but they'd still need to answer those questions.

At the hospital, he found that Cary had come in to be with Vicky and was waiting for him outside her room. "She's fine. She can come back with us in an hour," Cary told him. "Succinylcholine—it's a drug used in surgery to cause temporary paralysis. Thankfully, Vicky wasn't heavily exposed. She's in there."

Jude nodded. "You and Aidan. You saved a lot of people today."

Cary smiled at him. "You save a lot more—what that woman could have done if she had kept going is terrifying to imagine. And all to prove that she wasn't a pretty sidepiece, to… I don't know."

"I don't have a psychology degree, but it is frightening that someone so damaged could gain such an incredible amount of knowledge! But—"

"Go! Go to Vicky!" she said.

He rushed into the hospital room. She was already sitting up in bed, as if anxious to be out. He strode to the bed, sitting at her side, taking her into his arms, just holding her.

"I was so stupid—"

"I was so stupid!"

"But we were close, and—"

"It's over! It's really over!"

He pulled back just slightly, smiling with his incredulous relief. "It's over. But, partner, I'd like to think that we're never over."

She smiled at him.

"Never," she agreed.

They didn't know where they would take it from there, how they would make it work.

They just knew that they would. Of course, there would be a lot to tie up regarding the events of the day. Paperwork—and greater concern for the cyber teams going forward.

But for that moment.

They just held one another.

And it was all they needed.

EPILOGUE

"Hey! They are showing all kinds of classic movies tonight!"

Vicky turned to him, enjoying the soft warmth of the fire that emanated from the hearth at the ski lodge high in the mountains of California that they had chosen for their getaway.

"Classic?" she queried.

"You are going to love the lineup for the next few nights on one of the sci-fi channels the lodge gets. Starting with *The Matrix*. In one night! *The Matrix*, *The Terminator*, and *Blade Runner*. The next night starts off with fun for all ages—*WALL-E*. And that will be followed by *M3GAN*, *RoboCop*, and the very special Spielberg—ahead of its time—classic, *A.I. Artificial Intelligence*."

She smiled sweetly at him and warned, "If I weren't holding this delicious hot chocolate, I'd smash a pillow over your head!"

"Oh, but, hey, some good things came out of this. I had a chance to talk to Aidan when you were just in the ski shop."

She made a face. "You forget that while I was working in DC most recently, I grew up in Florida. I had to buy some warm clothing! But never mind that, what did Aidan say?"

"There's no way that it's not tragic that Marci and the others had to die, but Aidan believes they have been able to toughen up many systems—important security systems—that might have been in jeopardy if another Belinda Clay came along. An attorney in Tennessee, doing me a favor, has taken on the case of Victor Rodriguez and it appears he will be exonerated. And justice is being served—his father is locked up in the most secure criminally insane institution in the country. So, there's that. And here's a nice note: Samuel Hutchins and his wife are back together—it seems the threat and him being willing to die for her so readily straightened things out between them. Barton Clay, however, isn't being charged, but... Well, he's no longer wanted at the firm. Then again, we were there for the finale when he and Darla were grilled, and I don't think he suspected his wife for a second. I think he did believe that she was a 'dumb blonde' and it never occurred to him that she did anything on her computer except play her favorite gambling game. Clay does have money—he's moving out of the country. Alas, poor Darla is looking for another job. So, at least those we tried to keep safe were kept safe and... Well, it could have been a lot worse and gone on a lot longer."

"Still scary!" Vicky said.

"Hey, I knew a little about AI, but you were the one brought down to handle the field case!" he reminded her. "And with that said—"

She grinned at him, stood up, and yawned.

She wanted the privacy of their room. And the amazing whirlpool it offered.

"I may have some news. But you'll need to follow me and be patient."

"Oh?"

"Trust me?" she queried.

"With my life," he assured her.

She grinned. A few minutes later they were in the room.

She set the whirlpool to a deliciously hot temperature, stripped, and settled in.

"Okay."

Jude stripped and followed her lead.

"Well, the assistant director handled things for us," she told him.

"What?"

She grinned. "He was afraid that one of us would quit if we had to go to different states to work. I'm not sure how he knew or suspected, or… Who knows! It's Arnold. But I'm being transferred to your office! We will just be working with different teams, but—oh! I mean, I hope that's the kind of thing you wanted, I mean…"

He didn't answer. He moved across the water and pulled her into his arms.

His reply was physical.

And later, curled together on the plush bed of the lodge, he smiled and pulled her closer.

"AI. It may be the future, but you know what?"

"What?"

"Some things will always demand the human touch."

"Um, there are things out there…"

"No. To be amazing. To touch the heart, the mind, and the soul, to be everything in the world," he said. "And for that, I am grateful."

"And," she assured him, "deliciously human!"

"Oh, that I am!" he promised her. "I'll even prove it once again!"

★★★★★